BYE, BUY BABY

The Sisters, Texas Mystery Series
Book 11

BECKI WILLIS

Editing by SJS Editorial Services
Cover by Diana Buidoso dienel96

ISBN 13: 978-1-947686-20-5

CONTENTS

Who knew?

Whew! For a while, I wasn't sure I would make my deadline. It's been a rough year, in more ways than the obvious.

I set the debut date for Book 11 well into the new year. March should give me plenty of time, right?

Who knew I would have five extra people living in my house as I wrote this book?

Who knew I would fall victim to COVID-19, right at Christmastime? And it wasn't just me; half of our household came down with it. Thankfully, we all did great and recovered nicely, including my eighty-nine-year-old mother.

Who knew we would have not one, but TWO snowstorms in Texas in just over a month's time? Living in a rural area, we're accustomed to losing phones and electricity whenever there's bad weather, but we went for *days* without power in both January and February. I wrote a few chapters powered by a generator.

Who knew I would have TWO computers die on me last year? Even though I had almost everything backed up, a few things didn't make the trip to the cloud. This book required a lot of digging through handwritten notes, manuscripts, etc., to ensure consistency within the series.

Between the setbacks and the chaos of life in general, the plot didn't go exactly as planned. I didn't do all the in-depth research I had planned. I wanted to focus more on Genny's problems with infertility, as this is a subject near and dear to my heart. My own dreams of having a houseful of children were derailed by my personal battle with endometriosis, infertility, and a medical hysterectomy while still in my twenties.

Yet, as the characters discover in this book, God moves in mysterious ways. *He knew* that two children provided the perfect-sized family for my husband and me. *He knew* challenges only make me stronger. *He knew* that neither sleet, snow, lack of sleep, lack of power, lack of sanity, nor COVID-19 would keep me down for long.

HE knew, even when I had my doubts.

Thank you so much for reading my tales. I hope you enjoy this one, as it was truly a labor of love.

1

Camille Townsend gazed around the nursery with a satisfied smile on her face. Everything was perfect.

The walls were bathed in soft, buttery yellow. Playful zoo babies in various poses tumbled down the curtains and across the ruffled bed skirt. The velvet-soft crib sheet featured a giraffe print in muted colors, complementing the quilted baby blanket folded atop it. Stuffed koalas, pandas, and giraffes took up residence on a nearby hutch.

"Now all we need is a baby," she murmured softly.

Instinctively, her hand moved to her abdomen. It was an intuitive move, a protective gesture inborn in all mothers-to-be, even though her waist was as trim as it had been twenty years ago.

"The liaison said it won't be long now," her husband assured her, coming from behind to slip his arms around her waist.

After an involuntary start, Camille laughed at her own jittery reaction. "Doug! You scared me! I didn't hear you come in."

"Sorry about that, love." He nuzzled her ear, snuggling in close. He had loved this woman since he was sixteen years old, and there was nothing he wouldn't do for her.

Camille rested her head against his, breathing in the spicy scent of his cologne. Her hands traveled a familiar path along his arm, until she reached a spot that was unaccustomedly bare. Where she normally felt the cool, hard edge of eighteen-karat gold, she now felt bare skin. "What happened to your Rolex?"

When she would have turned in his arms, Douglas Townsend skillfully avoided her knowing gaze. Tightening his hold around her, he shushed her worries.

"I dropped it off at the jeweler's," he lied. "A couple of the links appeared to be coming loose."

"Thank Heavens you noticed in time. I would certainly hate for you to lose that watch. I know how special it is to you."

"My father gave it to me when I was named dean of the college," he mused softly.

"You've taken such excellent care of it through the years. I would hate for you to lose it now, especially over something as simple as a broken link."

"That was my thought." Steering the conversation to a safer subject, he added, "I may even get one of those smartwatches everyone is wearing these days. They do so much more than tell time. I hear you can even send pictures on it, so when the baby does something especially adorable, you can share it with me instantly."

"Maybe," Camille agreed, "but it just doesn't

seem like your wrist without the watch. That watch has become a part of you, somehow. As important as any appendage."

Douglas closed his eyes, the sting of its loss still raw upon his heart. The lawyer wanted another ten grand, claiming the adoption might not go through without filing this last, all-important paper. Douglas had come to hate seeing the name on his caller ID, knowing each call brought with it a new complication. The complications never came without a solution, as long as it was paid in cash and in a timely matter.

He stopped telling Camille about the calls several complications ago. The first time, he had the money in his checking account, so there was no need to worry his wife. She was busy converting her former sitting room into a nursery.

The next time, a quick call to his broker diverted the emergency funds to avoid a major setback in their schedule. The liaison from the adoption agency assured him this was nothing out of the ordinary; there were more prospective parents than there were babies, and timing was everything. If even a single paper weren't filed in time, the entire process would be delayed, and they might have to start all over again. It was best to take the lawyer's advice.

By the third call, cash was tighter, but Douglas managed.

By this last call, selling the watch was his only option.

"It is important to me," he admitted, "but not as important to me as you are. You know that, right? You're the most important thing to me in life. I'll do whatever it takes to make you happy."

Camille reached her hand backward to caress his face. "You. You make me happy," she assured him. "You and this baby we're about to welcome. We'll finally have a family of our own. Nothing could possibly make me any happier."

Douglas closed his eyes, breathing in the essence of her hair and her specially blended perfume.

Anything, he vowed again to himself. He would do *anything* to make her happy. Even if, somewhere deep in his soul, he suspected it wasn't quite legal.

This time, thoughts of his watch didn't sting so badly.

It was his conscience that smarted now.

2

"Derron, we're expecting a client this morning at ten. Please make sure the gate is open when she gets here." Madison deCordova didn't look up as she passed through the room, her attention on the day's mail she carried.

She shuffled the junk mail to the back of the stack as she walked. More to herself than to her employee, she murmured, "Thirty-second 'Final Notice' for an extended car warranty. Junk. No need for another credit card, so also junk." A colorful flyer promised amazing prizes if she visited its car dealership, which she promptly relegated to the back. "Not falling for the free Mercedes scam—definitely junk." Her eyes fell upon a familiar return address. "Ooh. My retainer check from Murray Archer. Not tossing this one."

The private detective firm out of Houston paid *In a Pinch Professional Services* a small monthly sum to remain on standby as its eyes and ears in the Brazos Valley. On the months they had an active case, like last month, it was an envelope *worth* opening.

She continued to sort through the remaining pile. "Notice from The Sisters ISD. Hope it's good news and not telling us the kids have done something wrong. Stays on top. Hmm. Not sure what *Cherubdipity Inn & Spa* is, but the cute envelope is worth a second look."

Derron Mullins broke into her musings. "Ten o'clock, you say? I'll keep an eye out, dollface."

"Thanks, Derron. Just send her back when—" The words died on her lips when she looked up and caught her first glimpse of the man behind the desk. She had been gathering the mail when he arrived for work, but he was now perched on the edge of his seat expectantly, clearly eager to see her reaction to his new hair color. "Your... your hair!" was all she could manage.

"You like?" He pretended to fluff the ends of the carefully manicured style. The tips of his naturally blond hair were like colors in the rainbow, each vibrant shade forming a stiff peak. Judging by the way he preened before her, she assumed the colors were intentional, and not some experiment gone terribly wrong.

"It's, uhm, very colorful," she hedged, not wanting to hurt his feelings with the truth.

"Ramon is studying hair design. I offered to be his first assignment."

"That was nice of you," she choked out. With any luck, the colors would wash out after a couple of shampoos. If not, now might be a good time to implement a dress code for the office.

She dared not look down at her own attire. Who was she kidding? Derron out-dressed and out-styled her any day of the week. Today, he wore a nubby knit sweater of dark amethyst over a crisp, white shirt with a starched collar. She couldn't see his feet but had no doubt his shoes were the latest trend and cost more than her entire outfit. Her own black slacks, simple, long-sleeved tee shirt, and lightweight cardigan didn't make much of a dent in her budget. Truth be told, they didn't make as much as a ripple in the fashion magazines, either. Derron, on the other hand, could easily be on the cover, even with his new rainbow hairstyle.

Now that she thought about it, the amethyst sweater did bring out the purple peaks.

Still, it wasn't quite the dignified look she was going for with her company's image. Maybe she would send him on a mission before their guest arrived.

A bing from the security cameras let her know it was too late. Her client was pulling into the driveway, ten minutes ahead of schedule. Without a plausible errand to send him on, she wondered if Lucy Nguyen, one of her first legitimate clients, might also be one of her last. Madison decided to treat Derron's new look like a bandage; best to rip it off all at once, than in small increments. If Lucy didn't run screaming when he greeted her at the door, the initial shock would be the worst of it.

Madison settled behind her desk and straightened a few papers as the security cameras showed Lucy stepping onto one of the old mansion's many front porches. The steps on the far-right side of the house had been designated as the formal entry to *In a Pinch*.

"Right this way, Mrs. Nguyen." Derron greeted

their client with his usual warmth and graciousness, somehow making his prissy ways even more endearing. "Can I get you something to drink? Coffee? Hot tea? Iced water with a wedge of lemon?"

"Thank you, but no." She eyed his hair warily as she eased past him into the spacious library turned office. "I have a daughter-in-law," she offered, motioning to the colorful peaks. "Wife of number one son. Work at salon. Get that color right out. Be good as new."

Derron appeared to laugh, but the sound that came from his mouth sounded more like one a horse might make. "I visit *Talk of the Town* on a regular basis," he acknowledged, flashing his manicured nails. "But Ramon would be crushed if anyone touched his masterpiece."

Noting the confused look on the woman's face, Madison quickly stepped in. She made it around the desk before Derron could say more.

"It's so good to see you again, Mrs. Nguyen. Would you be more comfortable here at the desk or by the fireplace?" She motioned to the cozy vignette arranged within the nook of the turret. The gas flames glowing in the paneled hearth offered more ambiance than they did warmth but put slightly more distance between them and Derron's desk.

Lucy Nguyen opted for the wing chairs clustered around the hearth.

"What brings you here today?" Madison asked as they settled into the cream-colored chairs. "You mentioned a problem at the chicken houses?"

"Yes. We need your help."

Madison paused, determined to make one fact abundantly clear. "You do understand that I no longer walk houses, right?"

When she opened her temporary services, Madison had envisioned filling in for secretarial tasks, or perhaps retail. Worst case scenario, she would expand her personal shopper services, pharmacy runs, and acting as chauffeur to and from doctors' offices. She hadn't planned on resorting to physical labor within the poultry industry, and she certainly hadn't been prepared for what 'walking' commercial chicken houses entailed. She assumed it was something akin to walking dogs, but nothing could be further from the truth. A crash course in poultry farming had followed, teaching her more about chickens than she ever wanted to know. First and foremost, 'walking' wasn't about exercising the feathered foul. It meant making at least four rounds through the five-hundred-foot, fully automated barns, looking for trouble spots that the computers and timers couldn't detect. Things like water and feed lines that needed adjusting as the birds grew, spotting broken fan belts and stalled motors, and, worst of all, retrieving and carrying out the dead birds.

At that point in her fledging new business, she had been just desperate enough to take the unsavory job. But things were different now. Even before her marriage to chief of police Brash deCordova, business had improved enough that she could be more selective in the jobs she chose. Walking chicken houses had been the first thing she marked off her list of services, and, God willing, it would never appear there again.

Lucy Nguyen nodded, her expression almost impatient. "Yes, yes. Not that. We need brain power, not muscle power."

Ignoring the snicker from across the room, Madison wondered if she were any more qualified for a mental challenge than a physical one. "I don't understand. What is it you need me to do?"

"*Barbour Foods* not playing fair. Threaten to jerk our contract if we not jump through circles. We stand up to them but need help."

"Circles?" she murmured, before clarity shone in her hazel eyes. "Ah. You mean jump through hoops. What sort of hoops are we talking about? What do they want you to do?"

"You name it, they want it!" Lucy threw her arms up in an exaggerated show of disgust. "Long list of upgrades, or we no get birds. No birds, no pay. No pay, no food on table or lights in house. They can't treat us like this!" she cried in outrage. Looking slightly less certain, she added, "Can they?"

"I... I don't know. I suppose it depends on your contract with them."

Madison knew that there were a dozen or more local contract growers for *Barbour Foods*, a major national supplier for the commercial food industry. Their poultry division even supplied meat and specialty products to international markets, where chicken feet were considered a delicacy. She wasn't sure of the exact legal arrangements between the growers and the company, but she knew a few of the basics. The company provided the chickens, feed, medications, and all transportation from the hatchery to the farm and from the farm to the processing plants, in exchange for the grower providing the land, the barns, and all the needed equipment to raise healthy, market-ready birds. It was a major investment of time and money for the grower, but a fifteen-year contract made it a lucrative venture for most.

"I brought copy," the other woman said, pulling a manila envelope from her over-sized bag. The tantalizing aroma of spicy pork and ginger wafted through the air, reminding Madison she had skimped on breakfast this morning. Their alarm clock hadn't gone off on the one day Brash had to make an early appearance at the courthouse. "And I brought lunch." Lucy added. "Fried rice and egg rolls."

"If you're trying to bribe me," Madison said with a sly grin, "it might just be working."

"No bribe. Just lunch."

Madison took the envelope, while Derron swooped in and offered to take the plastic containers of food. "I'll carry these to the kitchen," he said, but something in his face looked a bit too 'innocent' for Madison's liking.

"Do *not* open those," she ordered sternly.

"I wouldn't dream of it," he lied smoothly.

"I mean it, Derron," Madison warned. "I'll demand a breathalyzer test the minute you get back." Noting his smug expression, she added, "And you'd better not smell like toothpaste or breath mints, either. I mean it. No nibbling before lunch."

The smirk fell, replaced by disgust. "You're

cruel, dollface."

"I raised a pair of mischievous twins," she reminded him, "who are now manipulative teenagers. Along with their new stepsister, they can think of far more stunts than you, my friend."

"And I thought Dragon Lady was tough." He muttered the rare reference to his deceased mother as he trudged out of the room, his steps markedly heavier than they had been moments before.

Watching their interaction with amusement, Lucy shook her head. "Is he child, or grown man?"

"Sometimes I wonder," Madison admitted on a sigh. At least he was out of the room, and they could have a decent conversation. "Tell me more about your problems with *Barbour*."

"You remember competition."

Madison's mouth curled downward. "I remember. I never thought it was fair, making you compete with the other growers for better pay. So much of the outcome was out of your control."

"For sure," Lucy agreed vehemently. "When they built new complex in Crockett, even worse. We against brand-new houses."

"That hardly seems fair," Madison frowned.

"You telling me! Not fair! So, they say we need upgrade, make our old houses good as new."

"At whose expense?"

"Not theirs, for sure! All on us. And the list get longer every day. Cost go up. We just spend fifty thousand dollars on new computers. They say not good enough. Now they want another hundred thousand for something else. Neighbor had to spend two times that."

"That hardly seems fair. How can you pay for something like that?"

"Borrow more from bank, only way. One grower said no, so they said no more birds. Jerked contract, just like that."

"What do you mean by jerked contract?"

Lucy made a motion with her arm, imitating ripping the papers from Madison's hands and tossing them over her shoulder. "Make contract zero. Go away, just like that!"

"Can they do that?"

"That's why we want to hire you. You tell us!"

Madison looked down at the contract in her hands. "I'm no lawyer, Lucy." She forgot her best efforts to conduct this meeting in a professional tone. Since their first encounter over two years ago, Lucy made it her mission to feed Madison's family on a random schedule. She often dropped off a spur-of-the-moment dinner for the hungry crew, knowing Blake was especially fond of her fried rice.

Then again, the teenager was fond of anything that didn't eat him first.

"I think this is way beyond my area of expertise," Madison continued, shaking her head.

"But you our only hope," the other woman said. The genuine tears in her eyes tugged at Madison's heart. "Look at last sentence on last page. We signed, no sue company. Only way we could get deal. Hands tied. But maybe you could fight war for us."

"I—I don't know about that. Do I have your

permission to show this to an attorney I know and trust?"

"Sure. All we ask is chance. Meet with us. Hear our side before decide."

"I suppose I could do that," she agreed slowly.

"We have group of nine grower, want to come. You name time and place, we be there."

"I'll need to consult with Derron about my schedule." She didn't bother to add that she also wanted to discuss it with Brash. She didn't need his permission to take on new clients, but she did appreciate his support. "Can I get back in touch with you? It may be tomorrow before I can make arrangements."

"I offer my house to meet."

"That's very kind of you. Is any day best for you?"

"The sooner, the better."

"I'll do my best," Madison promised.

"I know this. So do the others." Lucy stood and turned toward the door but not before handing Madison another envelope.

"What's this?" she asked.

"Holding money. We pitch in to show you how important this is."

"I need to read over the contract, consult with the attorney I mentioned, and hear your stories before I agree to take you on as clients. I can't take this," Madison protested.

Lucy refused the proffered envelope. "Holding money," she insisted. "Meeting with us take up your time. We pay our fair share. Half now, other half when you say yes."

Madison couldn't help but smile. "You seem

awfully sure I'll say yes."

"You good woman. Fair. You and your husband. You'll do what is right, just like first time."

The first time, Lucy had come to her as a desperate mother, eager to prove her son's innocence when he was arrested for the murder of Ronny Gleason. The chicken grower had the distinction of not only being Madison's first real client, but also the first dead body she discovered. (Sadly, there had been others.) Lucy had come to her with an envelope full of cash and tears in her eyes, begging for help.

Madison made it clear she was no private investigator, but as a desperate mother herself—newly widowed, with two teenagers to care for, debt hanging over her head, and no real means of support—she had taken the case. Even though it put her own survival at risk, she had proved that Don Nguyen was innocent.

"I can't promise the same results this time, Lucy. It's simply too soon to say, and it may be completely out of my hands."

"No matter. You agree to try, and that's all we ask. You earn the money."

With a defeated sigh, Madison made one last stab at refusal. "I'd feel so much better if you took this..."

"So would we," Lucy insisted. "You keep."

After saying goodbye and thanking her once again for the surprise lunch, Madison carried both envelopes to her desk and sat down for a closer look. The contract seemed relatively simple, even for all its lawyer speak. The growers agreed to run the company programs and make the welfare of the birds their utmost concern, while the company agreed to compensate them accordingly. And just as Lucy said, the final article clearly stated that growers were expressly prohibited from suing *Barbour Foods* or any of their employees.

Madison's initial assessment wasn't good. From what she could see, the growers were at the mercy of *Barbour Foods*, with little recourse of their own to fight back.

Not that she was in any way qualified to make such an assessment, she reminded herself, she needed to consult with her friend and former client Shawn Bryant. He would be better suited to tell her what the contract said once the legalese was stripped away. She looked up his number and dialed, hoping he could squeeze her in later in the day.

While she waited, she pulled the money from the envelope, afraid she might find as much as four thousand dollars or more inside. Last time, Lucy ignored her very modest hourly rate and insisted on paying her one thousand dollars. Given that nine growers wanted her help, and Lucy had said 'half now, half later,' Madison wouldn't have been surprised to find $4500 inside.

She didn't find that amount inside.

Madison gasped when she found twice that much inside, all in cash. There were denominations in all sizes. Some bills were crinkled and worn, others crisp and new. Some were quite old, obviously stashed away during earlier mints. Madison couldn't help but feel she was staring at someone's hidden "mad money," or perhaps their coffee-can savings, tucked away a little at a time over the years. Simply holding the money made her feel inexplicably guilty.

"Lucy, Lucy, Lucy," she lamented. "*Half?* Do you think my rates doubled? And do you really think I'd accept nine thousand dollars for what is most likely an un-winnable objective? I wouldn't even feel right taking half that."

She was still shaking her head when the secretary at *Lone Star Law* answered her call and promptly placed her on hold for Shawn Bryant.

3

So much for fried rice and egg rolls. To Madison's delight, the attorney was able to meet with her over lunch. The irony of meeting at *New Beginnings* wasn't lost on either of them.

"You've done well for yourself, Madison," the man said. "Not so very long ago, we sat here and brokered a deal for your services. This very table was your so-called 'office.' Now you have that amazing space at the Big House."

"You know I can't take credit for that," she admitted ruefully. "Granny Bert sold me a drafty, old mansion for a song and then conned a national television show to remodel it on air. Some days, I feel so undeserving."

"Nonsense," he said, brushing away her admission. "Success is most often about being at the right place at the right time. Things may have fallen in place easily enough, but it took hard work and dedication to make your business successful. In this day and age, launching a business is hard enough, especially a temporary service in a small town. Don't belittle your achievement."

"Thanks in part to people like you, who were willing to give me a chance." She held her iced tea glass up in toast.

"So, are you taking my advice and incorporating?" he asked with a hopeful smile.

"No. Although I have considered it," she assured him. She reached into her briefcase and pulled out a file. "Actually, I'm hoping you can look over a contract and tell me if there's any wiggle room for my potential new client, or if this contract is as iron clad as it appears."

Slipping on his reading glasses, Shawn took one look at the names at the top and gave her a discouraging look. "I'll see if this one is any different from the dozen others I've looked at, but I don't hold much hope. Basically, *Barbour Foods* has worded the entire document in a way that leaves very little recourse for its contract growers. You either do it their way, or you're out."

"But that's not fair!"

"Maybe not, but the growers signed willingly."

"Only because if they don't, they won't be allowed to grow birds for the company."

"Exactly. *Barbour Foods* takes the position that they own the chickens and know what's best for them. Basically, all they're doing is paying the grower to take care of their animals for a set period. The grower agrees to follow their programs, their recommendations, use the equipment they approve, make the updates they say are necessary, etc., etc. If they don't, growers are in breach of the contract and subject to termination."

"But this is a fifteen-year contract, saying they agree to bring the grower a set number of batches per year. Doesn't that account for anything? According to my client, they can jerk a contract at will."

The lawyer shifted in his seat. "Yes, and no."

The waitress arrived with their meal, forcing Madison to wait for clarification to his ambiguous answer.

"What does that even mean?" she asked, digging into her taco salad. "Yes, but also no?"

"In some instances, the company does have the right to immediately sever the contract. Cases of bodily harm, for instance, or engaging in illegal practices, like violating environmental standards set by the EPA. Those are extreme cases and not the norm, but they do happen. The more likely scenario is that the grower is issued several warnings and given the chance to take corrective action. If they fail to do so to *Barbour's* satisfaction, the company has the right to end their alliance with the grower. Most people refer to that as 'jerking their contract,' but it has to be done through a legal chain of events."

"Even if the chain has a few weak links?"

"Even the flimsiest of links can hold up in a court of law," Shawn Bryant pointed out. "Much of it has to do with the precise wording and how vaguely or literally the words are interpreted. A company as large and powerful as *Barbour* pays big bucks to get the words right."

"That's hardly fair to the grower," Madison protested. "From what I understand, they're demanding that the growers update their farms at their own expense, just to stay in business."

"You'll find the precise wording for that in Section D, I believe it is. 'All equipment shall be kept in working order and compliant with the current company standards,' or some such phrase. It never addresses how often the company can change their standards or demand compliance. Technically, they could change their mind every week, and the grower would have to comply."

"Obviously, this isn't the first time you've looked at the contracts."

"I've warned more than one potential grower about the vagueness of the wording, but not a single one has heeded my advice. All they see are the dollar signs and the so-called 'guaranteed income' for fifteen years. Make no mistake, the growers are well compensated for their participation. Theoretically, they should put aside a portion of their income for routine upgrades and upkeep, but few people practice such discipline. They're too busy buying new vehicles and building new homes and enjoying their newfound wealth to save up for a rainy day. But mark my words," the attorney said, waving his fork for emphasis. "Even with a contract for an umbrella, the rain always comes."

"But don't the equipment and barns belong to the grower? Can't they just say, 'this is what I have; take it or leave it?'"

Shawn nodded his head. "They can. But *Barbour* will leave it, every single time. There's always someone else willing to take their place. Until and unless enough growers take a stand against them, losing a few farms here and there won't make a dent in *Barbour's* overall program. They are a huge company. They have office complexes bigger than even the largest chicken farms."

Madison thought about Ronny Gleason's old farm, which now belonged to Don Nguyen. There were six five-hundred-foot commercial barns, or 'houses' as they called them, along with the assorted outbuildings, well sheds, incinerators and such required to keep even a small six-house farm running. Several farms had twenty or more houses on them, each house containing about twenty-five thousand chickens inside.

"And don't forget most growers have a mortgage on the farm," the attorney continued. "The banks align them with the contract, so that about the time the loan is paid off, the contract has come to an end. At that point, growers finally have control of their destiny, but most find that there's little use for those long, old buildings. A few find a way to re-purpose them, but most simply sell to a new buyer. At which time new updates are required, and the cycle starts over again."

"I understand that. Banks won't shell out that kind of money—"

"Which can be several million, depending on the size of the farm," Shawn interjected.

Her eyes widened at the numbers, but Madison continued smoothly, "—without a contract. And I understand why there's no contract without updated equipment. It's starting the cycle over mid-way into the contract that I don't understand. That just doesn't make sense to me."

"Maybe not, but it makes sense to *Barbour*, and they're the ones pulling the strings."

Madison wrinkled her nose, clearly not liking the outcome of their conversation. She had known it wouldn't be good news, but she didn't realize how helpless the situation would appear.

Before she could ask more questions, her cell phone rang. She ignored it at first, until Shawn urged her to answer. As a businessman himself, he overlooked the breech of etiquette.

"Madison?" A voice crackled from the other end of the line. "This is your Aunt Lerlene. I think you need to come down to the Five and Dime. Bertha's down here, but she's not making a lick of sense. I think something's wrong with her."

Madison was already pushing back from the table. "Something's wrong with Granny Bert? What is it?"

"I'm not sure, but she's talking even crazier than usual. Can't seem to get her thoughts straight. She thought she needed to get home to cook dinner for your grandfather."

"But Grandpa Joe's been dead for almost ten years!"

"I know that. You know that. But for a few minutes there, Bertha didn't. I've got her lying down in the break room, but I think you should come down here. She may need to see a doctor."

"I'll be right there." She hung up the phone and stood in a single move. "I'm sorry," she told her companion, "but I have to go."

"You don't have to say another word," the

attorney assured her. He gathered her briefcase and helped her into her coat. "I hope Granny Bert is okay. Is there anything I can do to help? Do I need to drive you somewhere?"

"No, thank you. She's at her brother's store downtown and not feeling well." In her haste, Madison almost forgot to cover the check. She turned back to the table to ask a favor. "There is one thing you can do for me."

"Name it."

"Tell Genny to put this on my tab, and I'll settle with her later. Let her know I'm headed over to Uncle Jubal's to check on Granny Bert."

"I'll let her know, but lunch is on me."

"Absolutely not. I invited you."

"This is no time to argue. Go check on your grandmother. You know everyone in town loves her like she's their own granny. Make sure our favorite matriarch is okay."

The smile faltered on Madison's face. "Thank you for understanding. Tell Genny I'll call when I know something."

Madison drove from *New Beginnings'* parking lot in Naomi, over the railroad track, and crossed into Juliet proper. Together, the two towns comprised the community known as The Sisters. Even then, the duo barely scraped two thousand residents on the census. The 'downtown' area Madison referred to was exactly four blocks of storefronts, many of them now vacant and forlorn.

The entire process took a mere three minutes. In half that time, Madison was out of the car and rushing through the aisles of *Hamilton's Five and Dime Variety Store,* headed for the back room.

Her great-aunt put up a warning finger as Madison entered. "She's resting now," Lerlene Hamilton said in a whisper.

Madison ran a concerned eye over the eighty-two-year-old woman stretched out in the nearby recliner. The footrest was up, offering a clear view of her puffy ankles, uncharacteristically swollen to twice their normal size. Her face looked fuller than usual, too, even while her cheeks appeared to sink in, their color flushed upon an otherwise ashen face.

"Is she running a fever?" Madison whispered back.

"I think so. She feels mighty warm to the touch."

As she watched her grandmother sleeping, Madison's heart sank down to her toes. She didn't remember ever seeing Granny Bert look so old and feeble. She was normally full of life and energy—or, in Bertha Cessna's own words, 'piss and vinegar.' Right now, however, the older woman looked every bit her age. Her skin was wrinkled and marked with age spots and scars. Her normally neat hair was mussed and looked whiter than usual, even against her pale skin.

Not for the first time, it occurred to Madison that time with her grandmother was limited. If they were lucky, it could be another ten years yet, but life was never certain. Becoming a widow herself at the age of thirty-nine had taught her that.

"What's she doing?" Madison asked in surprise. In her sleep, Granny Bert reached her arms upward, her fingers working an invisible object.

"Earlier, she thought she was shelling peas. Looks like she's hanging out the wash now," said Aunt Lerlene.

After watching for a few minutes, Madison was prone to agree. With the ease of an old, familiar routine, her grandmother reached for an imaginary garment, shook the wrinkles out, and reached upward to hang the piece on the clothesline. She even took an invisible wooden clothespin from her mouth to secure her dream laundry in place. As she repeated the process a third and fourth time, Madison motioned for her aunt to follow her a few feet away.

"What do think is wrong with her? Was she complaining of anything hurting?" she wanted to know.

"Not that I recall. She came down about an hour ago to pick up a few odds and ends. I thought it was odd when she and Jubal squabbled over the price of something, but you know how the two of them fight like the brother and sister that they are. She accused him of price gouging and going up on prices, but the fact is, on the particular item, he had actually lowered the price."

Madison arced a brow in surprise. Her uncle was known to be a penny pincher, even though he expected his customers to pay a fair (and often inflated) price. Despite the name painted on the sign outside, there was nothing in the store that cost a dime or less.

Seeing her expression, Aunt Lerlene sighed with empathy. "I know. I tell him he can't take it with him, but he says he'll die trying to find a way. Anyway, it wasn't like Bertha to carry on like that, so I finally persuaded her to come back here and have a cup of coffee with me. She said something about laying off the caffeine—"

"Since when?" Madison broke in. "She drinks more coffee than Brash does, and I swear his blood is half-caff!"

"Said she was having some trouble with her bladder."

Madison looked back at her grandmother, still 'hanging out the wash' in her sleep. "Yes, I see how puffy she is. I wonder if she has a UTI."

"Could be. Jubal had one last year, and it made him powerful confused. That might explain what Bertha did next."

Almost afraid to ask, Madison did so anyway. "What did she do?"

"Started talking about Joe like he was still with us. Said she couldn't stay long. Had to get back and start dinner. Carried on about picking a mess of yellow squash from her garden, even though it's smack dab in the middle of winter." Her great-aunt sniffed with disbelief, but her concern seemed misplaced. "Ain't no crook-neck squash growing at this time of year."

"Is that all she said?"

"No. Then she started talking about avocados and dead bodies, before she switched back to making Joe's dinner. My sister-in-law is known to spin a tall tale or two, but even I couldn't keep up with the nonsense she was spewing."

Madison nodded in understanding. "She doesn't like to admit it, but that fiasco last summer really shook her up. It's not every day someone stuffs a dead body into your spare refrigerator. She acted like it wasn't anything she hadn't seen before, but I notice she still avoids going into the garage."

"But *you* were the one to find the body," her aunt needlessly reminded Madison of the gruesome fact, as if she could ever forget. "And it was Jubal's squash they threw out to accommodate the corpse! She didn't have to take it so personally." She threw her arms up in exasperation.

Madison had to remind herself that Aunt Lerlene and Granny Bert were roughly the same age, and neither were as poised and tactful as they once were. Granny Bert claimed such unveiled candor was an intangible right a person gained after a certain age, but Madison had trouble remembering her any other way.

"Did you call Aunt Trudy or Aunt Betsey?"

"Yes, but neither answered. So, I called you."

"I'm glad you did," Madison said, touching her arm in gratitude.

Bertha and Joe Cessna had been blessed with four sons, but only two still lived in or around The Sisters. While there were plenty of other helping hands to assist the independent matriarch when she needed it, Madison had stepped up to be one of her primary contacts. In many ways, she was more like a daughter to Bertha Cessna than a granddaughter. Granny Bert had taken Madison in and given her a home as a teenager and then again as a young widow, offering a solid foundation whenever she stood on shifting sands. Being there for her grandmother was the least she could do in return.

"I wonder if Dr. Seldon is in today," Madison murmured, thumbing through her phone contacts.

"Doubt it. It's Wednesday."

One of the drawbacks to living in a small town was the lack of available medical resources. Her best option was to take Granny Bert to Urgent Care or an emergency department in College Station, the nearest city. Even that was almost an hour away.

"I have a blood pressure cuff, if you want to check her numbers," Aunt Lerlene offered. "If I have to, I'll get a thermometer off the shelf. Just don't tell your Uncle Scrooge."

Madison gathered her supplies before gently waking Granny Bert. She called to her several times before rousing her.

"Maddy? Is that you? What are you doing here?" Granny Bert struggled to lift her head, then gave up in defeat and lay back against the headrest. "Are the little ones with you?"

Her brow gathered in concern, Madison stepped closer to her grandmother and spoke clearly. "If you mean Bethani and Blake, they're in school. With Megan."

"Megan?"

"Brash's daughter. These days, I feel like I have

triplets, not just twins."

The older woman still looked confused. "Brash? Brash deCordova, the football star?"

"He's the chief of police now, Granny. Remember? And he's my husband."

"In your daydreams!" the elderly woman snorted.

A smile touched Madison's lips. She could identify with the sentiment. She often felt as if she were living out a fairytale, marrying her high school crush after all these years.

"Brash and I were married last March, Granny. You remember. We had a small, intimate wedding down by the riverbanks, and then a big party afterward."

"A wildflower wedding," her grandmother murmured, as if it were all a vague dream.

"That's right." *Never mind the killer reception that followed,* she added to herself. *Just another dead body in a long list of many I've encountered over the past two years.* Blake jokingly called her a dead body magnet, but she considered it more of a curse.

"For a minute there, I thought you were still married to that good-for-nothing ex-husband of yours."

Madison's concern deepened, along with a new stab of pain. Not only was Granny Bert confused, she was being unusually rude. The elder woman always spoke what was on her mind, pleasant or not, but there was an unfamiliar edge to her blunt remark. Madison knew she had never been fond of Gray, but she had never been so openly hostile.

"Granny, I didn't divorce Gray. He died in an

automobile accident. That's why the twins and I moved back here to The Sisters."

"I remember. He left you broke and homeless, and on the verge of scandal. Even his hoity-toity mama couldn't hide what he had done, carrying on with his secretary and taking all that money."

Madison sucked in a sharp breath. What Granny Bert said may have been true, but in her right mind, she would have never said any of this aloud to Madison. Particularly not in front of Aunt Lerlene.

She glanced over her shoulder, relieved to see that her aunt had stepped away to find a thermometer. At least for now, she hadn't heard Granny Bert's outburst, but who knew what other secrets had slipped from her lips?

"Let's not talk about Gray, all right? And Annette and I have finally made peace. She's smitten with Brash and Megan and has accepted them into the family, so all is good."

"Of course she's smitten with that hunk of a man you have. Your grandfather likes him, too. He always says the deCordovas are good people."

Unsure of how to respond, Madison changed the subject. "How are you feeling? Aunt Lerlene said you were feeling poorly and turned down her offer of coffee. That doesn't sound like you. Is your stomach bothering you?"

Her wrinkled hands moved to her abdomen. She rubbed the area in a large, circular motion, tangling her clothes unmercifully.

"Does something hurt, Granny?"

With a slight moan, she admitted, "Little bit."

"I want to take your blood pressure, and Aunt

Lerlene's bringing a thermometer so we can take your temperature."

"You're not sticking it up my backside!" she said obstinately.

"No, of course not. Just relax and let me take care of you. The same way you've always taken care of me through the years."

"Lord knows that flighty mama of yours never would," her grandmother mumbled. Another thing that might be true but never mentioned when she was lucid.

By the time Madison saw her vitals and realized how weak and short of breath her grandmother was, she knew Granny Bert was truly sick. She sent messages to Brash and her aunts and let the kids know she might not be home when they got in from school. With Aunt Lerlene's help, she loaded Granny Bert into the car and left for College Station, promising to update the family when she knew anything. She had no doubt her great-aunt would contact the entire Hamilton/Cessna clan, as well as half the community.

"Hang on, Granny Bert. I'll get us there as quickly as I can."

"Tell Joe I might be late getting his supper on the table," she apologized weakly.

"He'll understand, Granny," she assured her softly, pressing her foot more firmly on the gas pedal.

A serene smile touched her face. "He's a good man, my Joe. Just like your Brash."

A moment later, a tear trickled down the same flushed, wrinkled cheek. Reality bumped into her fragmented memories, making the pain fresh and all the more poignant. "Lord, how I miss that man."

There were no cars coming as Madison pulled onto the highway. Ignoring the posted speed limit signs, she put the pedal down and sped toward the hospital.

4

"Genny, darlin'? You in here?" Cutter Montgomery rapped on the office door, looking for his wife after the lunch rush was over at *New Beginnings.*

"It's open," she called out, her voice muffled.

He walked in to see her going through a stack of papers, some of which she held between her teeth to sort them into orderly piles.

"Did your filing cabinet explode?" he asked warily.

"Something like that. Trenessa wanted me to give her more responsibilities, so I put her in charge of accounts payable. The problem is, she's terrible at filing. She keeps everything in a box and only sorts through it at the end of the month. So now, I'm doing her job for her, just so she can prove to me how responsible she is." The blonde shook her head in obvious disgust. "Not. Working."

"Lucky for you, I came to take you away from all this," her handsome husband announced with one of his sexiest smiles.

"Nice thought, but no way. I'm swamped." Genny sniffed the air. "I smell smoke. Did you have a call today?"

"A controlled burn that got out of control," the volunteer fireman replied. He dropped a kiss onto her lips before sinking into the chair across from her cluttered desk. "Can I help?"

"I don't even know where to start."

"A?" he suggested. "Work your way to Z?"

"Fine, Mr. Smartypants. Sort these."

"While I sort, I'll tell you my news. But first... What are your plans for next week?"

Genny consulted the internal calendar in her head, even though it sat in physical form in front of her. "I have a cake to make before Saturday, and a catering job week after next. Other than the matter of our first anniversary, I guess I don't have anything much planned. Getting married on Valentine's Day sort of took care of my plans for an annual community Valentine's party."

"Hey, we can have a party. We just aren't inviting anyone else to be part of it." His eyes twinkled with mischief. "When it comes to my wife, I don't share."

"Then we're on the same page. Private party," she said, her dimples appearing in her cheeks.

Cutter wagged his eyebrows suggestively before dropping his gaze to the stack of papers in his hands. He shuffled through them, rearranged them to his liking, and handed them back. "All done."

"No way. You couldn't possibly be done."

"Look through them and prove me wrong."

Genny ruffled through the papers, amazed to

find them in perfect alphabetical order. "How did you do that so fast?" she asked suspiciously.

"I was highly motivated to get through. I have news I want to share."

She set the papers aside and awarded him her full attention. "I'm listening."

"How would you like to go away for an anniversary trip? Stay at a quaint little resort and spa, with nothing to do all week but rest and relax?"

"Sounds like heaven, but there's no way. I have a business to run."

"Not next week, you don't."

"Her filing system aside, Trenessa has turned out to be a wonderful manager, but she's not ready to run this place by herself. There's no way I could go away for a full week. I can barely manage two days off in a row. And closing down for the week is out of the question."

"I've already talked to the staff. They've all agreed to take an extra shift or two, so we can go on a second honeymoon."

"A second honeymoon? Where? How? Did you hit the lottery and forget to tell me?"

Cutter pulled her from her chair and into his arms. "I hit the lottery the day I married you. You're my one in a million, Genny darlin'."

Genny accepted his kiss before snuggling against his chest and muttering, "You're crazy."

"Crazy over you. Do you want to hear the details, or not?"

"Sure. Let's hear your impossible dream."

"Not as impossible as you think, Mrs. Smartypants." He turned the moniker back on her. "I have a new job, and it comes with perks."

"What are you talking about?"

"Have you ever heard of *Cherubdipity Inn & Spa*, over in Robertson County?"

"I don't think so. Although it does sound vaguely familiar... Oh, wait! It was featured on the Texas Bucket List a couple of weeks ago. It's a little boutique bed and breakfast/spa and resort, hidden away in the middle of nowhere."

"Yep, that's the one. They're in need of an extensive project by an experienced welder and who, I ask, is the best welder in the Brazos Valley?" he preened in jest, knowing fully well how she would answer.

Genny played along with exaggerated batting of her eyes. "Why, you are, my modest and humble husband."

"Exactly. And I promised to give them priority status if I could bring my beautiful bride along for what promises to be at least a four- or five-day job. They threw in an all-expense-paid visit for a full week. Best room in the house."

Her jaw actually dropped. "You're kidding, right? I've heard that place is almost impossible to get into!"

"You forget. I'm a master negotiator."

"Oh, you are, are you?" she chuckled.

Cutter nuzzled his face against her neck. "I convinced you to marry me, didn't I?"

"As I recall, I was the one who made the actual proposal."

"You *think* you proposed. It was all part of my master plan. A simple negotiation on my part, making you think you couldn't live without me."

"I couldn't," Genny admitted shamelessly. "That week without you was the most miserable of my life. I thought I had lost you forever."

"I wasn't going anywhere, sweet darlin'. I was giving you time to come to your senses and realize our age difference was all in your head, not in my heart."

"I'll always be eight years older than you, Cutter. That means I'll age eight years faster than you. Women don't always age as well as men, you know."

Despite his best assurances, old insecurities reared their ugly head. Cutter had been the most sought-after and eligible bachelor in the entire county. Once *Home Again* hit national television, he received love letters and propositions from all over the country. One woman from Australia had even offered him a one-way ticket to come to her. How was a slightly over-weight, almost-middle-aged woman supposed to compete with the hot, young bodies flaunting themselves at him? Even with a ring on his finger, he turned down advances on a regular basis.

"I see it as eight years I missed out on, not knowing you from the very first," he said against her lips.

She scowled. "We've known each other three years," she reminded him.

"Doesn't matter. We have the rest of our lives together. But we're getting woefully off track. We were talking about my brilliant negotiating skills and the week I have planned for us. While I'm working during the day, you can read and get your nails done, or take long naps or long walks.

Whatever your heart desires," he promised. He moved to cup her face in his large, work-roughened hands. "But the nights," he said, his voice dipping to a sensual purr, "are for what my heart desires. And that's you, Genesis Baker Montgomery. Only you. Now and forever."

Their kiss heated until Cutter threatened to clear her desk in a single sweep of his hand and have his way with her. As tempting as it sounded, Genny was saved from deciding when her phone rang.

"Ignore it," Cutter growled.

"It might be important," she protested.

"*This* is important. Today might be the day we make a baby."

They had been trying almost since the first day they were married. Both wanted a houseful of children but so far, none of their efforts had been successful. It wasn't from lack of trying.

The reminder was like a splash of cold water on Genny's fire. "It won't be," she muttered, pulling away. "I started my period this morning."

"I'm sorry, darlin'," he said sincerely, refusing to release her. A mischievous smile replaced his down-curled lips. "But you know what this means." He wiggled his brows again. "Next week will be prime time."

"You're incorrigible," she scoffed, pushing on his shoulder to free herself.

"I'm insatiable," he corrected. "I can't get enough of my beautiful wife."

The phone had stopped ringing, only to start again. With a sigh, Cutter dropped his arms and told her to answer.

"Madison? What's wrong?" Genny asked the moment she heard her friend's strained voice. "How's Granny Bert? Shawn told me you might take her to the hospital."

"We're headed there now. She's talking out of her head, and her temp is getting higher every time I take it. Her blood pressure is all over the place. I'm no doctor, but I know that's not good."

"Do I need to meet you there?"

"No. We're headed to *Texas General* in College Station, but I can't reach Brash. He's in court and left his phone at the office for some sort of upgrade. Can you keep trying to get word to him?"

"Of course. Anything else I can do? You know Granny Bert is like my own grandmother."

"And she considers you one of her grandchildren. Let me get her to the ER, find out what the doctor says, and we'll go from there."

"Sounds like a plan."

As she hung up, Cutter was back at her side. "What's wrong with Granny Bert? Do I need to call the ambulance?"

"No, Maddy is taking her by car. We won't know anything until they get to the ER."

He saw the worry in his wife's blue eyes. "I don't know what it is, but Granny Bert is tough. She'll get through this, Genny darlin'."

"I know," she lied, but her smile looked anything but confident. After a moment of silence, Genny sniffed and offered him a genuine smile. "You know what? Assuming Granny Bert is fine, I think a week away with my adoring and handsome husband is exactly what I need. Nothing more strenuous to do than pick up my ereader and a glass of wine."

"Oh, we'll do something more strenuous than that, Mrs. Montgomery," he promised wickedly. "But you'll have the whole day to recuperate." He sealed his promise with a kiss. "So?" he asked, raising his dark blond head from hers. "Shall I call them back and accept the job?"

"Absolutely. This will be the perfect anniversary present for both of us."

"The first of many, Genny darlin'. The first of many."

5

An hour and a half later, Granny Bert and Madison were inside the emergency department at *Texas General Hospital*, waiting to hear from the doctor after her initial assessment. With a temperature of 101.8 and climbing, Granny Bert was feverish and talking out of her head.

Her trips down memory lane and her harsh criticisms had given way to fantasy. Now she saw quilt patterns on the ceiling, thought she was driving along the Texas coast in her motor home, and tried humming along to a tune that only played in her head. Occasionally, she would moan and cry out in pain but insisted that nothing hurt, except for a moment when she thought she was in a body cast. She fought to be free of the confinement, twisting her monitor wires and hospital gown into a mad tangle. Madison had to summon the nurse for help.

"May I help you?" the petite nurse asked, pushing aside the curtain. She immediately saw the problem and hurried forward, talking to her elderly patient in a calm but firm voice.

"Take it easy, Mrs. Cessna. These wires are delicate pieces of machinery and provide us with all sorts of important information. You don't want to send us the wrong signals, do you? We need your help to keep it all straight."

"I'm trying to get this dad-blame contraption off me!"

"The heart monitor?" the nurse asked. Her name tag identified her as Head Nurse Laurel Benson.

"No, this body cast! Fools thought I broke half my bones on that landing, but I came in smooth as you please. This wasn't my first time to jump out of an airplane, you know. I opened my parachute right as planned, but someone put all these wires in my way. Now they have me wrapped up like a mummy, when there's nothing wrong with me."

The brunette sent a sly wink toward Madison and took charge. "Here. I think I see what the problem is," she said. "Give me a minute, and I think I can get you out of the cast. Just rest your hands here and let me do something. You may want to close your eyes, so the debris doesn't get in them." After untangling the wires, she made a clinking sound with her tongue, tapped the bed rail a few times with her pen, and threw in a few convincing murmurs of 'almost got it,' 'hmm,' and 'nearly there,' before pronouncing her free. "All done! You can open your eyes now. You're free of the body cast."

"Finally!" the older woman huffed. "But that tuckered me all out. I think I'll take a little nap now."

"I think that's a very good idea." The words were hardly out of the nurse's mouth before Granny Bert was snoring softly.

"Nicely done," Madison commented. "I'm her granddaughter Madison deCordova."

The nurse snapped her fingers as recognition dawned. "That's where I know you from! You were on that television show, *Home Again,* where they remodeled that gorgeous old mansion you live in. I'm Laurel. Your grandmother was in here back in the fall, with one of her friends. Those two made quite the impression."

"If it was her and Wanda Shanks, I'm sure they did." Madison couldn't help but wince at the possible troubles those two could stir up.

"I do remember they kept us on our toes," the nurse said diplomatically.

Madison nibbled her lower lip in thought. "I suppose I should call Miss Wanda and tell her what's happening, but I don't know anything yet. Do you have any idea when the doctor will be back in?"

"She's ordered several tests. We're running the standard blood tests and urine samples, plus the doctor ordered a CT scan and an ultrasound of her abdomen. Someone should be in shortly to take her for the scan."

"Are you thinking it's a UTI?"

"Most likely, that's part of it, but sometimes when it's left unchecked, it can develop into something more. It's too soon to speculate at this point. Let's get the test results before we make a diagnosis, shall we?"

"She just seems so confused..."

"Quite common with a UTI," the nurse assured her. "We often see that in our elderly patients. The fact that she's resting comfortably and isn't sick to her stomach is encouraging."

Madison smiled weakly, knowing it took time to run the proper tests and make a correct diagnosis.

"Can I get you anything while you wait?" the kind nurse offered. "There's a vending machine in the waiting room, but I can bring you coffee and water, or juice. I may even scrounge up some Jello or peanut butter crackers, if you like."

"A bottle of water will be fine but thank you."

"I'll be back in a bit with the water," Laurel said. "I need to check with another patient before that, but if the techs come for her before I return, feel free to wait in here. They'll bring her back to the same room when they're done."

Madison sent out several texts while her grandmother slept. Granny Bert went back to doing her laundry and shelling peas, and occasionally she quoted laws and regulations from her years as justice of the peace. She never mentioned her late husband again, but more than once, she scolded her young sons for running across her clean floors or eating raw cookie dough before she got it in the oven. She even had a one-sided argument with Dolly Mac Crowder, her long-time nemesis since high school. Before she became too agitated, a technician came in to take her for x-rays and a scan.

Settling her long form into the molded plastic chair, Madison closed her eyes and took a moment to relax. Her day had been a blur of activity and information overload, and it was still early afternoon. She needed a few minutes to decompress.

The wall made an unforgiving pillow. Madison spotted a towel folded on the nearby metal bed tray, so she grabbed it, curled it into a roll, and stuffed it behind her head.

That was somewhat better but still not comfortable. After shifting into various positions, she found a semi-adequate pose by placing the towel behind her neck. She snuggled down for a moment of peace, trying to tune out the sounds around her. The curtained cubicles didn't provide much privacy, nor noise distraction.

She jumped involuntarily when something thumped against the wall behind her, followed by an angry hiss. "What were you thinking?"

The voice that answered sounded young and tearful. Madison could almost imagine one of her own daughters on the other side of the wall. "I wasn't, okay?" the girl all but whined. "I wasn't thinking!"

"Obviously! Do you realize you could have messed everything up?"

"I am well aware of that. You don't have to keep reminding me."

Madison imagined the girl was jutting her chin out about now, her jaw setting in a stubborn scowl. That's how Bethani and Megan would have done it, at any rate.

Still, the girl sounded genuinely sorry for whatever it was she had done. With a stab of empathy for the unseen teen, Madison felt guilty for overhearing such an intimate argument. She squeezed her eyes shut and tried tuning the conversation out.

No use. She could still hear the voices.

"You know you need that money for your future. This may be your only chance to go to college and make something of yourself."

"So you keep telling me."

The angry voice softened. "You know I only want what's best for you. You have so much potential. You don't need to throw your life away when you have your entire future ahead of you."

Madison rearranged the towel behind her neck, trying to find a more comfortable position. She tried hard not to listen to the conversation taking place in the adjacent room, but the next words caught her attention. In spite of herself, she strained to hear more.

"I still don't understand why having a baby is considered throwing my life away!"

Madison heard the girl spit out the angry words.

The older woman spoke in an even, no-nonsense voice. "You're young. Uneducated. You have no viable means of support for yourself or your child. Giving your baby up for adoption is the responsible thing to do. You know this. We've talked about it numerous times."

"But this is *my* baby!" Madison could hear the pain in the girl's cry. "It should be *my* decision!"

"No one forced you to sign those papers," the other woman reminded her coldly, "or to take the money."

Madison heard a sob from the other side of the wall. "But it feels like I'm selling my baby," the girl said brokenly.

It took great restraint to keep from storming into the next room and demanding an explanation. Madison knew it was none of her business, but she also knew that selling babies wasn't only illegal but highly immoral. Completely reprehensible. And apparently not something the young mother was doing entirely by choice.

"You're doing no such thing!"

She couldn't hear what else the woman said, her voice now hushed but urgent. Madison found herself already on her feet, ready to move toward the curtained opening, when the fabric suddenly pushed aside. The tech had returned with Granny Bert.

"Don't know where you got your license to drive one of these beds," her grandmother grumbled in a cantankerous mood. "Must have been at Wal-Mart, because you clearly don't know what you're doing."

"I'm sorry, Mrs. Cessna," the man said contritely. "These are bulkier than they look."

"I felt like I was riding my motorcycle down the railroad track," she snorted. "I probably have bruises all up and down my body."

Madison shot the tech an apologetic look. "But just think of the stories you'll have to tell your friends," Madison interjected, stepping up to her grandmother's side. She tried distracting their grumpy patient while the tech set the bed and all its paraphernalia back in place. "You'll have a fine tale for Miss Sybil and Miss Wanda."

The thought brightened her somewhat. "And Arlene Kopetsky," she snorted. "She keeps whining about the ordeal she had with her leg. Simple break, if you ask me, but not according to her! It was the worst orthopedic surgery known to mankind. She milked that injury for all it was worth. Not that her no-account, floozy of a daughter was any help. Look how *that* turned out!"

Madison would rather *not* recall the details of Lana Kopetsky's mental breakdown. Though the two of them had never been friends, it was tragic watching the other woman come unhinged, particularly when she was pregnant with her first child.

Her mind flitted to the conversation next door. Sometimes, adoption *was* the best option. Not just for the child, but for everyone involved. Rumor had it that before Lana was whisked away to a mental institute, she named her eighty-something-year-old mother as the legal guardian of her unborn child. Once the baby was born, Arlene Kopetsky realized she was unable to care for an infant and had put the baby up for adoption.

As for the baby's father... Madison shivered, blocking out thoughts of finding his dead body.

She deliberately concentrated on her grandmother, making sure she was as comfortable as possible. After a small squabble over the best position for her adjustable bed, Granny Bert drifted back to sleep. The least bit of talking stole her breath away and left her exhausted.

The doctor returned soon after that. Madison read through the thin smile on her face to see the underlying concern.

"It looks like your grandmother has a severe urinary tract infection. I don't see any hydronephrosis or kidney stones on the CT scan, but she's showing symptoms of pyelonephritis. I'd like to keep her overnight and see if we can find the source of her infection. We'll draw blood cultures and start intravenous antibiotics immediately. I think if we can get her fever down, she'll be much more comfortable."

Madison looked the doctor in the eye. "What aren't you saying?"

The doctor's hesitation was slight. "Especially in our older patients, it's easy for them to become septic. Once the infection gets into the blood stream, it spreads quickly and can go from bad to catastrophic in a matter of hours. It's very important that we find the right antibiotic to fight the right germ. In situations like this, every minute counts. I don't mean to alarm you, but your grandmother is a very sick woman. Sepsis is nothing to ignore."

"I—I understand."

"We're trying to get her into a room upstairs. You're welcome to stay with her if you like. There's a pull-out couch and a somewhat comfortable recliner in the room. We'll do everything we can to get her well and back home as quickly as possible."

"Thank you, Doctor. I appreciate your concern."

"It's what we do," the attractive doctor said with a genuine smile. "You have our best nurse at your disposal, so let Laurel know if you need anything. For now, sleep is the best medicine for your grandmother. She needs all the strength she can gather to fight this thing."

Long after the doctor left, Madison stood by Granny Bert's bedside, her hand resting lightly upon her wrinkled, feverish arm. She couldn't lose her grandmother. She couldn't begin to fathom a world without Bertha Cessna in it. The woman was bigger than life. Even Willie Nelson had written a song about her and her exploits with skydiving, motorcycles, and public office. Her outspoken candor was legendary, and her advice—though often not requested or even appreciated— was solid. She wasn't known for her flowery praise or gushy sentiment, but she was Madison's biggest cheerleader and the most influential person in her life.

"Brash," Madison whispered. Her husband of less than a year had quickly become her second anchor in the sea of life, alongside the woman in the bed. "I need you here with me."

As if sensing her words, her phone buzzed, flashing his name across the screen. She dropped back into the chair to take the call and talk in hushed tones, giving him a condensed version of the situation now that he was out of court and free to talk.

"I'll pack you a bag and bring it over," he promised. "I'll have one of your aunts gather some of Granny Bert's things and bring them, too."

"Be sure to bring a cell phone charger for both of us. Once she's more alert, I'm sure she'll be asking for her phone."

"Hard to rule her kingdom without one," Brash quipped. "You know your grandmother is the heartbeat of this community. What's that she says? 'If Bertha Cessna don't know it, it ain't worth knowing?'"

"Or so she claims." Madison chuckled wryly, but there was a catch in her laugh.

"It's going to be all right, sweetheart." Brash's voice was warm and reassuring, the deep tones willing her to believe.

"I certainly hope so."

"I love you, Maddy. I promise you; we'll get through this."

"I know. And I love you, too." As the curtain rustled and the nurse stepped back inside, she hurried to get off the phone. "The nurse just came back. I'll keep you posted. Love you. Bye."

Laurel smiled and nodded to the cell phone in her hand. "I didn't mean for you to rush on my account. I just came in to check on our girl."

"She seems to be resting comfortably. When she's awake, she's very irritable. More so than usual, at any rate."

The dark-haired nurse laughed. "I only know her from the reality TV show and our brief encounter last fall, but I have a feeling your grandmother is pretty outspoken. You know exactly where you stand with this little lady, a fact I happen to appreciate."

"You might not feel that way when her wrath is focused on you," Madison mused. "She raised me from the age of thirteen. There were times when I *did not* appreciate her strong and very vocal opinions."

"I can imagine!" They shared a laugh, and Madison immediately warmed to the friendly and personable nurse.

She only hoped all the staff at *Texas General* was as kind and gracious as the head nurse in the emergency department.

6

When Granny Bert's system didn't respond to the first rounds of antibiotics, the doctors called for another class of medication. With her grandmother showing moderate signs of improvement after the change, Madison breathed easier. Her Aunt Betsey relieved her on the second evening at the hospital, so on the way home from College Station, Madison called Lucy Nguyen and set up a meeting for the next week. She hoped by then, Granny Bert would be well on her way to recovery, and life would return to its normal brand of crazy.

'Crazy' was in full swing when she reached the Big House.

After their first baseball scrimmage of the season, Blake and a small group of players were in the media room, watching an amateur video of the game and critiquing each other's plays. The audio was at full blast, competing with music blaring from the stereo system and the raucous sound of seven teenage boys ribbing one another. Scattered across the end tables were three empty pizza boxes, empty soft drink cans, and the crinkled remains of a super-sized bag of candy.

Thank goodness for sound proofing! Madison thought, closing the door behind her to block out the racket.

She walked back into the kitchen and found Megan and Bethani in the middle of a rare screaming match.

"You *know* I like Jeff! We had an agreement. If one of us likes a boy, he's off limits to the other one!" Megan accused, eyes flashing angrily behind her stylish rhinestone frames.

"I can't help it if he sat down beside me!" Bethani defended herself. "What was I supposed to do? Move?"

"Yes! That's exactly what you should have done!" Megan stomped her foot. The animated movement sent her auburn hair flying in all directions. She glanced up and saw her stepmother. "Oh, hi, Mama Maddy. I hope Granny Bert's okay." Her tone was a complete three-sixty to the hurled accusations she flung at her sister.

Before Madison finished saying, "Yes, she's showing improvement," the teen took her smile as reassurance and assumed the crisis was over. She launched back into attack mode.

"Will you please tell your daughter to keep her hands to herself and to stop flinging her blond hair over her shoulder and sending the wrong signals to *my* crush? She knows I called him first!"

Bethani crossed her arms over her chest and jutted out her chin. "Would you please tell your stepdaughter that Jeff Adams is not a toy that we can simply call dibs on? Can I help it if he misinterpreted a toss of my head? My hair was in my eyes!"

"That's it?" Madison asked, nonplussed. "No 'hi, mom? Glad you're home?'"

"Oh, hi, mom. Glad you're home." The greeting was lackluster, at best, even though the teen brushed a kiss across her mother's cheek. She quickly stood back and returned to her argument. "Tell Megan that Jeff is free to sit by whoever he pleases. It's a free country, after all."

Almost wishing she had turned down Aunt Betsey's offer to take a night on the uncomfortable pull-out, Madison rubbed her head in confusion, not to mention exhaustion. "Okay, wait. I need a whiteboard to keep up with all this. I thought Jeff was taking your cousin Sara to the Valentine's Day Dance at school. Why are you two fighting over him?"

"I'm not fighting with her!" Bethani denied. "I'm asking Kevin to the dance, if Jeff will ever unglue himself from my side. And he and Sara broke up last week," she explained off-handedly. "Now she's going to the dance with Josiah."

Madison looked from the blonde to the redhead. "I thought you liked Josiah Burton," she told her stepdaughter.

"Not anymore," Megan said with all the drama only a seventeen-year-old could muster.

"So, here's a thought," their mother suggested. "Why don't both of you stay out of the media room and let the boys do the asking. Jeff can decide for himself which one of you he wants to ask to the dance."

"You're so old-fashioned!" Bethani accused. "We aren't living in horse and buggy days anymore. It's perfectly acceptable for a woman to ask a man out."

"But you aren't a woman yet, and those smelly, noisy boys in there certainly aren't men," Madison pointed out.

"M-o-m!" Bethani stretched the word into three syllables.

"And if he does ask you to the dance?" Madison wanted to know. "What are you going to tell him, knowing your sister likes him?"

Bethani rolled her blue eyes to the ceiling. "If I can go back in there, I can just ask Kevin and settle this once and for all."

"Assuming Kevin says yes," Megan smirked. "I heard he wanted to take Miley."

"That's not so!" Bethani cried.

"Is, too!"

Madison broke into their latest argument. "The dance is less than a week away. Why does everyone wait until the last minute to get a date? And where, by the way, is your father? Why isn't Brash down here playing referee?"

A deep baritone spoke up from the corner. "Because secretly, your husband is a coward."

Madison whirled around at the sound of his voice. "Brash! How long have you been there in the shadows? And why didn't you step in and stop this foolishness?"

"Hey," the big man defended himself, putting his hands up in surrender. "I'll go in there and take on that whole room of boys, smelly or not.

But girl fights aren't my specialty."

Hand on hip, Madison harrumphed. "Spoken like a man," she muttered. "And FYI. To whoever's making brownies, I think they're done."

Both girls flew to the oven, working in tandem to retrieve the pan from the oven. Just like that, their spat was over. They were giggling and plotting a new plan of attack by the time they carried a gooey, messy platter of brownies into the room of unsuspecting boys.

"That went well," Brash said, lumbering to his feet with a pop of his knee. "How's my lovely bride?"

"Exhausted," she said, sinking gratefully into his arms.

"Why don't you go upstairs and draw a nice, warm bath? I'll chaperone the mob." He gave her his signature look—part arched brow, part smirk—silently scolding her for doubting him. "I've been keeping an eye on them, you know. And Bethani is right. Jeff plopped down on the couch beside her, blatantly ignoring the daggers shooting from Megan's eyes."

Maddy sighed. "Whoever said parenting isn't for wimps was spot on."

"But you have to admit," he said with a charming grin. "We've got good kids."

"That, we do."

After issuing her husband a proper hello kiss, Madison made her way up the back stairway and into their suite of rooms. When *Home Again* remodeled and updated the century-old mansion, they turned the entire right side of the second floor into a sumptuous retreat befitting royalty.

She still thought double doors leading into the master closet and master bath were overkill, but on days like the past two, she considered the elaborate soaking tub a necessity.

Brash is right, she mused, pouring bath salts into the swirling water. *We do have good kids.*

Not all parents were so lucky. Her thoughts turned to the young girl in the ER. She wasn't suggesting the girl was bad, but she faced a serious situation. Teenage pregnancy was all too common and could easily happen to the best of kids.

She sobered with the realization it could even happen to their three, just as entanglement with drugs and alcohol could befall them. It was every parent's fear, and every parent's battle.

Madison stripped and stepped gingerly into the steamy water, easing down into its delicious depths. She felt the tension melt away from her shoulders and aching back. Those hospital pull-out beds were not designed for comfort!

After worrying about her grandmother and her arguing teenagers, Madison once again turned her worries to the unknown girl at the hospital. Maybe she would try to speak with Nurse Benson and see if she had any information on the girl. Again, it was none of her business, but it almost sounded as if the girl were selling her baby. Madison's conscience wouldn't allow her to ignore such an atrocious deed.

There could be another possibility, she told herself. *The money could be for her health care, which I understand is perfectly legal. Maybe she worked out a deal to save on her hospital bill, and she's using the excess to save up for college.*

Sinking deeper into the tub, she nodded her head lazily. Yes, that was probably it. She could live with that possibility.

That settled, she moved on to another worry.

Do the chicken growers stand a chance against Barbour Foods? She wondered. It appeared the company could do anything they wanted, dictate whatever demands they pleased, and their growers—the very people who provided the land and the labor to grow the flocks—had little or no control of their own destiny. *It just doesn't seem fair.*

Aloud, Madison chided herself, "Has anyone ever told you that you worry too much? Just let it go. Lie back and relax and accept these few stolen moments as the gift they are."

From the doorway, Brash's deep voice drawled lazily, "My sentiments, exactly." He held a thick, thirsty towel and a bottle of wine.

She gave him a cautious look. "I thought you were chaperoning the kids."

"The stragglers have all gone home, and the house is quiet. Shannon wanted Megan to have dinner with them, so the twins are in their rooms and lost in their own little worlds."

"Already? That was quick!"

"Quick? You've been up here forever."

"Come to think of it, the water is getting a bit chilly."

A sexy smile crossed his handsome face. "Then please," Brash said, his voice dropping to a delicious purr. He stretched the towel between his open arms. "Allow me to warm you up."

"I can't believe you're actually going away for a full week," Maddy told her best friend over coffee and Gennydoodle cookies. "But I think it's an excellent idea and, to be truthful, I'm terribly jealous."

"I know, right?" Genny's giggle sounded more like that of a teenager than a grown woman. "But it's the perfect opportunity, and we decided to just go for it!"

Madison reached out to pat her friend's hand. "I think it's exactly what you need."

"I'm a little nervous, leaving the restaurant in Trenessa's care, but she's been an excellent assistant so far. And most of the staff has been with me from the very first, so they know what to do. It's not like I'm just walking out on them and leaving them in the lurch."

"Of course not. You have this place running like a well-oiled machine. And you've taken off before. They managed without you then, and they'll manage without you now."

"Are you trying to make me feel better, or useless?" her friend teased.

"The sign of a great leader is how well they train others to take their place."

Impressed with her philosophical observation, Genny nodded her approval. "I like that."

"Thanks. I read it on a mug or in a fortune cookie. Can't remember which," Maddy admitted with a grin, "but it sounded like sage advice."

"You know," Genny said, settling more comfortably in the booth seat, "you'll have an anniversary coming up six weeks after mine. Do you and Brash have any plans?"

"I haven't thought about it. I don't know if either one of us can get off work."

"You own your own business, and he's chief of police. Surely, if anyone can pull some strings, it's the two of you."

Madison gave her a reproachful look. "Says the woman who owns her own restaurant but can't bear to leave it for more than two days in a row. And shall I point out that Franklin is less than an hour away from here? If worst comes to worst, you can come back to handle any crisis that might arise. Not that any will, mind you," she was quick to add. "But even if the ovens were cold for a week, the world would keep spinning."

Genny shook her head. "The townspeople would starve without me," she claimed.

"I still say that's half the reason Cutter married you," Madison teased. "I think he married you to assure himself of a lifetime of homemade meals and apple turnovers." She laughed at her own humor but noticed her friend didn't join in.

"Genny! I'm only kidding. Everyone knows Cutter adores you."

Her expression remained glum. "I know. Really, I do. It's just that..."

"It's not the age thing again, is it? You really do have to get over that!"

"I know. And I have." She toyed with the handle on her mug. "Mostly, anyway. But now I worry it's my age that's keeping me from getting pregnant. We both want a baby so badly. What if... what if I can't give him children? What if my eggs have shriveled and dried up, and now I *can't* get pregnant?"

"Has a doctor told you that?" Madison's tone was pragmatic.

"Not exactly. But there must be some reason it hasn't happened yet. It's certainly not from lack of trying!" Her face reddened at the candid admission, particularly when she realized there were diners around them who could possibly overhear their conversation.

Madison changed the subject without warning. "Remember that old Doris Day movie?" she mused. "The one where she was married to James Garner, and he was a doctor?"

"Is that the one where she was a spokesperson for a soap company, and he drove his convertible into the swimming pool he didn't know they had? We used to love watching that old movie!" Genny recalled.

"Yep, that's the one. Do you remember the older couple who were trying to have a baby?"

"Not really."

"Well, I do. Being a doctor, James Garner offered medical advice. Being a woman, Doris Day offered practical advice. If I remember correctly, she suggested they go away on a cruise and just enjoy themselves. I offer the same advice, my friend. Stop trying so hard, and let nature take its course."

Genny leaned forward in interest. "I think I vaguely remember that now. The woman came back pregnant, didn't she?"

"Sure did!" Maddy's hazel eyes glittered with mischief. She spread her palms out. "And, who knows? A week away, and you and Cutter may just come back with the same results!"

7

Back at the hospital the next day, Madison found her grandmother vacillating between moments of lucid conversation and those of fanciful musings. Weak but curious, in her lucid moments, she wanted to hear news from home. How were Brash and the kids? What was the outcome of the Juliet City Council meeting? Why in tarnation had Sticker wasted good money on a fancy bouquet of flowers that would just die within a few days? If she missed Tuesday afternoon Bunko, tell Sybil to keep an eye on Bettye Hooper; she suspected the Sunday School teacher had discovered a new way to cheat.

As her mind drifted in and out of clarity, she had trouble separating the past from the present. Today, she was preoccupied with the memory of an unsolved murder that still hung over The Sisters like a misty fog. Years ago, one of Naomi's most upstanding citizens was found dead in her home, and no one had ever been charged for the crime. It happened while Granny Bert was justice of the peace for River County, and Madison knew her grandmother still felt partially responsible for not seeing justice served. There had always been rumors and speculations about it being one of Alpha Bodine's family members who did the deed, but never enough proof surfaced to back the claims. Granny Bert rambled on about it now, lamenting the injustice of it all.

When Granny Bert groaned in pain and complained about anything that touched her skin, Madison buzzed for the nurse. She sat by her grandmother's bedside until the pain killers took effect, but with Granny Bert finally resting comfortably, Madison slipped from the room. She needed to stretch her legs and grab a bite to eat. Three cups of coffee and a complimentary pack of graham crackers didn't offer much in the way of nourishment.

The hospital's cafeteria was small but efficient, with a semi-decent offering of food. Madison made her selection and settled at a table to eat. Hoping to give her grandmother ample time for a long, uninterrupted afternoon nap, she decided to top off her meal with a cup of coffee.

A familiar face greeted her at the coffee machine. "Hello, Madison." Nurse Benson's friendly smile morphed into a look of concern. "Don't tell me your grandmother is still in the hospital?"

"I'm afraid so. They had trouble finding the right antibiotic to fight her infection, but I think we're finally on the right track."

"I hope so. Somehow, I don't see your grandmother as an exemplary patient." Her hazel eyes twinkled in mischief.

"Hardly," Madison scoffed. "However, right now, she feels so bad that she's semi-behaving. As she improves, I'm sure that will change."

"I suppose that's a good sign," Laurel said. Cup of coffee in hand, she lingered as Madison filled one for herself.

"Getting a moment away from the ER?" Madison asked.

"Yes. And unfortunately, the coffee machine in our break room is out of order, so I'm taking my break here."

"I have a table, if you'd care to join me."

"I'd love to, if it's not imposing."

"Not at all. I'm killing time while Granny Bert naps."

Once they were seated at the table, Madison asked conversationally, "How long have you been a nurse?"

"Are we counting the years I put bandages and splints on all my dolls, half of my friends, and one hapless but devoted dog? If so, since I was about three." Her smile was infectious. "I've been back here in Bryan-College Station for the past three years, after spending the first of my career in Houston."

"I'm sure it's been a change of pace. BCS is hardly the size of Houston."

"No, but this suits me much better. It feels more personable at a smaller hospital."

Madison warmed to the nurse, even more so than she had before. "It sounds like you love your job."

"I do. It may sound corny, but I've always loved helping people. I've been accused of being overzealous in my work, but it's just part of who I am."

"And I'm sure that makes you even better at what you do."

The women chatted for a few moments, until Laurel offered Madison the opening she was looking for. The nurse confided that one of the most frustrating aspects of her job was seeing signs of emotional and domestic abuse, and yet being unable to act upon it.

"I may be speaking out of turn," Madison said, leaning in to keep her words confined between them, "and I know you're limited to what you can tell me. But when I brought Granny Bert into the ER, I overheard a conversation in the room next door that made me very uncomfortable."

"Oh? And what was that?"

"I couldn't see the patient, of course, but she sounded young. Perhaps seventeen or eighteen. An adult was with her, but I didn't get the impression she was the girl's mother. Maybe her stepmother, or a court-appointed guardian. There didn't seem to be an emotional connection between them. It sounded almost like a business relationship."

"A teacher, perhaps?" Laurel asked, trying to recall someone who might fit that description. Often, a coach came in with a player if the parent wasn't available. "Did you feel there was something... inappropriate about their relationship?"

Madison frowned. "Probably not in the way you're thinking, but the conversation did strike me as disturbing. Apparently, the girl was pregnant, and the woman felt she had behaved recklessly, possibly endangering the baby."

Laurel's nod was solemn. "All too often, young mothers don't realize how their actions can impact the health and well-being of their unborn child."

"The thing is, I didn't get the impression it was the child's *health* that was foremost in the woman's mind."

"I don't think I follow."

Madison struggled with the best way to express her concerns. What she was about to suggest was a serious allegation.

"Please understand, I'm not accusing this girl of anything. Maybe I misunderstood or took things completely out of context. I wasn't deliberately listening, but the walls are rather thin..."

"I understand," the nurse reassured her. "What was it you heard that caused such concern?"

Blowing out a deep breath, Madison repeated what she overheard from the other cubicle. "I don't know, Laurel. It sounded a lot like the girl was... it almost sounded like she was selling her baby!"

The nurse was clearly as concerned over the information as Madison was. With furrowed brow, she leaned in closer toward the other woman. "You didn't see either of the people, or catch one of their names?"

"No. I was trying to catch a nap at first, until I overheard just enough to concern me. After that," she admitted sheepishly, "I confess to listening a bit harder, but I've told you everything I heard, which admittedly wasn't much."

"She wasn't my patient, but I do recall my co-worker mentioning a girl who had recently gone bungee jumping. She came in when she started spotting."

"Bungee jumping?" Madison asked, mouth agape. "Really? What was she thinking?"

"Like she told her companion, she obviously wasn't thinking. Not about her unborn child, anyway." Laurel tapped a finger to the side of her chin as she thought aloud. "Most likely, she would be under twenty weeks pregnant, or else she would have been sent to L&D." To clarify, she added, "Labor and delivery."

"I know adoptive parents paying for the medical bills is common, but this girl didn't seem comfortable with whatever it was she had agreed to. It seemed to me that the other woman was pressuring her in some way."

"Maybe the other woman was the prospective parent."

Madison shook her head in disagreement. "I don't think so. I didn't hear anything about the safety and welfare of the child. It was all about money. Almost like a business agreement."

"Maybe the woman was the adoption liaison. Maybe she thought the best way to reach the young mother was with the reminder of her future and what an education could do for her."

"It felt more like a used car salesman sensing a deal slipping through her fingers. It made me feel sleazy, just listening to their exchange." A shiver of revulsion squirmed over Madison's shoulders.

"You haven't come across other pregnant patients like this, have you? Something that just felt a little off? A girl with a companion that didn't seem to belong there?"

Mid-shake of her dark, loose curls, Laurel's head stilled. "Now that you mention it, this summer, there was a girl... She went swimming at the beach and came in after experiencing severe cramping and spotting. Unfortunately, she ended up losing the baby. But what I remember the most was her companion. A well-dressed woman who immediately left the room to make several phone calls. She didn't offer the girl much comfort, just criticism for being so careless." Laurel's hazel eyes clouded as she recalled more of the details. "I remember her saying something about how it had *cost* her, but I thought she meant mentally and emotionally. It never occurred to me that she may have meant financially."

"That's despicable! The poor girl!"

Laurel nodded in agreement, but Madison could tell by the look in her eyes that her mind was elsewhere, trying to recall specific details from this summer. "I'll dig around and ask a few questions," the nurse murmured, as if making a note to herself.

"I know you can't divulge personal information, but I would appreciate it if you could keep me posted. Whatever you can tell me to put my mind at ease."

"I'll do that." A glance down at her watch had the nurse pushing away from the table. "I hate to cut this short, but duty calls."

"I understand. I'm glad we had a chance to

visit."

"Me, too. If you'll give me your phone number, I can contact you when and if I know something."

Madison rattled off the number, and Laurel called it, so that her own number would show up on Madison's phone. With a beaming smile, the nurse said, "All done. Now we can keep in touch." She pushed in her chair before adding, "I have a friend who's a detective with the College Station PD. He speaks highly of your husband. If worst comes to worst and I discover something fishy is going on, we can bring him into this."

"I hope that's not the case, but it's good to know. It's always nice to have an open line with law enforcement."

"Detective Resnick is a good man," Laurel assured her. "We've butted heads a few times, but when it comes down to it, he's always fair and professional. We can depend on him to help, if need be."

Alone at the table, Madison checked her messages, sent out a couple of texts, and played a detective game on her iPad. *Hey,* she reasoned to herself when purchasing the game, *if people want to hire me for detective work, I may as well hone my skills.* She wasn't sure if finding hidden objects in a picture and piecing clues together counted much toward training but, then again, it couldn't hurt.

When she thought sufficient time had passed for Granny's nap, she gathered her trash, tucked her electronic gadgets away, and headed back upstairs.

She found her grandmother awake and full of

sass.

"And just where have you been, young lady?" the older woman wanted to know.

"I grabbed a bite to eat in the cafeteria."

"You were gone long enough!"

Madison consulted her watch. "About an hour," she agreed. "I wanted to give you plenty of time to rest."

Bertha Cessna harrumphed. "Hard to do when they came in and poked me with more needles and asked a bunch of senseless questions! Wanted to know if I felt safe at home and who my caretaker was. Caretaker!" Her snort was loud and disdainful. "Who do they think they're dealing with? An invalid? A baby? I don't need a caretaker. I can take care of myself, thank you very much."

"I'm sure you told them just that."

"Can a tadpole swim? Of course I told them that! Told 'em to stop pestering me with all their nonsense, too."

"I take it you didn't get a nap?"

"Maybe a few minutes," she admitted grudgingly.

"Are you still hurting?"

"Only because I feel like a pin cushion. They've poked me more times than a porcupine can poke a yappin' mutt."

Madison ran a hand along the back of her neck, praying for patience. Her grandmother was in rare form this afternoon.

She thought it best to change the subject. "Did Miss Arlene come by to see you yesterday? She said she would try."

"She called. Said her daughter was feeling up to having visitors, so Wanda drove her over. We all know Arlene is still using her leg as an excuse not to get behind the wheel, when it's her eyesight that's ailing. She's milked that injury for all it's worth, and then some! With all her newfound wealth, you'd think she could afford a pair of new glasses!"

"Newfound wealth? What are you talking about?"

Granny Bert waved her hands in the air. "All of a sudden, she's Miss Moneybags. She won't say where she got the money, but I suspect there was a lawsuit in there somewhere. I'd wager she sued someone over her daughter's distress and mental anguish, even though the girl's always been a couple of bricks shy of a load. That's what happens when you have an uh-oh baby so late in life."

"Maybe. But I saw enough to know that Lana's breakdown was real."

"Didn't say it wasn't," Granny Bert snapped. "Real or not, doesn't mean it was someone else's fault. Or that someone else should have to pay good money for it, just so Arlene can live the high life. Did you know she's taking Wanda on a cruise this spring? Offered to pay for the whole thing if she'd come along."

"That was nice of her."

"Nice?" scoffed the woman in the bed. "She offered to pay for Wanda but said if Sybil and I wanted to come along, we'd have to pay our own way. Does that sound very nice to you?"

"Cabins are double occupancy," Madison

pointed out. "She'd probably pay just as much going alone as she would taking a friend."

"And what are Sybil and me? Chopped liver?" Madison made light of the supposed snub. "You didn't care much for cruising anyway. Remember? You said the boat rocked too much."

"It did. Sloshed melted butter all down my new blouse. Had to take it to the cleaners, who tried taking *me* to the cleaners!"

Madison realized the error of her ways even before her grandmother went off on an age-old tirade. "That danged fool dry cleaner wanted to charge me more to clean the blouse than what I even paid for it. I told him I wasn't going to do it, and by golly, I didn't!"

Granny Bert spent another five minutes reliving the event that eventually resulted in the dry cleaner issuing a public apology to her grandmother. She had used her influence in the community to boycott the dry cleaners one town over and encourage Mitzi Wynn to open a rival business in Juliet. The new upstart hadn't lasted long, but it hurt *Riverton Dry Cleaning* enough that they not only took out a half-page ad in the local paper to apologize, but they also gave Granny Bert free dry-cleaning for life. As a matter of principle, she snubbed their offer and now took her dry cleaning to Navasota.

When the nurse came in to start a new bag of IV meds, Madison followed her out.

"My grandmother seems extremely irritable today," she explained. "Is that normal?"

"Unfortunately, that does tend to be a side effect of this antibiotic," the nurse informed her.

"The good news is that it doesn't last. As soon as we finish the dose, she should be back to normal."

"Not that normal is much better," Madison muttered beneath her breath. "I'll try to keep that in mind, even though I may need something for my own nerves before that bag drains dry."

"Another plus is that Carter will be her nurse this evening, and she seems to be partial to him. He always has a special way with the ladies."

"That sounds about right. Even at eighty-two, my grandmother still likes to flirt."

8

"Look at this place," Genny murmured in awe.

Cutter turned off the highway, driving beneath the arched header identifying the property as *Cherubdipity*. A long, black-top road wove a crooked path across a grassy field, still green despite the date on the calendar. It led to a large house perched atop a hill, its many statues visible from the road.

"The gate will be the first thing I work on," the welder informed his wife. "They want a more impressive entrance, with elaborate ironwork and insets for those concrete angels we just passed."

"Cherubs," she corrected absently, still staring at the house with its many gables and roof lines.

"Whatever. They need some clothes on. The only thing covering their privates is a ribbon made of stone."

Genny laughed, running her hand over her husband's strong forearm. "I think those are supposed to be loin cloths, or possibly diapers. Cherubs are baby angels."

A dubious frown appeared on his face. "That's

morbid."

"Not really. According to biblical angelology, cherubs are angels of the second highest order in celestial hierarchy. They're the symbol of innocence and eternal youth."

"Because they're dead," he muttered, still unconvinced.

She gave him a playful shove. "Behave yourself. I'm *this* close to a week of heaven on earth." She held her thumb and finger together, almost touching. The inn loomed large as life in the background. "You and your smart mouth aren't about to get me kicked out now."

Twenty minutes later, Cutter hauled the last of their suitcases into their cottage. "Why did you bring so many suitcases? I told you I wanted to see you in as little as possible for the entire week. Nothing at all would please me just fine."

"Maybe so, but I imagine our companions at the breakfast table will have another opinion," she retorted.

"Breakfast table? I thought this was our own private cottage."

"It is, silly. But it's still part of a bed and breakfast. We can request private meals, but you heard the woman at check-in. They serve a full breakfast in the dining room every morning from six till nine, and a five-course dinner at the same time every evening."

"I vote for breakfast in bed," he said with a wicked grin. "Dessert first."

"Hmm." She pretended to contemplate his suggestion. "I did see a handsome waiter through the dining room doors. Maybe he would deliver our meals."

The smile fell from Cutter's face, replaced by an exaggerated scowl. "You'll pay for that comment, woman. Just for that, I may keep you in bed for an entire day."

"And this is punishment?" she teased back. She squealed in delight when Cutter lunged for her, chasing her all the way into the bedroom.

Later, as they lay in one another's arms, waiting for their breathing to return to normal, Genny murmured, "I think this week is going to be perfect."

"It's certainly started out that way," he agreed, running his hand along her curves.

"This room is perfect. I like the murals painted on the ceilings and the heavy drapes on the windows. The sunken living room and the overstuffed couches give it a decadent feel, don't you think?"

"I guess that's one word for it," he said noncommittally.

"And did you see the size of that Jacuzzi tub? And the walk-in shower? There's room for at least four people in both of them!"

"I told you. I don't share."

Genny ignored his cynical comment. She continued to gush about the room. "I love the white-washed furniture and the color palette of the entire suite. It's so soothing and relaxing. I can see why this place is so hard to book. Don't you just love it?" She all but squealed, squeezing his arm in her excitement.

"Honestly? I feel a little guilty."

"Guilty?" she asked in surprise. "You think it's

too fancy for the likes of us?"

"No, not that. You're a fancy-schmancy chef, after all, trained in France. You're accustomed to all this grandeur and fuss."

Her voiced softened as she guessed, "But you're not?"

"Nah, that's not it," he denied. "I'm accustomed to you, so I figure I've earned it by default."

She tilted her blond head to look at him curiously. "Then what do you feel guilty about it? This is part of your payment for a job, right? A job you know will be well done."

"That's not it, either."

"Then what is it?"

"After what we just did? Those are God's little angels looking down at us. They saw every intimate detail, and I have more planned for later. I don't like an audience, especially of little angel babies."

Genny's laughter filled the room, ringing as clear and delightful as a crystal bell. "I'll let you in on a little secret," she whispered in his ear. "We didn't do anything wrong. And I'm sure the little guys closed their eyes when we got to the best parts."

"You think?" he asked, eying the tasteful mural above them.

"It's better than a mirror," she offered.

"I see your point." He gathered her close, tugging her beneath him once more. "This time keep your eyes open to make certain they close theirs," he murmured.

Genny squealed again in laughter.

It was shaping up to be a fine week, indeed.

They had breakfast the next morning in the dining room, before most of the other guests were up and about. Cutter wanted to get an early start on the day, and Genny insisted on seeing him off to work, just as she did at home every morning.

"The waffles are good," he said, leaning over to speak in a confidential tone, "but not nearly as good as yours. If you get too bored this week, maybe you can give them a few pointers in the kitchen."

She shook her head, making her blond curls dance around her face. "Nope. I'm on vacation. I'm not cooking a thing."

"Are you sure? Because I saw a stove and refrigerator in the cottage."

"Nice try, but no cigar."

He smiled at his wife indulgently. "Just kidding you, darlin'. I want you to put your feet up and relax this week. This is well-deserved time off."

"I just feel guilty that I get to goof off all day, while you have to work."

"I'll let you make it up to me," he offered. "You can have that big ole tub filled with hot water when I get in this afternoon. I could do with a back rub, too. Maybe a foot massage."

"I'll see if a masseuse is available," she teased.

He drained his coffee cup. "If you're done, I'll walk you back to the cottage. I'd like to get started as soon as possible. The earlier I start, the earlier I'll get off."

"If you don't mind, I think I'll stay here and look around the inn. I have my key to get back in the cottage."

"Whatever you want. The day is yours."

"It's a lovely house. I know the guest rooms are upstairs, but I'm anxious to see all the public spaces."

"I'll be in for lunch. And I'll have my cell phone on me, if you need anything." He stood and pushed his chair in, offering to help her with hers.

She shook away his gallantry. "I think I'll have another cup of coffee first."

"You just want another scone," he teased.

"Too dry," she whispered from the side of her mouth. "They didn't freeze and grate their butter."

"You should know. You make the best." He dropped a kiss on the top of her blond hair.

She lifted her face for proper placement of the next kiss. "You're starting with the front entrance?" she asked.

"That's the plan."

"Be sure and keep your shirt on," she teased. "We don't want to cause a traffic jam."

"Funny," he shot back. But his cheeks colored when a server overheard her words and gave him a suggestive once over.

Good thing Genny's back was to them, or she may have 'accidentally' spilled her coffee when the girl refilled her cup.

"I don't believe we've met. I noticed you wandering around, and I wanted to introduce myself." An attractive black woman with gray at her temples approached Genny with a friendly smile and an outstretched hand. "I'm Marcella Durant, proprietor and innkeeper here at *Cherubdipity*. Welcome to my home."

"I'm thrilled to be here! I'm Genesis Montgomery, but my friends call me Genny."

"Then may I call you Genny?"

"I'd be offended if you didn't. Please. Join me." Genny motioned to the sofa beside her. She was curled up in a big, comfy chair near the fireplace.

As the other woman accepted the invitation, Genny asked, "How did you become an innkeeper? I'm not sure I'd want to share such a lovely home with strangers."

"Ah, but once they've been here, they're no longer strangers," Marcella replied smoothly. "See how easily you and I became friends?"

"Touché."

The innkeeper eyed her a moment before saying, "I know who you are."

"You do?" Genny laughed at her own surprise. "Why, of course you do. You're the one who hired my husband and offered us that amazing cottage. It's absolutely perfect, by the way."

"Thank you. And, yes, it's true I hired your husband. But I meant other than my business arrangement with him."

Genny winced. "I suppose you mean the television show." While the Big House had been the focal point of the season-long program, *New*

Beginnings had enjoyed more airtime than Genny had been comfortable with. Not only was it the most popular restaurant in The Sisters and where all the locals gathered, but her relationship with the show's star had made her one of the main players, alongside her best friend. *Guilt by association*, she often joked.

"That, too," Marcella nodded. "But I met you before, several years ago. In Boston while you worked for the Morgans."

"You did? You knew my friends?" Genny asked in surprise.

"Not well, but I attended a few parties they hosted."

"That's amazing! And such a small world! Are you from Boston?"

"No, but for a while, I was... involved with a man from there. He was a business acquaintance of Ralph Morgan, and I would come as his plus one."

"I'm sorry that I don't remember meeting you. I promise, if it happens again, I'll definitely recall our meeting!"

"I hope so, now that we're friends," Marcella said with twinkling eyes.

"You must have some fascinating stories, running an inn like this."

"You could say that," Marcella smiled.

Genny waited for her to pick up the conversation starter and say more, but that was her only comment. A moment of uneasiness passed between them, until Genny saw a teenage girl carrying a stack of fresh towels up the stairs. She made another attempt to keep the dialog running.

"I can't help but notice that several of your employees are quite young. Are you associated with some sort of vocational program through the local high school?"

"No. Most come to me on their own, looking for a job."

"Do you find you have a higher turnover rate, hiring high school students?"

"Not really. Much of the staff has been with me for a while."

"Really?" Genny was surprised, her eyes going back toward the stairway. "Some of them seem so young."

"Yes, that's true. But some are seasoned veterans." With a noncommittal smile, the subject was closed.

Genny made a final stab at conversation, something vague about a nearby cherub painting. Marcella sparked to the topic, saying the most Genny had heard so far.

Even though Marcella was personable, Genny soon realized she wasn't *personal*. Though always polite and graceful, the innkeeper smoothly avoided answering specific questions. She skirted around any reference to her personal life. The smile stayed in place, but the gesture never quite reached her eyes.

Later that evening, Genny pondered the topic with her husband.

"She's hiding something."

"Are we still talking about Marcella?" he asked, adding more wood to the fire pit. Even though it was February, with no wind or bone-chilling humidity to keep them indoors, it was pleasant enough to enjoy a glass of wine by the fire pit. There were three other pits scattered about the inn, but this was on their private terrace, assuring they had the space to themselves.

"Yes, we're still talking about Marcella. Something's off with her," Genny proclaimed.

"You've been playing detective with Maddy for too long. You're starting to see mysteries when none are there."

"Really? Then why won't she answer any of my questions?"

"Maybe she's a private person."

"She runs a public business! She invites strangers into her home. That's not the hallmark of a private person."

"No, it's the hallmark of a smart businessperson. She's capitalized on her assets. Doesn't mean she has to tell guests her life story," Cutter reasoned.

"But why wouldn't she? She volunteered the fact that she met me in Boston, but when I asked who her friend was, she clammed up. She wouldn't even tell me how he was connected to the Morgans, other than to say they were business acquaintances. How vague is that?"

"Maybe her 'friend' didn't share those details with her."

"What are you talking about?"

"Maybe they didn't have that sort of relationship. For all you know, maybe she worked for an escort service and was just there for appearances."

"Seriously? You think our hostess was a

hooker?"

"It sounds classier when you say she may have been a professional escort."

Genny paused. "Which I suppose would explain her reluctance to discuss the past. But why would she even bother mentioning the connection, if she didn't want me to know the truth?"

"Simple," Cutter said, pulling her to lean back against his chest. "She was afraid you might recognize her and wanted to make the first move. Looks like she has nothing to hide."

"When she so obviously does."

He nuzzled her neck. "Are we really going to talk about Marcella all night, or are we going to talk about us?"

"I must admit. I like the subject of us much better."

"So do I." With deliberate redirection, he changed the subject, "So. Other than sniffing out an imagined mystery, what else did you do today? And what are your plans for tomorrow?"

After pretending to give it thought, Genny decided, "I think I'll do the same thing tomorrow as I did today." She flashed a dimpled smile. "Absolutely nothing."

9

After having breakfast with Cutter early again
the next morning, Genny treated herself to a
leisurely walk around the grounds. A light jacket
was required this morning, but the brisk, frosted
air felt good as she traversed the rolling
landscape.

Even though she and Cutter lived on a ranch,
and she was accustomed to seeing domesticated
and wild animals roaming about, Genny still
appreciated the pastoral view from *Cherubdipity*.
The hilltop inn offered a sweeping vista of the
area. Houses and the sprawl of nearby towns
dotted the horizon, but the immediate area was a
patchwork of dead, dormant grasses, green fields
planted in winter oats, and clusters of barren
trees amid the evergreens.

Scattered about the property were angel
statues in all sizes, shapes, and forms, marking
the general perimeters of public spaces. The
concrete sculptures stood as silent guardians
around the various seating areas and fire pits,
leading the way to picnic tables and garden

vignettes, and lined, now-empty flower beds to the little white chapel among the pine trees.

A large pond beckoned from the bottom of the hill, a well-worn path lined with stones and intermittent statues guiding the way to and from. Closer in, an in-ground swimming pool, covered now for winter, awaited warmer weather. No water flowed from the presiding angel's ewer, but a fountain near the front entrance, lined with dancing cherubs and winged doves, still bubbled. To the side of the swimming pool, the hot tub was a welcome treat on chilly days, and a nearby stone building was marked *Spa* in fancy letters and elaborate graphics. It came as no surprise to see the likenesses on either side of the doorway were cherubs.

As Genny walked down to the pond and back up the hill—it was a good way to work off this morning's pancakes— she realized the property was larger than she first thought. Beyond the statues and tucked discretely behind a row of cedars and a semi-manicured hedge, she saw a cluster of out-buildings. One was a two-story, utilitarian styled structure.

Maintenance buildings, she assumed. Maybe even a caretaker's residence.

She glimpsed two women leaving the taller of the buildings. When they turned in profile, the breeze pushed against their clothes, exposing the swell of both their bellies. Though she couldn't say why, their pregnancies surprised her. Perhaps because she had noticed another worker was expecting, as well, and the odds of such a small staff with concurrent pregnancies struck her as odd.

What were the chances? She muttered the thought beneath her breath.

She pondered the thought as she made her way back up to the inn. Perhaps she was hyper-sensitive, noticing other women's expectant status because she longed for the cachet herself. Maybe she could go into any business or any public place and see the same quota of expectant mothers versus non-pregnant women.

Maybe, she thought. *But doubtful.*

She would make a point to be more vigilant in the future, noticing that sort of thing. Maybe her own business at *New Beginnings* was the oddity, not the norm. After all, most of her female staff was older or else part-timers still in school, either at The Sisters High or at one of the nearby or online colleges. Just because she hadn't had a pregnant employee in the three years of her role as a restaurateur didn't mean other employers had the same experience.

And what if Marcella did tend to hire expectant mothers? *Kudos to her*, Genny decided. These women were pregnant, not helpless.

Thoughts of having a baby of her own were never far from Genny's mind. It was something she had considered long before she met and married Cutter, but she'd never been brave enough to join the ranks of becoming a single mother. She had watched Maddy rear her twins and was often an active participant in the process. Even when their paths had taken the best friends in different directions, they still lived in one another's lives, never spending more than six months apart. Even when Genny was in Europe, Madison had come to visit. That was back when she and Gray were still in love and happy, before the pressures of his job and climbing the ladder of success had inadvertently led to his crashing descent. And when Madison became pregnant, Genny swore she went through a false pregnancy of her own.

Genny had been there when the twins were born. She had helped plan their first birthday party. Stayed up at night with one teething or feverish baby, while Madison coaxed the other back to sleep. She had taken pictures on their first day of kindergarten, bandaged more than her fair share of scraped knees and bruised hearts, and had attended their school programs and applauded their achievements like the doting aunt that she was, blood or not.

Not once had Genny been jealous of the family Madison had, but she had been envious. She wanted the same for herself, but she was old fashioned enough, and practical enough, to know she didn't want to go it alone. As Gray became more distant and spent more time at his office, she saw the hardship it placed on her friend. She heard it in her voice, saw it in Maddy's weary countenance as she shuffled two active youngsters back and forth to games and practices and programs with little to no help from her husband. When Blake's appendix ruptured and Gray was away on a business trip, it was Genny who stayed at the house to see that Bethani was taken care of and tucked in at night.

Genny was smart enough to know that

motherhood was never easy, especially when done alone. She had almost given up hope of ever having a baby of her own, but then she had returned to The Sisters and met Cutter Montgomery, the handsome firefighter and welder who had all the women's hearts aflutter. It seemed every female from the age of two to ninety-two were smitten with the man, and it hadn't taken Genny long to follow suit, even though she had denied it at first. It was almost too good to be true when she realized he was smitten with her, too.

At first, she swore that was all it was. A passing crush on both their parts. But Cutter had been not only patient, he had been persistent, until finally she realized that what they had between them was real, and that it was forever. Now, she couldn't imagine life without him. And while she could be happy building a future that consisted of just the two of them, a baby would make her world even more perfect. She could think of no greater joy than having Cutter's baby.

Sorrow seeped through her at the thought of their many failed attempts. She had seen three different doctors, two of them fertility specialists. All had agreed that, in the grand scheme of things, twelve months wasn't so unusual when trying for conception. One, however, had expressed concern over her age, admitting that at forty-one, her window of opportunity was narrowing.

He had suggested several possibilities, starting with simple things like creating a fertility chart. Genny dutifully took her basal temperature each morning before getting out of bed, knowing to look for patterns. A sustained rise in temperature over a three to four-day period could signal ovulation, thereby indicating the best time to become pregnant.

After a series of in-office tests, the specialist diagnosed Genny as having endometriosis and suggested a laparoscopy. Just before Christmas, she had the out-patient procedure done and was now fully recovered, with only a tiny scar as a visual reminder of the process. The inner scars, around the walls of her diseased ovaries, and deep within her soul, were harder to see. And to heal.

The doctor had suggested more aggressive measures. She could take fertility shots or consider in vitro fertilization. It was a decision only the couple could make, but when and if she was ready, he was there to help her.

Her feet as heavy as her heart, Genny sank into the first chair she came to. Their cottage was only a few hundred feet away, but it suddenly seemed too far to walk. She needed to sit and gather her strength, both physically and mentally. Most of all, she had to gather emotional strength.

For whatever reason, she had avoided taking the next steps in their fertility journey. A low sperm count wasn't the issue; Cutter had undergone his own series of tests. Genny knew that meant *she* was the weak link. The inability to conceive lay squarely on her.

What if her age really were the problem? Could she bear to know for certain? She had come so far, overcoming her insecurities about her body and her age, only to have both betray her now. Her husband was young and virile, and incredibly sexy. He deserved a wife who could give him children. When he knew the truth, would he still feel the same about her?

Genny immediately felt guilty for thinking Cutter could ever be so shallow. She knew he would stand by her and love her, no matter what medical complications she faced. He had been nothing but supportive; how could she ever doubt him?

Determined to repay his support and faith with a show of her own, Genny knew it was time to see her doctor and take the next step. Before she could wimp out, she scrolled through her contacts and dialed the number. If she waited until she reached the privacy of their cottage or to discuss the matter with Cutter, she might lose her confidence. It was time to act.

She spoke with the nurse. The office was experiencing computer issues and couldn't readily pull up her file, so she explained her situation and the tests she had already taken. It was hard, saying the words aloud. Hearing her own voice admit that her age might be the reason she couldn't conceive. She had put off having children for so many years, and now it might be too late.

At last, they set a date for an appointment and ended the call.

Emotionally drained, Genny put her hands over her face and wept. Hope, excitement, and dread all roiled in her gut, making her feel queasy. Right or wrong, she had taken the next step.

It was a beginning, she congratulated herself.

Or possibly an end, a traitorous thought

intruded, *depending on the results.*

Either way, she would finally know for certain. That was possibly the most frightening thought of all.

After a few moments, a soft voice spoke at her side. "Ma'am?"

Genny sniffed and attempted to wipe away the tears.

"Ma'am, are you okay? Are you ill? Can I help you in any way?"

Embarrassed to be seen in such a state, Genny was slow to open her eyes. She saw a dark-haired girl bending close, her touch soft upon Genny's shoulder and her voice kind. "Can I get you anything?" the girl asked.

"Thank—Thank you, but I'm... fine." Her voice faltered on the obvious lie.

Brown eyes flickered over her, silently doubting her words. "I'm Tatiana, one of the staff here. Is there someone I can call?"

Genny didn't want to disturb Cutter. He was working so hard, trying to squeeze in as many daylight hours as possible so he could spend the evenings with her.

"No. Truly, I'm fine." She sniffed again. "But thank you."

"Tatiana!" The harsh bark of her name made the girl jerk away. She pulled herself into a stiff position as Marcella Durant swept their way.

"I am so sorry, Genny," the innkeeper apologized, her expression softening as she focused on their guest. "Was Tatiana bothering you? Did she say something to offend you?" Without waiting for an answer, she returned her attention to the frightened young woman. "I've warned you, Miss Gomez. Staff is expressly prohibited from fraternizing with our guests."

"No!" Genny broke in, placing her hand on Tatiana's arm as if to ground her from flight. She felt the girl trembling in fear. "She didn't upset me. She was only trying to help me."

Marcella looked doubtful, her suspicious gaze going from one to the other.

"Truly," Genny said, her voice taking on conviction. "Tatiana was very kind, offering to get me anything I needed, or even to call someone for me." She smiled warmly up at the younger woman, trying to offer her reassurance.

"If you say so," Marcella murmured, still unconvinced.

Genny didn't like the fact that her hostess doubted her. She didn't know the dynamics between the two, but this obviously wasn't the first time Tatiana was on the receiving end of her boss' wrath. Afraid this last interaction might cost the girl her job, Genny made her position clear.

"Not only did Tatiana handle the situation with professionalism," she insisted to the other woman, "but she handled it with compassion." Her smile held an edge as she added, "You've trained her well. As a friend recently reminded me, that's the true sign of a great leader."

The reverse psychology worked. Marcella's rigid face softened with the flattery, and beside her, Tatiana released a grateful sigh.

"If there's nothing I can do for you..." The girl's voice trailed off as she offered a small curtsy, carefully averting her eyes from Genny's.

Marcella spoke for her guest, clearly dismissing her, "That will be all, Tatiana."

"And thank you again," Genny said sincerely, determined to have the last word with the tyrannical boss. "I won't forget your kindness. I hope to see you around again."

She murmured something inaudible, her dark eyes darting toward her boss before she scurried off.

Marcella turned questioning eyes back to Genny. "Are you certain she didn't do something to offend you? Are you trying to protect her?"

"Of course not. Nothing could be further from the truth, in fact." Genny took a deep breath and admitted, "I had just made a difficult phone call, and she heard me crying. She came to check on me and make certain I wasn't hurt or ill. As I said, she offered to help."

Believing her at last, Marcella nodded with acceptance. "That's good to know."

"As I said, you've trained her well. She seems to be a true asset here at *Cherubdipity*."

Marcella watched the girl's hastily retreat. A sigh slipped through her lips.

"I know I may have appeared harsh," she admitted. "Some of the girls..." She paused, as if trying to find the correct words.

With an expectant look, Genny encouraged her to go on.

"Some of the girls forget their place," Marcella continued. "They forget they are here to serve, not form friendships."

Genny cocked her blond head. "Can't they do both? I like to think of my customers as friends.

Even though we have a business relationship—my food, in exchange for their money—I hope they consider me as a friend."

"But you're the owner. We have a different position from our subordinates."

"Then we aren't doing our jobs right," Genny said quietly. "I never ask something of my employees that I'm not willing to do myself. It may be naive of me, but I would hope that all employees feel that way."

The black woman looked as if she wanted to laugh at such a foolish notion, but something held her back. Genny watched as a grudging light of appreciation sparked within her dark eyes.

"I hope your telephone call wasn't too upsetting?" she inquired. It was a small peace offering, signaling the other subject was now closed, and she was moving on.

Genny didn't immediately answer. "It was," she said slowly, "but it needed to be done."

"I hope it won't ruin the rest of your day."

Genny looked around, appreciating the feel of warm sunshine upon her skin, and the brisk air teasing her hair. It made her realize how much she had to be grateful for, baby or not.

Her smile was confident.

"It won't."

10

Temperatures warmed during the afternoon, presenting the vacationing couple with another mild and pleasant evening.

"Where did all this come from?" Genny wanted to know. She had disappeared inside the cottage to fetch a bottle of wine for her and a beer for Cutter, plus a throw to cuddle beneath. When she came back out, he had the makings for s'mores waiting for her.

"I made a request at the front desk," he said with a nonchalant shrug. "I know how much you like them."

"You know me too well." She sank onto the bench across from him, arranging the throw around her legs. "You also know they're one of my many weaknesses."

She looked up with a playful grin, surprised to see the serious expression on his handsome face. "Wh—What's wrong?" she asked, her heart stalling. Her mind raced in a dozen directions.

Had something happened at the restaurant? Had Granny Bert gone back to the hospital? Was it his parents, Tug and Mary Alice? Or his grandfather? Had one of the many women from Sticker's past (including Granny Bert) made good on their threats and strung him up on a limb? Maybe Cutter had burned his hands while welding today. Her eyes raced over him, looking for signs of injury.

Only a few seconds had ticked away while her mind created the morbid scenarios. She was stunned when a lopsided grin appeared on her husband's face, and he reached out a hand to cup her face.

"You're my weakness, Genny darlin'." He leaned forward to breathe the words against her lips. "I'd do anything for you. You know that, right?"

"Of—Of course."

"Sometimes I wonder what I did to deserve you. You're my whole world."

She cupped his chiseled face within her own hands, searching his hazel eyes. "I feel the same way about you. Of all the women you could have, I still can't imagine why you chose me."

He looked slightly uncomfortable. "You saw that, did you?"

"Saw what?"

His quick answer drew her suspicion. "Nothing."

"Don't give me that, Cutter Montgomery," she said knowingly. "Another woman made a move on you again, didn't she?" She was more amused than she was threatened.

"I swear, I did nothing to provoke it. I never do."

"I know that. You can't help it if you have such an adorable face and irresistible body." Genny applied slightly more pressure than necessary as she squeezed his face in her palms and kissed him with pursed lips.

"Ouch!" he protested, pulling slightly away. "I mean it, Gen. You're my whole world. I don't want you to ever see how foolish those women act and think I encourage it. I can't even look at another woman without seeing your beautiful blue eyes and your sexy little dimples."

"Good," she said with a satisfied nod. "Because if you ever do encourage them, I will haunt you with these eyes and make you wish you'd never seen my dimples." She did the forked finger thing from her eyes to his, as if putting a curse on him.

Cutter wasn't amused. "I mean it, sweetheart. When she kept bringing me 'refreshments' out to the gate, I finally had to set her straight. I made it plain I was here with my gorgeous and loving bride, and I planned to come back here to celebrate our twenty-fifth anniversary and, God willing, our fiftieth, too."

"Awww." Her heart melted on the spot, just like a gooey s'more. "I think that's one of the sweetest things you've ever said to me."

He touched her face again, his touch tender. "I mean it, darlin'. I plan to grow old with you by my side." He traced the path of her earlier tears. His voice was low as he confided his worries to her. "I heard you were crying earlier. It wasn't because of me, was it?"

"No. No!" She scooted closer to the edge of the bench, leaning close so that he understood her words. "Sometimes you do make me cry, but it's because I'm so happy being married to you, and because I love you so much. Never because I doubt you. Never because of another woman."

"Then why were you crying, Genny darlin'? I thought you'd like it here. I thought a week away would make you happy."

"I do! It does. That had nothing to do with why I was crying." A frown darkened her face. "How did you even know about that?"

"That girl that kept flitting around me," he said in disgust. "She made some crack about how our marriage wouldn't last that long, considering how unhappy you seemed. She said she saw you crying."

"Tatiana told you that?" she asked, surprised and oddly hurt at the girl's betrayal.

"No, I think she said her name was Cindy or Wendy, or something like that." A dismissive wave of his hand showed how little thought he had given her. "Who's Tatiana?"

"A staff member who saw me crying and was kind enough to offer help."

"So why *were* you crying?" He pushed for an answer.

Genny took a steadying breath and released it slowly. She lifted the blanket and patted the seat beside her. "I think we need to talk."

Looking mildly worried, Cutter did as she requested. He stretched his arm along the back of the bench and pulled her in against his side. "I'm listening."

"I called Dr. O'Hara's office today and made an appointment."

If she thought the announcement would concern him, she was in for disappointment. He nodded as if pleased. "Good. I'm glad you did. When do we go?"

"Uhm, at the end of the month."

"Send a reminder to my phone so I can block off the day and time. I want to go with you."

"Really?"

"Of course. We're in this together."

"But what if... what if they tell us I can't have children?"

"What if they tell us you can?" he countered with a smile.

"Aren't you scared? Because I'm terrified," she admitted.

"There are a lot of things in life that scare me," he answered slowly. "That you might become sick, and I won't be able to help you. That one day I'll go to a wreck, and it will be you, or one of our family members trapped inside a burning car. I'm scared of tornadoes, or that a spark from my welder will cause a grass fire that gets out of control. I'm not too fond of snakes, either," he confessed, "especially ones with rattlers. But one thing that couldn't possibly frighten me is the thought of having you all to myself for the rest of my life."

Tears pricked at her eyes as she smiled and laid her head against him. Somehow, he always knew exactly what to say.

They spent several minutes staring into the fire, each lost in their own thoughts. After a long while, Genny mused aloud. "Cutter? Is it just me, or have you noticed that several of the women that work here are pregnant?"

"I told you, darlin'. I hardly notice other women. I can't even tell you what color hair that Mindy-girl had. She makes a pretty good peanut butter and jelly sandwich, but I have no idea what color hair she has."

"Ah-ha!" Genny cried softly in triumph. "So, the way to your heart truly is through your stomach. I knew you only loved me for my cooking."

"That is part of it," he admitted, pressing a kiss into her blond head. "But it's also because of your smile. And your disposition in life. You see the good in other people, and you definitely bring out the good in me. I love you for your passion and your compassion. To be honest, I'm crazy about the whole package." A teasing tone slipped into his voice. "And if that package happens to come with the best apple turnovers in Texas, all the better for me."

"You and your apple turnovers," she muttered, playfully jabbing her elbow into his side.

"Can't help it. They're as sweet and delicious as my little wife." He tickled her, causing her to squeal with laughter.

Movement from behind them drew their attention. Stiffening in alert, Cutter turned to peer into the darkness.

"Is someone there?" he asked.

"It's me," a timid voice said.

"Step out here where we can see you," Cutter demanded.

"I—I can't."

Cutter looked down at his wife with a frown.

On a hunch, she asked lowly, "Tatiana? Is that you?"

"Yes, ma'am. But if the missus sees me talking to you, she'll fire me. I can't lose this job."

"Why don't you come into the cottage," Genny suggested, "and we can talk there?"

"I don't dare. If she ever found out..."

"That's fine," Cutter said smoothly, trusting his wife's judgment. "We'll join you in just a moment. Wait for us behind the cottage."

Acting as if nothing were out of the ordinary, Cutter gathered up their blanket and foodstuff, talking about how tired he was. His voice was slightly louder than need be. Soon, he had ushered Genny inside, turned out the interior lights except for those in the bedroom, and opened the back door in stealth.

"Are you here?" he asked lowly.

The girl stepped from the shadows. "Yes, sir."

"Are you okay, Tatiana?" Genny asked worriedly. "Are you in some sort of trouble?"

"I don't know," she said honestly. "I hope not. But I do need your help."

Cutter sent his wife a questioning glance. Did the girl want money? She looked innocent enough, but he knew that even sweet young girls could get involved with drugs, or worse. Was she playing them? What was her angle?

"You'll have to give us more than that," Genny urged softly. "We can't help if we don't know what the problem is."

It was dark behind the cottage, with night hovering in the tree line and pressing down from the cloud-shrouded sky. Tatiana's raven hair and olive skin tones blended in well with the shadows, but Genny saw her look over her shoulder, making certain no one was nearby.

"I'm pregnant," the girl said on a sob.

The words sent a jolt through Genny. Was it a jolt of sympathy? The girl could easily still be in her teens. *Or,* she asked herself candidly, *was it envy?* She and Cutter wanted a baby so badly. She longed to say those very words herself.

Cutter, too, seemed stunned, but he recovered first. He prodded with an encouraging, "And...?"

"And—And I'm too young to have a baby! I can't have an abortion. My family is Catholic. They would never understand, and, frankly, I couldn't live with myself." Her whispered words were frantic. After sobbing quietly again, she continued, "I don't want to give my baby up, but what choice do I have? I'm barely nineteen."

Genny found her voice. "The baby's father?"

"We love each other, but our families... I'm Hispanic. He's Asian. It would never work."

"How does he feel about the baby?"

"Scared. Sad." Her voice was hesitant. "He's younger than I am. A senior in high school. His parents control his life. They have forbidden him to see me. If I lived at home, my parents would do the same." Her voice came out on a whimper. "We cannot be together."

"I'm sorry, Tatiana. I truly am," Genny said, her voice filled with compassion. "But what are you asking from us? How could we possibly help?"

"You seem like good people. I've watched you. You're kind to everyone, and your husband is a

hard worker. You would make excellent parents."
A bittersweet smile touched Genny's lips. "I'd
like to think so."
Tatiana wiped away her tears. Then she nodded
and blurted out, "I want you to adopt my baby!"

11

Lucy Nguyen's house was filled with a dozen or more extra bodies, with a few stragglers still arriving. Madison recognized a few of the faces, but most were unfamiliar.

Clapping her hands over her head, Lucy called the crowd to order. Her husband spoke limited English, but he sat beside her with a big smile on his face, obviously proud that his wife could command respect from the group consisting primarily of men.

"People!" Lucy said. "You listen. My friend Madison speak. She good woman. She help us."

After a round of polite applause, Madison stood and introduced herself.

"We know you," one man said. "You helped Don get out of jail. We'll hear you out."

"The truth is, I'm not sure what good I can do you, but I promise to try," Madison said. Lucy shushed the disgruntled crowd with another wild wave of her arms.

"Hush, now. Listen," she commanded.

Madison was impressed when they did just

that.

"I'm not saying it's useless," she started over. "I need to know more specifics before I can help come up with a plan."

"See!" Don Nguyen said enthusiastically, jumping to his feet. "She'll go to battle for us, just like I told you she would!"

His mother quietened the crowd again. "One at a time. Back of room first. Go."

Madison recognized Earl Ray Irwin, a longtime resident of Naomi. She understood he was one of the first to go in business with *Barbour*.

"I've been with the company for over ten years," he said. "Made a good living at it, too, especially in the beginning. I knew there would be upkeep. Can't run that many birds through every year without wear and tear on the equipment. Too much dust and ammonia. But the company has done gone loco," the older man complained.

"I've been a top grower for them," he went on. "Run the same ventilation program for years. I know my birds. I know my equipment. I know how to raise a healthy chicken, but suddenly, they tell me I'm doing it all wrong. I tried their new program, and it cost me twelve grand in propane in only a few weeks. Darn fools were sucking all the heat out of the houses with their newfangled timers! Some pencil-pusher sitting behind the desk, thinking they know better than the grower. I told them I wouldn't do it. I'd go back to my own program and still place in the top five slots. Guess what they did? They gave me four FDs. One more farm deficiency, and they can pull my contract. I paid extra on my loan through the years and owe less than eighty grand. They want me to invest three times that to finish out my contract. It just ain't fair!"

A murmur of agreement swept through the crowd.

A second man stood, his English broken but plain. "Same for me. I grow big bird, win bonus. I proud of my farm, take good care. Now they say I do it all wrong. Need new fans, new timers. Where I get that much money? I spent two hundred thousand last year for new cool cells. Bank say no more money for now. *Barbour* say then no birds. I caught between rocks."

A rock and a hard place, Madison translated in her head.

A woman was the next to speak. "Same story here. No offense to my fellow growers here, but it's hard for a white grower to get the money these days. Most of it comes from China. They can't wait to control our food sources and own a bigger chunk of America. *Barbour Foods* is selling us out for easy money. They don't care what it does to the people who helped them build their empire. All they see is dollar signs, and they'll find any way they can to push us out. Their latest tactic is to issue FDs and jerk our contracts."

A Vietnamese man stood and nodded vigorously. "She right. Dirty money moving in, pushing us out. I work hard for what I got, don't want to lose it to a government that wants to take over. I got FD for not mowing grass. But too much rain to mow. Keep getting stuck. *Barbour* don't care. Someone else waiting, fresh off boat from China with suitcase full of money."

The next person took his turn, a younger man Madison recognized from around town. She thought he was some kin to Wanda Shanks.

"I built my houses six years ago, exactly to their specs. They wanted me to use a new line of equipment from Chickadee, so I did. Now they say Chickadee is out. I need to put in HighRollers. The problem is, it's going to cost me almost three hundred thousand dollars, and they refuse to help cover costs. They've given me three months to make the transition, or they'll pull my contract. I just can't do it," he admitted. "I spoke to a realtor about selling. Six months ago, my farm was worth 3.4 million dollars. Now there are so many farms on the market, I'll be lucky to get 2.25. They've flooded the market with growers desperate to get out from under loans with no contract." With a stubborn set to his jaw, his voice strengthened. "It's time we stood up to them and tell them they can't treat us like this. It's not right."

A ruckus spread throughout the room, as everyone agreed and tried to add their own sentiment of outrage and unity. Even Lucy's frantically waved arms couldn't calm them.

Madison resorted to a trick she had seen Brash use on their teenagers. She put her fingers in her mouth and gave a loud, shrill whistle.

The crowd stilled immediately.

"I believe Lucy said one at a time," she said with quiet aplomb.

Lucy looked pleased. Beside her, her husband beamed and gave Madison double thumbs up.

The rest of the stories were much the same. A new manager had taken over the Rockdale

Division, and he was making sweeping changes throughout the complex. No one, not even their best growers, were safe. With his sights set for higher management at the national headquarters in Arkansas, he couldn't be bothered with something as insignificant as a clear conscience. He had ladders to climb, people to crush, and records to break. Only the stockholders mattered. If they were happy, his dream of upper management was within reach.

After hearing all their stories, Madison addressed the crowd again, "I think I understand what the problem is," she said. "But I'll be honest with you. I don't know what to do about it. I've spoken to an attorney, and he agrees that the contract is worded so precisely, it will be difficult to fight. That doesn't mean it can't be done, but *Barbour* has deep pockets. They can afford to see this stalled in the courts for an indefinite period. Meanwhile, you have bills to pay and banks to answer to. This isn't going to be an easy fight."

"But you try, won't you?" a woman named Wanda Wong asked.

Madison looked out at the crowd of desolate faces. As hopeless as it seemed, she couldn't say no.

"I will try," she heard herself promise. "But I don't think I can take your money. It's too iffy."

"We pay in good faith," someone said.

"I understand that. But faith may not be enough. I may not be able to help."

"But you try. That enough for us," someone said from the back of the room.

"You our only hope," another grower agreed.

"They're right," Earl Ray Irwin said. "We can't take them to court. We can't even openly challenge them. But we can pay you to kick up some dust. Cause a stir. Start one of those internet campaigns. Get a boycott going. Hit them where it hurts. In their pocketbook. It's the only thing they understand."

"I'll do what I can," Madison promised lamely.

But she doubted it would be enough.

"How was your meeting?" Brash asked over dinner that night. "Did you take the job?"

Her voice was small. "Yes."

"You don't sound very enthused about it."

"What?" Blake broke in with jest. "No dead bodies to catch your interest?"

"More like too many dead bodies," Madison muttered. "Feathered bodies, that is. A group of chicken growers wants to hire me."

Both twins shuddered in horror. "Not that again!" Bethani wailed. "Do you have any idea how much you reeked back then?"

"Yeah," her brother pitched in. "You borrowed a pair of my boots, and I had to throw them away, they smelled so bad."

"And you *know* how bad his feet stink," Megan added, stabbing her fork in his direction.

"I won't be working in the houses," Madison told the naysayers. "I'll be working behind the scenes."

"Doing what?" Bethani wanted to know.

"Keeping books, or something?"

"Or something," she replied. "It seems *Barbour* is making some radical changes, and their growers can't afford to keep pace. Some of them have been forced to sell their farms to get out from under their loans."

"Like we had to do with our Dallas house," the teen said solemnly, her blue eyes luminous and sad.

"Oh, honey. I never wanted you kids to know the sordid details," Madison said, reaching out to cover her daughter's hand with her own. Grayson had made such a mess of things before his untimely death, leaving his widow and children to pay the price of his foolishness.

"We knew more than you gave us credit for, Mom," Blake reminded her once again. "But I get what you're saying about *Barbour*. Riverton High lost their best pitcher this year, because Ky Beaver's family had to sell their farm and move away."

"I heard Elle Lomax talking about something like that at school last week," Megan nodded. "Her mom is a service tech for *Barbour*. She said they're putting so much pressure on her, she's thinking of quitting."

"What kind of pressure?" Madison asked.

"Something about making her growers do things that don't make sense." The teen waved her fork again. "Something about computer settings and timers on the fans. Or maybe it was heaters. Or maybe both." She turned to her stepsister. "Do you remember?"

"I hardly know her. She's friends with Miley

and her little clique." A roll of her eyes summed up Bethani's opinion of the group.

"Hmm," Madison said. "If any of you hear anything else, let me know. You never know when the tiniest little detail will turn out to be a big lead."

Brash's lips twitched with humor. "Recruiting our kids again? Next thing I know, you'll have Granny Bert and Genny on the case."

Madison wagged a finger in the air. "I won't bother Genny this week, but you know she hears all the latest gossip down at the restaurant."

"Second in line only to your grandmother," the lawman pointed out.

"True. That's why I've already called her. She still didn't sound like she felt very good, so I only asked vague questions. Not enough to start the next great inquisition."

"So, she'll only round up half her posse, not the whole crew," he said with skepticism.

Madison shrugged. "Hopefully. She sounded tired. Maybe she fell asleep before she made all her calls."

Brash shook his auburn head in amazement. "I swear, the FBI needs to hire that woman. She could cut through all the bureaucratic red tape and make half the agents obsolete."

"Too bad all her methods aren't legal," Blake snorted.

"Not to change the subject, but did you remember to order Danni Jo's corsage for the dance?" his mother asked.

"Picking it up after practice," he confirmed.

"Girls? Did you get your dates boutonnieres?"

"Guys don't wear those anymore. Not to Valentine's Dances, anyway," Bethani informed her mother. "Half the girls don't even wear corsages."

"Really?"

The teen nodded. "Just to be sure, I asked Derron. You know he's the closest thing we have to a fashion guru around here."

"Speaking of Derron," Blake said. "What's with all the weird colors in his hair? And how does he make it stand up like that? He must put glue in it or something."

"I don't ask," Madison was quick to say. "I don't want him to mistake it for interest. And certainly not for approval."

"You do need to have a talk with him," Brash said, gentle rebuke in his eyes. "Someone actually called down to the station to file a complaint. Claimed he was a distraction and caused a fender bender."

"I'll see what I can do," she promised glumly. Her sigh spoke volumes. "Just another thing to add to my list of impossible tasks."

"Since you brought it up..." Bethani said slyly, seeing the opening she needed. "I might need your help with an upcoming project at school. And by 'might,' I mean totally. This one is a real mother."

"Bethani!" Madison chided. "Watch your mouth, young lady."

"No, really. I have to become a 'mother' for my health class. We'll draw straws and see which of us has to pretend we're pregnant, which of us has to pretend to adopt a baby, and which of us has to pretend to have an infant. It's a lame project, but our teacher seems all excited about it. She'll drop the bomb next week on who's paired with who, and which straw we draw. I hope I get Russell for a husband. Or Jamal. Anybody but Trenton Torno." She rolled her eyes with exaggerated scorn.

"Oh, yeah," Blake commented. "I think I have to do that, too."

"Megan? What about you?"

"I don't take health until next year," the auburn-haired teen said. She flashed a bright smile. "No baby for me this year."

"And let's keep it that way," her father said with a stern look.

"Ooh, yuck! There's no way I'm having a baby while I'm still in high school. And, please. Spare me 'the talk.' Mom and I had it a long time ago." She tossed her head saucily and darted a covert look at her father. "Taught her everything I knew."

He reacted like the over-protective father that he was. "Which had better be absolutely nothing!"

"Relax. I just wanted to see that little vein pop out on the side of your head," she teased.

"That, and to watch a few more hairs turn gray," Bethani added mischievously.

Brash turned to his wife. "These two are grounded until they turn twenty-one," he deadpanned.

"Oh, goodie," his daughter feigned excitement. "We get to crash Friday night date night with you and Mama Maddy. And just think. The first one is on Valentine's!" she said with false brightness.

"The grounding starts first thing Saturday morning," Brash amended.

"Got it." Madison nodded dutifully. "One question. Does that go on the list above or below toning down Derron's flamboyant personality? Because both are impossible, you know."

Brash huffed out a rueful sigh. "A guy can always dream."

12

Genny spent a restless night, tossing, turning, and replaying the conversation with Tatiana in her head.

After the girl blurted out her surprising statement, she disappeared. She claimed to hear a noise in the darkness and became frightened. After looking at one another in surprise, still shocked by her suggestion of adoption, the couple had turned to see if anyone came from the direction of the main inn. When they turned back around, Tatiana had melted into the shadows.

The teen's obvious fear had worried Genny as much as anything else. Was Marcella Durant truly so tyrannical that she spied on her employees? In case Marcella did lurk nearby, Genny couldn't very well call out the girl's name and ask her to return.

But she *could* formulate a plan to speak with her today.

After having breakfast with Cutter (who was particularly attentive whenever a certain blond-haired server with a name tag of Lyndie came into the dining room), Genny tried acting as nonchalant as possible. She curled up in an out-of-the-way reading nook and did a bit of surveillance, both in person and on her phone.

Covertly watching for Tatiana, she also took note of other staff members. As the inn came to life, and more guests came in for breakfast, servers milled in and out of the kitchen, while other members of the staff slipped up the stairs carrying stacks of fresh towels. From where Genny sat, she had a decent view of the short hallway between the kitchen and formal dining room, as well as the back stairwell.

As Marcella claimed, her staff was a mixed bag of young and old. One server was a nice-looking young man, but the other two were young and female. Through the swinging kitchen door, Genny caught glimpses of a middle-aged man at the grill, a white-haired woman pulling dishes from the ovens, and a young woman at the triple-basin sink. Three other young women traveled up and down the back stairwell, arms laden with laundry. She recognized the person at the front desk as the one who had checked them in on Sunday, a friendly woman seemingly in her early sixties.

Except for Lyndie, all the younger women had some degree of swell within their bellies. For all Genny knew, flirty Lyndie could also be pregnant and, like Tatiana, not showing yet. It hardly seemed coincidental that of the six younger women she could see from her vantage point, five of them were visibly with child.

When she wasn't watching the buzz of activity

at the back of the house, Genny browsed through her phone. She stalked the social media sites, trying to find profiles for nineteen-year-old girls named Tatiana. She couldn't remember how Marcella had addressed her. Miss Gonzales? Galvez? Gomez? Guzman, perhaps? She thought there had been a 'g' and 'z' involved.

With no luck on social media, she pulled up the nearby local high schools. It took patience and a good chunk of her phone's battery, but she finally found a link to their old yearbooks. Another five minutes, and she pulled up the smiling face of one Tatiana Gomez as a graduate last spring. Another twenty, and she found a few random group pictures of the girl among friends. Two of the pictures showed her with a nice-looking boy who could have been Asian, so she presumed it was the baby's father. Another picture showed a group of smiling girls, Tatiana among them, in front of a restaurant named *Antonio's*.

Just as Genny punched the restaurant's name into the map app on her phone, she heard the click of high heels approaching. She looked up to see Marcella coming her way.

"Genny, dear! What in the world are you doing tucked back here in this dark hallway?"

"Just enjoying some downtime," she returned with a smile.

"In the noisiest spot in the house? Wouldn't the library be more relaxing? How can you even concentrate with all that clatter from the kitchen?"

"Most people would probably agree," she

answered ruefully, "but I find the sounds oddly relaxing. They're the sounds I know."

Marcella laughed. "Yes, I suppose I can see that."

"And this is a very comfy loveseat," Genny added, bouncing a little for effect.

"I'm glad you're enjoying it. I trust you have everything you need at the cottage? No troubles I should be aware of?"

Is it my imagination, Genny wondered, *or does she look suspicious? Was she spying on us last night, trying to catch Tatiana 'fraternizing' with the guests?*

"Everything is perfect," Genny assured her, laying it on thick. "It's very quiet and secluded. Even though we're within easy walking distance of the inn and all its conveniences, it's almost like we're in our own little world over there."

Her answer seemed to appease the innkeeper. "That's wonderful to hear and exactly the vibe we were going for," Marcella said.

"It's been an amazing week so far, and it's only half over. I'm anxious to see what the rest of the week holds in store."

The other woman's eyes sparkled, as if she knew a secret. "Yes, Valentine's Day is coming up. And as I understand it, your anniversary."

"Our first."

"That explains the dreamy expression in your eyes!"

"I am married to a wonderful man," Genny pointed out. She assumed that much was obvious to anyone who met him.

Before she could say more, Marcella's phone

rang. The innkeeper pulled it from her pocket, frowning when she saw the name on her caller ID. "If you'll excuse me," she apologized, "I must get this."

"Of course. In fact, it's probably time I head back to the cottage."

As Marcella hurried away, Genny heard their hostess hiss into the phone, "Why are you calling again?" Her voice was anything but gracious.

Despite claims to return to the cottage, Genny pulled her own phone out again. The little red locater dot showed that *Antonio's* was only a fifteen-minute drive from the inn. She smiled, thinking this gave her the perfect cover to speak to Tatiana again. She would pretend to ask for directions, or recommendations for dining. She wouldn't tip her hand that she had seen the photo, but it stood to reason that a local would know the best places to eat.

Now, to run into Tatiana again...

Marcella closed the office door behind her to ensure privacy.

"What do you want?" she asked impatiently. "I thought we finished this conversation last night."

"Not quite," the other person replied. "One of our investors is having trouble coming up with the cash."

"I have bills to pay!" Marcella spat. "Supplies to buy. Payroll to meet. An atmosphere to maintain. I can't afford to have unstable investors. That's your part of this partnership."

"I'm aware of that. The investor assures me he'll have the money no later than Friday."

"Friday is payday. I *will not* have my people's paychecks bounce. Do I make myself clear?"

"Abundantly," came the crisp reply.

Marcella didn't bother with a goodbye. She clicked the end button, silencing any further argument.

She stared out the window to the rolling landscape beyond, for once not feeling the serenity it normally provided. Some days, she felt as if things were spiraling out of her control.

When Gregory had banished her to Texas, she thought her life was over. But she found a way to scrape her existence back together, using her pitiful 'compensation for services rendered' to survive. Not just survive, but to flourish. She had turned her life around. More importantly, she was turning around the lives of others, too. She was doing a good thing here.

The trouble was, the more prosperous *Cherubdipity* became, the more money it required. The adage that it took money to make money couldn't have been truer. It seemed the more their reputation grew, the more her guests demanded. That last remodel hadn't come cheap. In desperation, she had turned to outside investors. It was the only way she knew to make ends meet. The influx of cash gave her the capital needed to upgrade the inn and take her services to the next level of luxury. The downside, however, was that she now had a partner, and they didn't always see eye to eye on matters.

Her phone rang again, but this time she smiled when she saw the name.

"Hello, Father," she greeted in a warm tone.

"Hello, Marcella. How are you today?"

"Busy, as usual. But I always have time for you. How can I help you?"

"I may have another candidate for your program."

Marcella closed her eyes for the time it took to draw in a deep breath. "As always, the thought fills me with equals parts sadness and joy."

"It's a good thing you're doing for them, Marcella," he assured her.

"That's the thought that keeps me going. Now, tell me about this candidate."

"Seventeen-year-old girl, most likely a runaway. I'm sending her file to your email now."

"What's her name?"

"She calls herself Britney, but I noticed she has several things embroidered with the initial 'D.'"

Marcella's computer binged with a received message. "I've got the file. I'll look over it and get in touch with you."

"That's all I can ask. Bless you, Marcella."

"Thank you, Father. Have a nice day."

As Marcella opened the file, she prayed the investor came through with the money. With another mouth to feed, she most definitely needed it.

Genny returned to the cottage to charge her

phone and do some research on her laptop. The first thing she googled was Marcella Durant.

She found several hits for the woman. Her background was impressive. She had graduated with honors from a public school in Baltimore and earned an academic scholarship to Harvard, where she received a bachelor's degree in business management. She minored in Renaissance Studies, which could explain her fascination with the era and her excessive collection of cherub statues. Her resume included positions at several prominent firms in the greater Boston area, roughly correlating with the time Genny worked for Ralph and Suzanne Morgan.

After that, there was a two-year absence of information on Marcella. When she appeared again, it was as a resident of Texas. Six years ago, she had filed for a permit to operate a bed and breakfast out of her home. As the inn grew in popularity, her name appeared more often. *Cherubdipity* made the local paper quite often, via pictures and flattering articles each time the establishment was named Business of the Year, Best of the Brazos Valley, claimed a spot on the Top Ten Spas in East Central Texas, or whenever they made a generous donation to a local charity or organization.

The more Genny dug, the more good deeds she found associated with Marcella Durant and the *Cherubdipity Inn and Spa*. Each Christmas, the business sponsored a Cherub Tree, their own version of an Angel Tree for underprivileged children. Near Mother's Day, Marcella treated the moms of those children to free massages and mani/pedis.

Even more surprising, Genny discovered that *Cherubdipity* was listed as a safe haven designation. Marcella Durant worked in tandem with a local church to sponsor disadvantaged and troubled teens with temporary housing and employment.

That, she decided, explained all the young people working here, and the industrial-type building out back. Most likely, it was a dormitory of sorts.

It didn't, however, explain why so many of her employees were pregnant, unless that was the true meaning behind 'disadvantaged and troubled.'

Something to ask about, she noted.

Her snooping concluded for the day, Genny walked back toward the inn in hopes of finding Tatiana.

Along the way, she pondered these new, conflicting feelings about her hostess.

On the one hand, Marcella was doing good deeds, caring for those less fortunate than herself. Not only did she devote time and resources to worthy causes, she gave generously of her profits, too. But Genny still had trouble understanding her secretive nature and the way she treated her employees. For all her pretense of treating those less fortunate as equals, she went to great efforts to separate her workers from her guests. When it came to business, social status ruled.

Genny considered it a stroke of luck when she caught a glimpse of Tatiana as she approached the inn. The dark-haired girl was collecting abandoned containers and paraphernalia from around the hot tub and nearby fire pit, stacking them on a tray to carry back to the kitchen.

"Hello, Tatiana. How are you today?" Genny smiled. By the time she reached her, the girl had made her way to the main fire pit.

"Fine, ma'am. And you?" Her manner was polite but stiff as she glanced around to see if anyone watched their interaction.

"I'm good. Do you think we could find a minute to talk?"

"I—I don't think that's a good idea."

"After last night, surely—"

"That was a mistake, ma'am," the girl said quickly. "I don't know what I was thinking, coming to you like that. Please, don't tell the missus."

"Of course not. Your secret is safe with us, Tatiana."

"I can't be seen talking with you," the girl said, sending furtive glances around them for signs of being watched.

"I simply want to ask for directions to a local restaurant," Genny said smoothly. She pulled out her phone, already queued to *Antonio's* profile.

Keeping a proper distance, she extended her phone toward the girl and pretended to ask for recommendations. "Can you come to our cottage again this evening?" she asked lowly.

"Too risky."

"Where, then? We want to talk to you."

"I'll get you word."

"Do you have a cell phone?"

"No, ma'am." She saw movement from the side

of her eye. "Uh-oh. Follow my lead," she hissed.

She waved toward the woman stepping onto the patio. With a motion of her hand, Tatiana beckoned Marcella Durant their way.

"I'm sorry to bother you, Mrs. Durant," she said, taking a pro-active approach to the situation. "Our guest is asking for a recommendation on a restaurant in town, but I'm afraid I can't help her. Maybe you can answer her questions?"

"Why, yes. I would be delighted." She smiled at Genny before flicking her hand toward the girl. "That will be all, Tatiana."

Genny played along, dutifully turning her full attention to her hostess. "Do you have a recommendation for dinner? Everything we've had here at the inn has been delicious, but we were thinking about going into town and checking out the local flavors. Is this *Antonio's* good, or do you suggest somewhere else?"

"You're looking for Mexican food?"

"It sounds good." Genny nodded, even though her stomach had been upset the past few days. She thought it had more to do with the chef's heavy hand with the spices than it did with any stomach bug she may have picked up.

"*Antonio's* is good," Marcella allowed, "although I prefer the national chain next door to them."

"Really? You've been so supportive in the community, I thought you would recommend a locally owned mom-and-pop restaurant." When the innkeeper looked startled by the observation, Genny flashed a dimpled smile and explained, "I confess. I've been checking up on you. You have a very impressive resume, I must say."

She accepted the compliment awkwardly. "I do what I can to help my community."

Genny took a seat on the nearby bench and patted the spot beside her. "Please. Do you have a moment to visit?"

After the slightest hesitation, Marcella took a seat.

"The other day, I asked you about all the young girls that worked here. I asked if you were affiliated with a school work-program."

"And as I said, I'm not."

Not understanding why she still seemed so stiff, Genny offered a gentle, encouraging smile. "You never mentioned you have a program of your own established. That, in fact, is so much more impressive."

"Well, I..." Again, she seemed uncomfortable with the praise.

"I don't mean to embarrass you. I think it's wonderful that you're helping those less fortunate. But... I can't help but notice that many of the girls are pregnant," Genny dared to press on. "Is that part of your program? Do you only help expectant mothers?"

Marcella's answer was slow, her "No," stretched with meaning. After a resigned sigh, she seemed to realize Genny wouldn't give up so easily. She may as well answer her questions. "But you are correct. Most of the girls who seek my help are expecting a baby and have no means of supporting them. No support system at home. I offer them shelter and temporary employment."

"That's very commendable of you. How did

you get started in such an endeavor, if you don't mind me asking?"

Marcella looked down at her hands, which were twisted into a nervous knot. "When I was younger, I found myself in the same situation," she admitted. "I didn't handle it well. My family had already disowned me and when I came up pregnant, so did the baby's father. I was suddenly homeless, jobless, and with child. I refused to have an abortion or give the child up for adoption. I loved my baby, but I behaved selfishly. And then..." Her hands tangled even more, and her voice dropped an octave. "And then, the state stepped in and declared me an unfit mother. I still had no home, no job, no viable means of support for myself and my baby."

"I—I'm sorry. I didn't know. I shouldn't have pried," Genny apologized, her eyes filling with tears.

"It's all right. I tell this story every time I welcome a new girl to *Cherubdipity*. It keeps me focused and reminds me of the importance of what we do here."

"And what is it you do here, exactly?"

"We offer the girls a chance. They work here and earn a fair salary, complete with room and board. If they choose to give their babies up for adoption, we put them in touch with agencies that can do that. If they wish to keep their babies, we do what we can to give them a head start. They may stay here until the beginning of their third trimester, at which time our arrangements come to an end."

"Wow. That's very impressive." The awe in her

voice bespoke her sincerity.

But it still doesn't explain the secrecy and rather tyrannical control of the staff, a nagging voice said inside her head.

Clearly wanting to change the subject, Marcella smiled. "It's almost lunch time, and that handsome husband of yours should be in at any time. He's doing an excellent job, by the way."

"Then maybe we'll go out this evening and celebrate!" Genny decided.

"You can't go wrong with *Antonio's*," Marcella granted, even though she preferred the chain restaurant.

Genny allowed her this one slight to a locally owned small business. Marcella did good in other areas of the community, so she could hardly fault her for her food choices. Besides, the innkeeper wasn't originally from the South. Her taste buds probably weren't geared for authentic Tex-Mex cooking, which the restaurant was known for.

After Marcella excused herself and went inside, Genny's phone buzzed with a message from Cutter. He would be at a good stopping point in about an hour, if she could hold off eating for that long.

His message offered a perfect excuse for her to request a picnic basket for their room.

And with any luck, Tatiana would be the one to deliver it. She seemed to work the cottages and outdoor areas, rather than inside the inn itself.

Thirty or so minutes later, Genny heard a knock on the cottage door and hurried to open it. Tatiana did, indeed, stand there with a basket and a smile, but she was in an obvious rush.

"I believe this is everything you requested," the girl said with a polite and professional smile. "Two sandwiches, bottled water, a pint of mixed fruit, assorted cheeses, and crackers."

"Yes, I believe it is. Thank you, Tatiana."

"I just need you to sign for it here," she said, pulling a small receipt book from her apron.

"Do you have a minute to visit?"

"I'm afraid not. I can't be seen here longer than it takes to deliver and sign."

Disappointed but understanding, Genny added a generous tip to the receipt and singed with a flourish. "Can we meet later?"

"I have a doctor's appointment tomorrow afternoon, so I'll be going into Franklin. If you can get away, we could meet at *Cup o' Love*, a nearby coffee shop." She glanced down at her watch. It was a simple, no-frills off brand, so unlike the fancy smartwatches most teens wore these days. "About four o'clock. Act surprised to see me there."

With that, she took the signed ticket and departed, barely sparing a glance back over her shoulder.

13

There's no time like the present.

Taking the advice she heard so often from her grandmother, Madison wasted no time digging into the situation surrounding *Barbour Foods* and their growers.

She knew corporations had an obligation to their investors and stockholders. They were in business to make a profit, even when it meant taking a hard stand and enforcing company policies.

She also knew that, without the farmers, the company would have nothing. No chickens to sell and no profits to make. People who thought their meats came from the grocery stores were woefully out of touch with reality. It took real people and real animals on farms and ranches to provide enough food to feed an entire nation. She often worried what would happen in the future, when the highways, railways, shopping centers, and housing developments spilled from the cities and gobbled up the countryside. It was already happening at an alarming rate. When there was no land left for farming, how would people eat?

There had to be a common ground between *Barbour Foods* and their contract growers, but where? Loyalty was earned, and if *Barbour* didn't stand behind their people, they could hardly expect to build a profitable operation dependent upon their essential players. It took a sense of unity and loyalty to create a strong network.

Madison couldn't very well call up the company and ask questions. If they bothered to answer her at all, it would be with a sales pitch and the same rote statistics and jargon she found on their website.

There were two sides to every story and, so far, she had only heard one of them. She knew the tales she had heard were understandably biased. Likewise, the company's website and public information was biased from the opposite perspective. What she needed was someone with a neutral opinion. This called for a hands-on approach and a road trip.

Poultry Pickings was a huge farm supply company with special emphasis on the poultry industry. Their main headquarters and flagship store was in Rockdale and within easy driving distance of The Sisters. Just a few miles down the road, *F&R Depot* offered similar services on a much smaller scale, so she could hit both places in one afternoon.

She came to the latter first, so she grabbed a yellow tablet from her seat and walked into the farm and ranch store under the pretense of being a reporter.

"Come on back." The man at the counter

seemed more than happy to welcome a reporter into their midst, clearly hoping for his own chance at fame. With his permission, Madison even snapped a few pictures of him at the register with her phone, gushing about what a great cover it would make for her magazine. "The boss is in his office."

"Shouldn't you ask if he's willing to talk with me before we barge in?"

"Nah," the man assured her. "We're always looking for a way to get a leg up on the competition. He'll be tickled pink to know you chose us over them." Just before rapping on the door, he peered down at her. "You ain't interviewing them, too, are you?"

She flashed him a smile. "Being a new publication, we're a bit of an underdog, too. I think it's nice if we all stick together. Don't you?"

"Sounds like a winner to me." He knocked and immediately pushed the door open, not waiting for approval.

"Hey, Bill. This little lady is here to do an article on *F&R*. I figured you'd want to give her a tour of the place and answer whatever questions she has."

"Oh, really?" A man with sandy-red hair lumbered to his feet, stretching his arm out beyond his extended belly. "Bill Gladstall, owner and operator here at the *Farm and Ranch Depot. F&R* for short."

"It's a pleasure to meet you, Mr. Gladstall."

"What is it I can do for you? Are you with the Farm Digest?" He practically salivated at the thought of snagging an interview with the industry's leading publication.

"No, I'm with Poultry Potpourri. We're a new publication just getting started. So new, in fact, that our business cards aren't even ready yet." She offered an appropriate look of exasperation. "We're still working on our debut issue, and with any luck, *F&R* may just make the cover."

Bill Gladstall swelled up like a banty rooster. He strutted around the desk with an air of importance, hitching his blue jeans up around his wide hips. "Well, now, don't that just sound fine and dandy. I do believe we'd make a fine cover story. What is it you'd like to know, hon? I don't think I caught your name."

She ignored the 'hon' remark, intent on coming up with a suitable moniker. The first man hadn't asked, and Madison hadn't thought to make up an alias beforehand. She finally went with something easy to remember and at least half true.

"Josie Cessna." The name listed on her birth certificate, in fact, was Madison Josephine Cessna.

"Well, Miss Josie, come with me, and I'll tell you all about supplying the farm and ranch industry."

"We'd like to focus on the poultry houses in the area, and the changes you've seen over recent years."

"I reckon you mean all the new specs *Barbour* has come out with, demanding growers update their houses to keep up with the new Crockett division. Fine business for us, mind you, but a slap in the face to the farmers who signed on first.

They helped to build the company when it was still just a chick in an eggshell." He grinned, quite pleased with his own little joke. "Did you see what I did there? Chick in an eggshell? You can use that in your story, if you like."

"Oh, absolutely." She jotted it down in her notebook with an exaggerated nod.

"Yep, those farms who started out ten or so years ago helped build the company's poultry division. *Barbour Foods* started out packing frozen vegetables and canned goods. Branched into dairy, and then poultry. The Rockdale Division was the first chicken complex they built, so these growers are pioneers. Don't seem fair to be tossed away now, just because the company built shiny new houses in another area."

"It sounds like you know all about the poultry industry. Can you tell me more?"

"I can tell you anything you'd like to know, little lady," the big man beamed.

Having learned from a first-class schmoozer, Madison knew to play to the man's ego, just as Granny Bert always did. She jotted down an indecipherable note on her yellow pad. She added a few exclamation marks and underlines for good measure. "I can see this article is going to be a big hit. Tell me more about these updates and new specs."

"Follow me. I'll tell you about it on the way to the warehouse."

He led her down a hallway as he talked. "You see, when these houses were built, *Barbour* called for top-of-the-line everything. That meant Chickadee. They're simply the best there is. A couple of the other companies give 'em a run for their money on things like motors and fans, but on poultry-specific equipment, like feeders and water lines, no one can beat Chickadee. That's one of the reasons these new specs just don't make sense. HighRollers offers an inferior product, but that's what *Barbour* is calling for these days. Nothing but HighRollers."

"Maybe they offered a break on equipment if they used them for everything?" Madison suggested.

"If they did," Bill snorted, "it's sure not to the grower. Or to us supply houses. HighRollers is a good fifteen percent higher across the board, and I've got to pass that cost along to my customers if I want to stay in business. If anyone is getting a break, it's somebody at *Barbour*, and it's under the table."

Stunned, Madison stopped in her tracks and stared at him. "Are you suggesting someone at the company is getting a kickback for using HighRollers?"

"I ain't naming names, mind you. And I ain't making flat-out accusations. I'm just saying it don't make sense to use over-priced, under-performing equipment when the product they're replacing is better made and better priced. *Barbour Foods* didn't become a leader in the industry by making fool decisions."

"You mean the current equipment is still in good shape?"

"Not always. But eight times out of ten, we're ripping out equipment that still has a lifespan of several years, only to replace it with new product that will probably last the same amount of time. Don't make sense," the man insisted.

He led her out to the warehouse, where he showed her replacement feed pans for both brands. He pointed out the difference in the materials and to the moving parts on the HighRollers example that were likely to break. For the most part, Chickadee featured solid construction.

After they had toured most of the warehouse, and Bill had rattled on until Madison's head threatened to explode, they returned to his office.

"Do you think what you mentioned earlier is possible?" she asked as he opened the door for her. "Do you think someone at *Barbour* could be padding their own pockets by pushing HighRollers products? And if so, who would it be? Someone in accounting, maybe?" she suggested.

"Nah. It would have to be someone in upper management. The broiler manager or higher. Maybe the planner for this complex. Maybe the division manager. Who knows? Maybe even somebody at corporate. It has to be someone who has the authority to make decisions and see that they're carried out."

Back at his desk now, the depot owner asked, "Did you need to take a picture? Use my good side, if you don't mind." He turned his face to the left.

Having almost forgotten about her ruse as a reporter, Madison pretended to ponder the question. "On second thought, I think I'll send a staff photographer to take photos. We need a true professional to do you and your business here justice."

Bill Gladstall was all smiles as they parted amid handshakes and a vague mention of having their prospective offices coordinate dates for a photoshoot. Madison bit back a tinge of guilt as she hurried out to her car and slipped behind the wheel.

It's for a good cause, she assured herself. Lucy Nguyen and the rest of the chicken farmers, complex-wide, deserved justice. *Barbour Foods* must be stopped. They weren't just ruining the growers, they were ruining the supply houses, too. I saw all that useless Chickadee product piled to the ceiling. Who would buy it now, when only HighRollers was allowed?

Just down the road was a complex three times as big and busy as the one she had just left. The name *Poultry Pickings* was lit up with a big neon sign.

This time, she pretended to be a potential chicken farmer, there to gather prices and information for her prospective business. She turned to a fresh section of her yellow pad and jotted down a few specific items she remembered seeing not only at the last warehouse, but also at Ronny Gleason's farm when she worked for him those fateful few weeks.

She wandered into the expansive building which, at first glance, looked like an average hardware store. There were rakes, shovels, wheelbarrows, all sorts of small hand tools, and some that were quite a bit larger.

A few rows past the potting soil and seed, she found the poultry-specific products. Bags of layer mash, wire for chicken coops, and an assortment of goods for raising backyard chickens.

Beyond that, the aisles grew wider to accommodate the needs of commercial farms. She was halfway down an aisle filled with replacement feeder pans when a salesman found her.

"Hi. I'm Jody. How can I help you today?"

"My husband and I are considering buying commercial chicken houses, and I need some information."

"You've come to the right place," Jody assured her with a bright smile. "What kind of information do you need?"

"What can you tell me about replacement pans for the feed lines? I see the yellow ones are quite a bit cheaper than the purple ones."

"Yes, the yellow are Chickadee. By far the best product, but if you're growing for *Barbour Foods*, you'll need to use the HighRollers brand."

"Why not use the best, especially if they're cheaper?" Madison asked.

"Because *Barbour* has decided to go exclusively with HighRollers."

"That hardly makes sense, if the other brand is better," she argued. "It even looks sturdier."

"Hey, I don't try to understand the rules, and I definitely don't make them. But what *Barbour* wants, *Barbour* gets. There's a handful of farms around here that grow for *Chicken International* and even a few turkey farms with *Miller Meats*, but by and large this is *Barbour* country. If they say they want HighRollers, then we'll clearance out our older lines and stock HighRollers."

Madison frowned. "It sounds like they have a

monopoly on the market."

"Something like that," the salesman agreed. "How big of a farm are you looking at buying? Does it have yellow or purple equipment?"

"Yellow. Which is good, right? That means we have the better ones." She pretended not to know about the required upgrades.

"Not exactly. To bring your houses up to spec—sort of like up to new building codes, if they were residential houses—you'll need to change everything out to HighRollers."

"That sounds expensive!"

"Depending on the size of your farm, it can be. Didn't the seller tell you all this? Or the front office at *Barbour*, when you went in for your interview?"

"What interview?" Madison asked.

"*Barbour* has the right to accept or reject anyone they want. Before you can buy or build a farm, you have to pass their background checks and an entry interview."

"No one ever mentioned that," she said, which was true.

"Yep. The company controls your fate, so to speak."

"But I understood we would be contract growers, in business for ourselves."

"Maybe on paper," Jody said, "but *Barbour Foods* is really the one in control." He spread his hands in a helpless gesture. "You know the old saying. It's their way or the highway."

Madison asked a few questions about pricing, but her notes weren't about numbers. She was jotting down reminders to herself.

Find out if HighRollers is a subsidiary of Barbour Foods.

See who the stockholders are for both companies.

Find out who's in control here in Rockdale and at the national headquarters.

Call it a hunch, but as Granny Bert would say, something about the entire situation smelled like a mud cat caught three days ago and left in the sunshine.

Something smelled fishy.

14

Cutter quit early the next day, his project almost done. They spent the afternoon in town, browsing the shops before and after meeting Tatiana at the coffee shop. They would conclude their outing with dinner at *Antonio's*.

Just before four, the couple wandered into *Cup o' Love* and perused the menu board while they stood in line at the counter.

"I see they have apple turnovers," Cutter mused. He leaned in close and murmured, "I won't even bother. They can't be anywhere as good as yours."

"You should really broaden your horizons. Try someone else's for comparison, or, if you really want to step outside your comfort zone, try something else for a change," his wife teased. "A cupcake, for instance. That strawberry and cream one looks nice."

"See, I don't get why everyone is all gaga about cupcakes. They're too messy. Plus, I'd look ridiculous in a pink mustache," the macho man proclaimed. "At least apple turnovers just leave a few crumbs." He flicked his fingers across his western shirt to brush away imaginary crust.

"Again. Broaden your horizons."

From behind them, a timid voice spoke. "The fudge brownie delights are good here."

Whirling around, Genny truly was surprised to see Tatiana. She hadn't realized anyone came in behind them. Plus, she almost didn't recognize the girl out of her starched uniform. Face scrubbed free of makeup and her dark hair now cascading freely down her back in loose waves, the girl wore jeans, a simple t-shirt, and a ragged denim jacket for warmth. Genny had to wonder if the frayed edges and rips were a statement of high fashion, or of low necessity.

"Tatiana! Imagine running into you here," she beamed. "You must have the afternoon off."

The girl shrugged. "Running a few errands and decided to drop in for a cup of coffee and a treat."

"Do you have a minute to join us?" Genny asked with a friendly smile.

"I... I really shouldn't." Tatiana's eyes darted around the mostly empty room, ferreting out eavesdroppers.

"And miss seeing this guy try something new?" Genny said, hooking a thumb toward Cutter. "Not a chance."

After ordering— Cutter chose a huge peanut butter cookie and, with a defiant gleam in his hazel eyes, a not-so-scrumptious-looking apple turnover—to Genny's fudge brownie delight. He suggested she grab a table while he waited for Tatiana to order. He paid for it all, and then the two of them carried their coffees to the middle back table Genny had chosen.

"I thought you could sit facing the door," she murmured, motioning to the open seat snuggled against the wall.

"Thank you," the girl said, sliding her slight form into the chair. "I'm afraid I don't have long to talk."

"Warm up with a few sips of coffee, and then we'll visit," Cutter suggested. "It's turning colder out there."

Genny blew on her vanilla latte and broke off a bite of her brownie. She forced herself to taste both before she barged into the conversation, even though curiosity had her on edge.

"I can't help but notice how nervous you are about being seen talking with guests. Is it really against the rules?" she all but blurted out.

Tatiana took a gulp of coffee, wincing when it burned its way down her throat. It also bought her time to find an appropriate answer. "The missus strongly discourages social contact between the staff and the guests."

"How much trouble do you get in?" Cutter asked quietly, setting aside his cup. His scalding-hot coffee was already half-gone. He claimed that, as a firefighter, the heat didn't faze him.

"At first, we lose privileges. Repeat offenders lose their jobs."

"Privileges?"

"Television time, book check-outs from the in-house library, free airtime on the internet. That sort of thing."

His low whistle wasn't of admiration. "Sounds like she runs a tight ship."

Unwilling to speak ill of her boss, the girl compromised with, "She does believe in discipline."

"I spoke with Marcella a bit today about the program she runs," Genny said. "I must say, I was surprised. And impressed. Quite frankly, judging merely by her interaction with you and the rest of the staff, I didn't know she had such a compassionate and caring side to her personality."

The girl toyed with her own brownie. Another sip of coffee delayed her response. "She says it's because of her own past and the choices she was faced with. Or maybe it was the lack of choices she had back then. She wants to offer more to today's generation."

"And that's very commendable of her. But I still don't understand why you're so afraid to be seen talking to us." Genny glanced at her husband before continuing. "Are you... Are you there of your own free will?"

Tatiana looked shocked at the suggestion. "Yes. Yes, of course! She doesn't run a cult. She just has rules. Boundaries." Her voice turned into a sulk. "Something most of us were obviously lacking, or we wouldn't be in the situation we're in now."

"So, you're free to leave, anytime you like?" Cutter pressed.

"Sort of?" Squirming in her seat, she went on to explain, "We sign a Commitment Pledge before we're hired. We make more than minimum wage, plus we get free room and board. The missus keeps part of our wages in a high-yield, interest-bearing account, which she returns to us when we graduate from the program."

Genny frowned in confusion. "Program?"

"Part of the agreement says that we'll complete a ten-week educational program. She gives us a tablet, and we take online classes on personal finances, time management, childcare, how to look for a job and fill out a resume, and electives in whatever field we think we're interested in. If we pass the classes with good grades and perfect attendance, the tablets are ours to keep."

"That's very impressive," Cutter said, finishing off his coffee. The cookie was gone in just a few bites.

"There's more. We must attend mandatory group counseling twice a week, with private sessions available if we need them. There's also chapel, meditation time, and etiquette classes."

Which explains Tatiana's impeccable manners and good diction, Genny thought. *She doesn't talk like most nineteen-year-olds.*

"And," the girl continued, "depending if we choose to keep our babies or place them with an adoption agency, there's hands-on classes in childcare or meetings with prospective parents and agency liaisons."

A crease divided Genny's forehead. "So, these are private adoptions? You get to help select the parents?"

Tatiana looked uncertain. "I guess." She toyed nervously with the brownie, most of which was untouched.

Cutter and Genny exchanged a loaded look before he spoke. "I have to admit, it sounds like

Marcella Durant is offering you ladies a first-class opportunity. It's hard to believe she's being so generous, when all she gets in return is six to nine months of guaranteed workers."

"Make no mistake," the girl said, her dark eyes flashing with a spark of passion. "We work hard for our money. Those little luxuries may not sound like much, but we pretty much live in isolation out there. Not by force, but by necessity. Between work and classes, we don't get a lot of time to come into town. I'm one of the lucky few who has my own car, even though it's not much to look at, and it has a terrible knock in the engine. Every time I drive over fifty miles an hour, I wonder if she's gonna make it. With nothing much else to do at the inn, watching television, reading, and getting free airtime becomes a real treat. Our tablets are for school and hooked to the main server, so we can't use them just whenever we feel like it."

It went without saying that their log-in history could be traced.

With a heavy sigh, Tatiana went on to admit, "But I suppose she gets our loyalty, too. Like you said, not many people would go to so much trouble for a bunch of messed-up girls. Obviously, our own families don't, or we wouldn't be here."

Glossing over that glum thought, Genny changed the subject. "I understand you must have a firm plan of action in place by the end of your second trimester?"

"Yes. If we decide to keep our babies, we must leave well before we give birth. We have to take the money we've earned and the money that she's saved for us, and go out into the big, cold, scary world to become single mothers. She gives us letters of recommendation and has a list of contacts for us, like places to apply for a job and look for housing, or, if we're lucky, the confidence to go back to our parents or boyfriends and beg for a second chance."

"And if you choose to give your baby up for adoption?"

"We can stay here until delivery. And beyond. The arrangements are the same, except the classes must be with an accredited college or work force. That way, we're more prepared to go out into the world and make something of ourselves."

The Montgomerys were stunned with the thought and care Marcella had put into her program.

They were also confused. Genny said so.

Reaching gently across the table to touch the girl's hand, she kept her voice low and gentle as she asked, "I have to ask, Tatiana. With such a generous and well-thought opportunity being offered, why did you approach us? Why not go through the agency Marcella recommends? Why us?"

"You seem like a nice, stable couple. You could offer my baby the life I never could. I see what a hard worker your husband is. He's done a fine job of the fence." Her voice dropped to a whisper. "Too fine, maybe. Now it feels a little more like a fence to keep us in, rather than to keep trespassers out." She shook the thought away, determined to be upbeat. "I see how much he adores you. And you him. You're devoted to one another, and you'll be devoted to your children. I see how kind and compassionate you are. I can't think of better parents for my baby." She laid a protective hand over her stomach. She wasn't showing yet, but the doctor said she was progressing on schedule, and soon she'd sport a baby bump.

Soon, Tatiana knew there would be no denying the truth.

"We're flattered, of course," Genny said, patting her hand, "but you don't know us."

"I don't know those other people, either," the girl asserted. "Sure, I can take one look at them and see they have money. They can raise my baby with the best of everything. But most of the people who come here are old enough to be *my* parents." Emotion glittered in her dark eyes. "I want my baby to have parents who can sit on the floor with her and show her how to put together a puzzle. I want her to have parents who'll take her to softball practice and teach her how to throw a spit ball, not just sit in the stands on game days, leaving the nanny to do all the dirty work. Parents who can not only afford to send her to college, but who will still be alive and mobile when she graduates."

Genny sent a helpless look to Cutter, her heart already a puddle of empathy and emotion.

"You look like the kind of people who won't care about the color of my baby's skin. The other people who come here, they can *buy* her way into the right schools and the right circles, but they can't buy other people's respect. But you." She waved between the two people sitting across the table from her, both obviously caught up in her vision. "You'll teach her to *earn* people's respect. To deserve their respect. I know you're the kind of people who will give her the confidence to rock her looks, not try to cover them up with bleached hair and too much makeup."

Overwhelmed by the huge compliment the girl bestowed upon their characters, Genny touched her hand to her heart and bit back a sob. Even Cutter choked up.

Misunderstanding their quiet response as hesitation, Tatiana quickly added, "Did I mention one of my grandmothers has mixed blood? One of her grandmothers was from Norway. My mother's twin brother inherited her bright, vibrant blue eyes. Like yours. So did two of my sisters and one of my brothers. There's a chance my baby will have them, too."

Genny gave a most unladylike snort, louder than she intended because of her tear-clogged throat. She pulled her long-sleeved blouse up at the wrist, exposing her lily-white skin. "I was thinking what a wonderful complexion your baby will have, with your Hispanic coloring and your boyfriend's Asian skin tones. He or she won't have to worry about burning and freckling out in the sun the way I do."

Beside her, Cutter scoffed, making fun of his own weathered skin. "Between ranching, welding, and fighting fires, my skin's so tough and leathery, I've forgotten what color it is. My freckles seared over long ago."

"So, a child of color won't matter to you?" the girl reiterated.

"It might offer the perfect balance in family photos," he mused. "What was it Kiki called it? An anchor color?" He hadn't paid a lot of attention to what the flamboyant designer called things when she redecorated the Big House on TV, not until Genny used the same terms while decorating the farmhouse he restored especially for her.

Tatiana leapt at the hint of acceptance. "You'll consider adopting my baby?"

"I..." Genny looked at her husband helplessly, but he saw the hope that had already sprung into her blue eyes. "We'll have to discuss this at length, Tatiana. This isn't something we can make an immediate decision about."

"I understand," the girl mumbled, but she dropped her eyes in disappointment.

"There's still plenty of time, right? You aren't even showing yet. How far along are you?"

"Only seven weeks. But..." She blew out a deep breath before admitting, "I'm starting to feel a little pressured. I need to develop my plan, submit it for approval, and then work toward my goals. If I'm keeping my baby, I'll have to be out in four months. That's not enough time to plan out our entire future."

"But she offers you resources, right?" Cutter pointed out the positives. "People who can advise you and help you along the way?"

"Yes. But I only know of a couple of girls who took that route. The rest choose to give their babies up. Somehow, it not only seems easier, but they make us feel like it's the only responsible thing to do." She rubbed at her skin, which was now covered in gooseflesh. She didn't meet their eyes as she continued in a not-so-proud voice. "I don't know. Somehow, it feels like I'm selling my baby," she admitted lowly. "The adopted parents pay for all the medical bills, but the girls..." She looked around, making certain no one was near enough to overhear her words. "Somehow, the mothers always have enough extra cash to buy new clothes and new shoes. I guess they found a way to cut medical expenses and keep the excess money for themselves. A lot of the girls move out and ditch the program after their babies are born, but there's one girl here who's pregnant for the third time."

"Tatiana." Genny's low voice was filled with shock. Fear. Horror. "Are you suggesting these girls are actually *selling* their babies?"

She jerked her dark head up, her eyes wild with a different kind of fear. "No! No, not at all. That would be... No. I'm just saying... I don't have a good feeling about it. I'm just not sure I can do it, not with people I don't know and trust." Her face lost all color when her nervous gaze landed upon the people just entering the coffee shop. She sucked in a gasp. "Oh my God. I have to go. They can't see me talking to you." She was already standing, keeping her face carefully covered by a curtain of dark, tangled hair as she franticly consulted her watch. "I'm sorry. I'm sorry, but I have to go."

The newcomers stalled in the doorway, discussing something in low voices and effectively blocking the girl's means of escape. She opted for the restroom in the back, darting off before the Montgomerys could say another word.

"What in the world..." Genny murmured in horrified mystique. "That poor girl is frightened out of her mind!" She sat back in indecision. "Should I go to her?"

"No. She strikes me as girl who can get herself out of a scrape." A sly smile lifted one corner of Cutter's mouth. "That doesn't mean we can't help create a distraction, though, once they're seated, and she's ready to hightail it out of here."

After ordering their coffee, the incoming trio took their seats two tables away. They were just far enough away that the couple couldn't hear their conversation, but they could read their body language.

Genny thought she recognized one of the newcomers as a girl from the inn. She wore casual clothes similar to Tatiana's, but her stomach was swelled large enough to roughly accommodate a basketball. Her face was pale with apprehension, and a high, nervous pitch carried in her voice.

This girl, too, was clearly filled with fear, Genny realized.

The two people in suits carried briefcases and spoke in calm, professional tones. Their precise words were unintelligible, but their mannerisms spoke volumes. The man facing Genny looked slightly more uncomfortable than his counterpart, once even sloshing coffee from his stoneware cup into the saucer beneath it. While the suits opted for true coffee cups, the girl had chosen a clear, throw-away and straw that revealed the colorful, fruity concoction with no caffeine.

Should Tatiana have been drinking caffeine? Genny wondered. *And when and if I became pregnant, will I be forced to give up my addiction to caffeine?* It was a downside she hadn't considered yet, but a small price to pay for carrying a healthy child.

The coffee slosher pulled an envelope from his briefcase and slid it toward the other suit. The flash of a shiny, new smartwatch caught Genny's eye, bringing to mind the simple timepiece Tatiana wore. A quick glance at his companions confirmed they all shared his taste in the latest gadgets.

The other suit took the envelope, peered inside, and nodded briefly before pushing the envelope to the girl.

For a moment, the girl stared at the envelope as if it were a snake. When Genny saw her lick her lips, she amended the thought. Perhaps she stared at it like she would a big, juicy *steak*. Her hand trembled as she reached out and whisked it off the table, tucking it safely within her backpack.

The suit said something, and the girl dutifully pulled out a manila file.

Genny didn't know if it was part of his plan, but Cutter's timing couldn't have been better. Just as he bit into the over-cooked apple turnover, Tatiana poked her head out from around the corner. As he coughed in regret for choosing any turnover other than one made by his wife, he caught sight of the girl from his side vision. He made a sound of protest and kicked out a long leg, silently objecting to the inferior pastry. As a true gentleman, he had tucked his hat away beneath his chair, resting it on its crown like any revered cowboy hat should be treated. Now, however, it sailed neatly across the room, coming to rest at the feet of the girl with the stretched-out shirt.

He lumbered to his feet, issuing an apology and causing quite the commotion, as Tatiana ran for the door and disappeared down the street in the opposite direction of the plate-glass windows. He stood for a moment beside the girl and her companions at the other table, demanding their full attention with his charming smile and old-fashioned manners. When he finally turned back to Genny, hat in his hands, his eyes twinkled in self-satisfaction.

"You are so bad," she giggled so that only he could hear.

"Why don't we get out of here, and I'll show you just how bad I can be," he suggested with a provocative waggle of his eyebrows.

"You owe me supper, Mister. Don't think a simple brownie is going to cut it."

"But it was the deluxe, *delight*ful model," he pointed out. As he stared at the abandoned turnover, his mouth curled down in distaste. "Unlike that sorry excuse of an apple turnover over there. They need to take lessons from you on how to give proper homage to a quality pastry and American favorite like the apple turnover."

"Let's just hope *Antonio's* lives up to its hype." She let him assist with her chair and help her into her coat. She flashed her trademark dimples in appreciation, flipping her short curls over her collar. "After we visit that cute little dress shop on the corner, of course."

15

The restaurant was already busy and quite noisy, but Genny spotted a table being set up for a large group in the backroom. After speaking with the manager, she flashed Cutter a big smile and followed the server to the booth tucked into a quiet, secluded corner.

"The party doesn't start for over an hour, ensuring us the better part of a quiet, intimate conversation over a couple of margaritas and another meal I didn't cook," she told her husband as she slipped off her coat. "Win-win."

They ordered quickly, knowing the quiet bubble around them was limited. As the server delivered frosty mugs of frozen margaritas crusted with salty rims, Cutter eyed his wife with knowing eyes.

"You're considering it, aren't you?"

Over the tip of her straw, she looked appropriately innocent. "Considering what?"

"Adopting that girl's baby. That's what."

She didn't answer right away. After a moment

of silence, she gathered the strength to say, "It's not an option I ever allowed myself to consider. But, the very truth of the matter is that I may be unable to get pregnant. Even if we go the in vitro route, or I take fertility shots, there's no guarantee either will work. And with shots," she reminded him, "there's always the chance it may work *too* well. We could end up with quadruplets! Even octuplets!"

"That's eight at once, right?" he asked, stretching out the collar of his shirt as it tightened around his neck.

"That's momma in a nut house, and all of us in the poor house!" she quipped.

"I'm not sure a private adoption is much cheaper," he mumbled. "The way Tatiana talked, only the high rollers can afford to play that game."

"We're not exactly hurting for money," she reminded him. "*New Beginnings* is a very lucrative business, as is *Cutter's Torch*. And even though it took you forever to tell me about it, those two little inventions of yours bring in a nice cash roll of their own." She kicked him playfully beneath the table, still slightly miffed at his oversight.

"It was just a couple of gadgets that made sense for the chicken industry," he said with downplayed modesty.

"But you had the good sense to patent them, and now we're reaping the rewards. Just the royalties alone could make a sizable dent in the cost of a private adoption."

Behind a big swig of margarita, minus the dainty straw, her husband muttered something that sounded a lot like, "Who needs a retirement fund, anyway?"

"We'd need to know the particulars, of course," Genny was quick to point out. "But it's something to consider, isn't it?"

"Sure. But don't you think we ought to hear what the doctor has to say, first? There may be some new procedure we don't know about. Some new medical breakthrough just discovered. We may can get pregnant on our own."

The server brought their plates, bringing a temporary lull to the conversation as they dug in.

"But you heard how distressed Tatiana was," Genny said after a moment. "This is very good, by the way." She pointed to the food with her fork but kept talking. "And that other girl. She was as frightened and upset as Tatiana. Mark my words, something more is going on at *Cherubdipity*. Marcella seems sincere enough, but there's something she's hiding. I just can't put my finger on it."

"Clearly, she's pressuring the girls to give their babies up for adoption."

Genny shook her head. "I didn't get that impression from her at all. I think she regretted losing her own child, and she truly wants to make a difference for these girls."

"Maybe she regretted having the child taken from her, instead of simply giving it up from the beginning. Maybe she's trying to do a good thing and save them the same heartache, but she's going about it the wrong way. You can't force someone, especially a scared young girl, to make such an impossible decision without time to think it through."

"Even under the best of circumstances, the time for a decision is limited to nine months."

"True."

As her mind switched gears, Genny mused aloud, "I'm sure there was a nice, fat check in that envelope today, but I wonder what was in the manila file?"

Looking quite satisfied with himself, Cutter supplied, "I happened to get a good look at it as I was talking to them. It was the mother's full medical history, along with a few details about the father. I know he's Caucasian with brown hair, eyes that start with a b, and that he has no venereal disease. Either his name is Cameron, or he was born in Cameron."

"You saw all that?" His wife was duly impressed.

"I pretended not to meet their eyes because I was embarrassed. I read as quick as I could."

Genny beamed as she patted his hand. "Good job, honey. Maddy and I may let you join Snoop 'n Scoop yet. Did you see anything about the girl?"

"His file was on top, so I couldn't see much of hers. I saw 'Medical History for' and the name Bailey, but I don't know if it was a first or a last. I caught St. Mary's Hospital and the year 2001, presumably where and when she was born. That's about all I could see."

"It's probably more than I could have gotten in such a short time."

As they continued eating, the conversation never strayed far from the expectant mothers and the woman for whom they worked. Despite their suspicions of her, they were impressed by the innkeeper's initiatives to help the girls plan for their futures.

"Still," Genny said, pushing away her plate, "I can't help but think of the sheer panic in Tatiana's eyes when she saw those people come in the coffee shop today. She's afraid of something."

"Or of someone."

"So, can you blame her for not wanting to hand her child over to someone she can't trust? Someone she's so obviously frightened of?"

Cutter's nod was slow. Thoughtful. His plate followed hers toward the center of the table.

"You're truly considering this, aren't you?" he asked in a quiet voice.

"Aren't you?" she challenged.

The server appeared to whisk their plates away and offer dessert. After ordering sopapillas, Cutter reached out to take Genny's hand in his. "I have to admit, the girl made a strong argument. And she's right. We *will* make great parents."

"But you want a baby of our own." Disappointment thickened her voice, making it heavy and low.

"Yes. A baby of our own." He jiggled her hand, forcing her to look up at him. "But that's not to say it has to be a baby we *make* on our own."

Her voice caught with hope. "You—You'd consider adopting?"

His smile was indulgent. "Genny darlin', I've been in love with you since about ten minutes after I first met you. From the very beginning, I knew I wanted to marry you. I wanted to settle down and have a family with you. I dreamed of having little blond-haired babies with big, blue eyes, just like their mama, who would grow up to be amazing human beings, also just like their mama."

"But if we adopt...?"

"They may not have blond hair and blue eyes." His answer was simple, just like the shrug of his broad shoulders. "But if you're their mama, I know they'll become amazing individuals. The outside is all cosmetic, anyway, and it never stays the same. The outside changes with time and has nothing to do with the goodness inside a person, or the integrity of their character. Those are things learned. Things taught. Things experienced and emulated because of the people and the environment around them. Even if we don't share the same blood with our babies, we'll share something more important with them. We'll share our lives and our values, and you'll somehow know just the right thing to say and do to make our children as awesome and amazing as their mama." A sheen of moisture misted his hazel eyes. "So maybe our babies won't look exactly like us. That doesn't mean we'll love them any less. It doesn't mean we won't be a family."

"Have I told you how much I love you? Just when I think I can't possibly love you more, you say something like this." At a loss for words, Genny squeezed his hand even tighter and tried hard not to cry.

Judging from the server's look when he returned with the plate of warm sopapillas, she wasn't very successful.

"Should I wrap these to go?" the man asked,

his eyes darting back and forth between the two of them.

"We're good," Cutter assured him, never looking his way. He kept his gaze on his wife. "Better than good. In fact, we're perfect."

"Perfect," Genny echoed. "And we'll have the perfect family, no one matter how it comes to be."

The server ducked away, wary of the flowing tears and somehow feeling as if he had intruded on a very private and emotional moment.

"And who knows?" Genny said with a smile. "Tatiana said someone in her family had blue eyes. Maybe our first baby will have black hair and blue eyes."

"Makes no difference to me," her husband assured her. He shifted in his seat, his mood seeming to shift with him. "But Genny," he said, his voice holding a note of caution. "Don't get your hopes set too high. We need to sit down and talk openly with Tatiana. There's something more to her story than she's telling us. Some reason she's afraid to be seen with us and was so scared in town. We need to know more before we can even think of adopting her baby."

"I agree."

The words sounded as if they were grounded in reality, but the starry look in her eyes said differently.

In her mind and in her heart, Genny was already knitting baby booties and reading bedtimes tales to a little dark-haired, olive-skinned bundle of joy.

Spending Valentine's Day at *Cherubdipity* exceeded all of Genny's expectations. It was the perfect place to celebrate their one-year anniversary and spin dreams of many more yet to come.

With only final details to finish, Cutter took the day off from work and spent it with his wife. They had breakfast in bed, lunch at the inn, and a romantic, candle-lit dinner prepared in their cottage by a professional chef. Cutter made the arrangements himself, requesting special treatment for his special lady. Bouquets of roses and other fresh-cut flowers sweetened the air and set the stage for their romantic meal. Champagne, dark chocolate truffles, and an intriguing trail of rose petals promised even more love and romance for dessert.

They kept their conversation light and upbeat during their meal, but later, as they followed the rose petals to the soaking tub made for two, candlelight reflected off the tears swimming in Genny's blue eyes.

"What's wrong, Genny darlin'?" Concern made Cutter's voice low and slow.

"I'm just so happy. Everything is perfect. This whole day, this whole trip." She squeezed the arms surrounding her as she leaned back against his chest. "This whole past year."

"It has been perfect," he agreed.

"I don't have a single complaint. Not a single regret. It's been happier than I ever dreamed possible."

She couldn't see it, but she heard the smile in his voice. Felt his mouth curl upward against her blond hair. "But let me guess. You feel almost guilty for wanting more."

A tear slipped down her face as she nodded. "You know me too well."

"I know how you feel, darlin'. The only thing that could make things more perfect is for us to have a baby and start a family together. Whether that baby comes from here" —his large hand covered her waistline, then moved upward to her heart— "or here makes no difference. We'll be good parents, Genny. We'll have a family and leave a legacy for future generations."

"I want her baby, Cutter," she admitted. "Tatiana seems like a very smart young woman. She has her head on straight and wants what's best for her child. I believe with all my heart that *we're* what's best for her baby."

"I can't say I disagree."

"We'll tell her we accept her offer?"

Hearing the hope and excitement in her voice, Cutter couldn't bear to dampen it. "We'll talk to her," he promised.

"Tomorrow?"

"Tomorrow."

The opportunity to talk with Tatiana the next day never came. New guests were checking in, departing guests were checking out, and current guests had the inn and surrounding grounds buzzing with activity. Cutter finished the final details of his handiwork and despite hanging around the inn all day, Genny caught only one glimpse of the dark-haired worker.

The couple even lingered outside that evening, hoping the girl would appear in the shadows. They gave up by midnight, knowing the day had slipped away without their plans being fulfilled.

As they prepared for checkout the next morning, disappointment lay heavy upon Genny's heart. How would she find a way to contact the girl? If Marcella censored her calls—and somehow, she knew that was the case— she couldn't very well call the inn and ask to speak with her, nor could she show up for a face-to-face visit. She didn't have her contact information. Today could very well be her only chance, but how could she make that happen?

The answer came with a soft knock at the door.

"Cutter? Can you get that, babe?" she called from the bathroom as she packed her toiletries.

"On it."

A few moments later, she heard his voice, slightly louder than necessary. "Tatiana! What a surprise. Come in."

Genny flew from the bathroom in time to see the girl step over the threshold, a basket in hand. "I wanted to drop off this thank-you basket as a little reminder of your time here with us." Her voice sounded as strained as her smile appeared.

"Don't worry, we'll always remember this trip," Cutter assured her, taking the offering from her hands.

Hoping her words didn't sound as accusing as they felt, Genny couldn't help but say, "I tried finding you all day yesterday, but I never could."

"Saturday is one of our busiest days," the girl replied without apology.

"We really need to speak with you, Tatiana. There are so many questions we want to ask. So many things we need to know."

The girl was already shaking her dark head. "Please. Forget I even said anything."

Genny was flabbergasted. "How could we forget such a thing!"

"We don't want to forget," Cutter said, his voice more reasonable. "We want to know more. We're very interested in your proposition."

"I—I should have never said anything. I wasn't thinking. I know better than to go against the missus."

Genny stepped closer and took the girl's hand. "Why, Tatiana?" she asked in a gentle voice. "What would happen if you did go against her?"

"I don't know for sure, and I don't want to find out! I've heard too many stories..." Her eyes were wild with fright.

"We want to help you. But you'll have to talk to us and tell us what's going on."

The girl still looked uncertain. Her eyes darted back and forth between the couple, but she allowed Genny to still hold her hand.

Cutter's voice was strong and reassuring. "Genny's right. We can help you, Tatiana. If you'll just talk to us, we'll help you find a solution. But first, we have to know what the problem is."

After a long moment, the girl nodded. She swallowed a gulp of faith and bravery before saying, "I have Thursdays off. If you could meet me—"

"We can!" Genny interjected, even before the girl named a time and place.

"There's a small city park two blocks from the coffee shop. We could meet there around noon."

Noon was the worst possible time for Genny, but that didn't stop her from nodding in agreement. "That's fine. We'll meet you there."

Pulling her hand from Genny's, Tatiana jerked toward the door. "I have to go. I've been here too long as it is."

She was gone in an instant. Cutter pulled his wife to his side for a one-armed hug. "I don't know what's going on," he said, staring at the slammed door, "but that girl is scared out of her mind."

16

With Granny Bert home from the hospital, Valentine's Day all but a sweet memory, and a busy weekend behind her, Madison devoted her attention once again to work.

A deep dive into *Barbour Foods'* upper management roster had provided her with a long list of potential people to consider. When the corporate offices relocated to Quincy, Massachusetts three years ago, there had been quite a shake-up within the company. All six of their poultry complexes—scattered from South Carolina to Texas—saw realignment within their management teams. Each time a new complex was created, or someone quit or retired, another shake-up occurred.

With the addition of the East Texas division in Crockett, the Rockdale manager took the helm of the new facility, thus making room for new leadership in his old position. According to the website, that manager was David Davison, formerly in lower management at the Georgia division. Not only was he brought in to manage the Rockdale unit, but he was now over both Texas divisions. No doubt, he was the one local growers had complained about. They claimed he cared more about making a name for himself than he did about the company and its growers.

In a way, Madison couldn't fault him. Every leader wanted to leave their mark by creating something newer and better than the version they acquired, but there was a right way and a wrong way to go about it. Stepping all over people on the way to the top was the wrong way.

A quick search told her that David Davison was originally from Rhode Island but studied business management and poultry sciences at Texas A&M University. After graduation, he had gotten a job with a nationally known poultry producer before eventually landing in management at *Barbour Foods*.

From what she could tell, the Texas divisions were the only ones mandating what brand of equipment could be used. The Georgia, South Carolina, and Louisiana divisions allowed their growers to choose from multiple suppliers.

So why, she wondered, *had the Texas divisions decided to go exclusively with one company? Was Davison starting a company-wide trend?*

Before she could do more digging, she heard the familiar ding alerting her to the front gate opening. That meant school was out, and she would soon have two, possibly three, hungry teenagers barging through the kitchen door. Megan split her time between parents, so she could pop up at either place, as long as she let the other parent know her whereabouts.

Saving her progress on the computer, Maddy pushed back from her office desk and started for the opposite side of the sprawling old house.

"Mom? You home?" Blake tromped through the kitchen's side door, dropping his backpack as he headed for the refrigerator.

Bethani grumbled as she came in behind him. "Way to go, Mr. Slob. I nearly tripped over your bag."

"Watch where your big feet are going," her twin shot back.

"And hello to you, too," Maddy said, sensing the teens weren't having the best of days. "Rough day at school?"

"Not really." Blake shrugged, chugging back what was left in the orange juice container. "Just hungry. I missed half my lunch period because the coach had us running bases."

Bethani's dramatic sigh all but drowned out her brother's words. She slung her backpack onto the bar and plopped down on the first stool. "I had. The. Worst. Day. Ever." She blew out an exaggerated sigh, disturbing the blond hair around her forehead. "Mom, you gotta call the school and complain. Can you believe that Miz Hathaway paired me up with Trenton Torno? It's not fair! She's playing favorites! Blake got Danni Jo and Addison Bishop got Kevin. Can you believe it? Addison and Kevin? And me, stuck with Dork Face?"

"Bethani! What a rude thing to say," her mother chided her.

"You haven't seen him, Mom. He's a total

nerd."

"Who is he again? I don't think I know the name."

"He's new this semester. He has metal all in his mouth, a citified haircut, and glasses that are like an inch thick. He's really smart and spends all his time with his nose stuck in a book, instead of hanging with the rest of us."

"Maybe because the rest of the kids are as critical and judgmental as you. Keep in mind, young lady, that not so very long ago, *you* were the new kid at school. Remember how hard it was for you to fit in at the time. If it hadn't been for Megan, you could have been tagged the citified dork."

"But he's so lame," the girl complained. "The teachers all think he's the grandest thing ever, but he always keeps to himself. Outside of class, I haven't heard him say a dozen words. Now I have to be 'married' to him for two full weeks."

"A quiet, smart husband? Hardly sounds like a bad thing," Madison pointed out.

"But we have to spend time together outside of class, coming up with our 'adoption plan.'" She rolled her eyes as she used more air quotation marks. "That's the straw we pulled. We have to pretend we're adopting a baby and make a detailed plan of what to do."

"Then I advise you to invite Trenton here, work on your assignment, and bring home an 'A.'"

"But Mom!"

"Don't three-syllable mom me," Madison warned, wagging her finger to silence her daughter's protests. "And I insist on meeting my future son-in-law before you make me a grandmother." That decided, she turned to her son. "How did you manage to get paired with Danni Jo?"

His sister spoke up before he could. "Besides being the teacher's pet?" she sneered.

"Besides that."

Ever modest, Blake put his hand across his chest. "I suppose I won her over with my exceptional charm, smarts, and good looks." Flashing a smile, he added, "That, plus she paired couples the best she could. Said it would be a good life lesson and safety measure, whatever that meant."

"What straw did the two of you draw?"

"We're expecting a little bundle of joy sometime this summer." The teenager grinned. "We have to make a budget, schedule doctor's appointments and daycare, decide what we need to buy for a baby, where we'll live, look at getting into a good preschool—as if that's even a thing here in River County but, hey, you never know— plus a whole bunch of other stuff."

"It's that *other stuff* that will get you," his mother acknowledged. "With a baby, there's always some expense or some complication you never expected."

Bethani rolled her eyes again with a loud groan. "I'm going to my room and FaceTime my friends while they're still talking to me. Being 'married' to Dork Face is going to ruin my social life."

"If your friends ditch you for who you're partnered with at school—or even in real life—

then they aren't really your friends. I thought I'd raised you better than to be so shallow, and I had hoped you would look for the same traits in your friends, as well."

"Please, Mom. No lectures. I'm depressed enough as it is, without you laying a guilt trip on me." Bethani pulled her backpack from the bar and headed for the stairs. "And if it's okay with you—" her tone couldn't have been any less enthusiastic than if she were planning to pull all her own teeth— "Trenton will be here on Thursday to start our assignment."

Madison smiled sweetly. "I'll look forward to meeting my future son-in-law," she teased.

As Bethani stalked away in a grumble, Blake took a parting shot at his twin. "See you later, *Mrs*. Dork Face."

Madison reproached her son. "I wish you wouldn't torment your sister that way."

"She deserves it. She gave me grief all the way home." He shrugged indifferently, pulling out ingredients for a sandwich. "Like it's my fault the teacher paired me and Danni Jo together. I had nothing to do with it. That's not to say I'm unhappy about it, but it still wasn't my doing."

Maddy's phone rang, and she saw her best friend's name flash across the screen.

"Hello, Miss Queen of Vacation. How was your trip?" she greeted her.

"Amazing. I have so much to tell you! I was thinking of dropping in to see Granny Bert. Want to meet me there?"

Madison glanced down at her watch. "Give me fifteen, and I'll be there."

With half of his sandwich already gone, Blake nodded to her phone as it went dark. "Where are you meeting Aunt Genny at? Are we going to *New Beginnings* for dinner?"

Hearing the unmistakable ring of hope in his voice, she shook her head in wonder. "You're eating a double-decker sandwich, and all you can think about is dinner? Where do you put it all?"

"I'm a growing boy," he reminded her with a grin. "Daddy D says I have two hollow legs."

"And a rot-gut stomach. But in answer to your question, Genny wants me to meet her over at Granny Bert's. Can I trust you not to eat us out of house and home before I get back?"

He eyed her as if weighing his options. "What's for dinner?"

"Since it's warmed up a bit today, Brash is grilling salmon on the outdoor grill."

"I think a few cookies and fruit should hold me till then," he decided. "Tell the two G's I said hello. And tell Aunt Genny if she'd like to make me some Gennydoodle cookies as a welcome home present, that'd be great."

"You goofus," his mother said affectionately. "Welcome home presents are for those returning, not those left behind."

"Yeah, but it's good to shake up tradition every now and then."

"I'll be sure and mention it to her."

Twenty minutes later, Madison relayed the

message to her best friend. With hugs and greetings out of the way, they settled around Granny Bert's kitchen table as the coffee brewed.

"That boy," Genny said, shaking her head. "Tell him I'll see what I can do." She turned to Granny Bert and gave her a no-nonsense look. "You gave us all quite a scare, young lady. I trust you're better now and following the doctor's orders?"

"For the most part," the older woman agreed. "Sometimes, you have to sift through those orders to find the best parts."

"She's referring to her caffeine intake," Madison explained. "The doctor told her to limit her coffee and tea consumption, but Granny's having a little trouble following through."

"I beg to differ," her grandmother argued. "He said limit, not eliminate. I'll have you know, yesterday I drank two cups less coffee than normal, and only had one glass of sweet tea all day long."

"Two less than how many? Two dozen?"

Granny Bert sniffed at Madison's suspicious tone. "Doesn't matter. What matters is that I cut back. Now, enough talk about me. I can tell by that glow on Genny's face that her second honeymoon was a humdinger. Give us all the details, girl."

A pretty blush stained Genny's cheeks. "Maybe not *all* the details," she giggled, thankful of how quickly Cutter had overcome being intimidated by the cherubs. "Let's just say it was a wonderful week. The accommodations were very posh and luxurious, with an eye for detail. In my book, a truly first-rate hotel has four things. A good bed, good water pressure, a good chair to sit in, and good food." She ticked off all four factors on her fingers, before pressing a hand to her stomach. "They had all four, although the chef was a little too free with the spices. My tummy has had a bit of trouble adjusting." She clicked her tongue as she lamented, "I don't know why people think they have to over-season food, when all they really need is the correct cooking technique."

"Overall, four stars or five?" Maddy asked as she got up to pour coffee.

Genny hesitated with her answer. "Hard to say. The inn itself was fantastic."

"But?"

"The staff was lazy, weren't they?" Granny Bert guessed. "That's the trouble with young folks today. They don't understand the concept of a hard day's work."

"No, the staff was amazing. They were all very well trained, from their level of service to their presentation. Marcella Durant runs a tight ship. On the surface, it was hard to find fault with hardly anything."

After serving the others, Madison slid back into her chair with her own cup. "Beneath the surface?"

Genny blew on her coffee before answering. "Something is going on there. We can't put our finger on it, but both of us got the impression that something more was happening at *Cherubdipity* than meets the eye."

"*Cherubdipity?*" scoffed Granny Bert. "That's your first hint right there. What kind of name is that?"

"It's a play on the words 'cherub' and 'serendipity'. The owner has a thing for cherubs. It kind of freaked Cutter out at first, knowing 'dead angel babies,' as he called them, were staring at us from every angle and every surface."

"Hope it didn't intimidate the man," the older woman grumbled without finesse, "or you'll never get a baby."

Genny blushed. Madison frowned. Granny Bert waved away their expressions and continued, "What, exactly, do you think is going on behind the angels' backs?"

Genny fingered the handle of her cup. "It's hard to say. The first thing I noticed was that most of the staff was very young and, for the most part, female."

"Nothing wrong with supporting young women," Granny Bert insisted.

"I agree. I asked Marcella if she used some sort of program in tandem with the school or the Texas Work Force Commission, but she said no. Then I noticed that most of the girls I saw were pregnant. That time when I asked, she admitted it was a program of her own making, designed to help young girls—particularly young, expectant mothers—get back on their feet and plan for their future."

Madison spoke up, "That sounds like a very commendable project. Why does it concern you so?"

"Let me back up. It's a very well-thought out, impressive program. The girls commit to a ten-week work and education program, taking classes on a variety of life skills and prepping for their future. If they choose to keep their babies, they can live and work there up until their third trimester, at which time Marcella gives them references for places to live and places to work. If they choose to give their babies up for adoption, she helps them make arrangements and even allows them a say in the adoption process. They can continue working and living at the inn but must take accredited college courses. Again, on the surface, it's an incredibly generous and amazing program."

"It does sound that way," Madison said. "But I take it there's more?"

"The girls must follow very strict guidelines. They're punished and/or rewarded with time on the internet, movies, books, that sort of thing."

Granny Bert harrumphed from behind her coffee cup. "Sounds like a cult to me!"

"That was our first thought, too, but I don't think cult is the right word. They're free to leave after they complete their ten-week program. And they must leave if they keep their babies."

"My first thought," Madison broke in, "is how does she pay for it all?"

Genny squirmed in her seat. "I think that's what concerns us the most."

Granny Bert rapped her knuckles on top of the table. "Follow the money," she said. "If you think there's something shady going on, follow the money. It will lead you to the answer. Every time."

Another shift in her seat. Another trace of her cup's handle. After a significant pause, Genny admitted, "We met a girl there..."

Madison and Granny Bert exchanged a knowing look. They were finally getting to the crux of the matter.

"Her name is Tatiana, and she seems to be wise beyond her years. She really has her head on straight, you know? She wants what's best for her baby, but she's torn on what to do. But the thing that struck us both is how absolutely frightened this girl is."

"Frightened? Of what?" Madison asked.

"That's what we want to know. She refuses to say anything negative about Marcella. Her loyalty is commendable, but I can tell she's suspicious. I think she's convinced there's something going on behind the angels' backs, as Granny Bert called it, but she won't tell us what it is."

"A prostitution ring?" the older woman suggested.

"I don't think so. Although," she recalled with a frown, "Cutter has already suggested she may have been a high-priced call girl, herself. Oddly enough, Marcella tells me that we met once, back in Boston. The Morgans threw a party, and she came as someone's date." She gave a brief recap of why her husband suspected as much.

"But," Genny concluded, "I don't think that's it. Most of the girls are pregnant when they get there, so how sexy can that be? To someone other than the baby's father, I mean."

"There's some real weirdos in this world, girl. You never know how some perverts get off."

Genny's blond hair danced around her face as she shook her head. "I still don't think that's it."

A sense of unease slithered through Madison's mind as she recalled the girl from the hospital. "You don't... you don't think it's a baby trafficking ring, do you?"

"It's occurred to us. The thing is, Marcella seems so sincere in her desire to do good things for these girls. She's rather vague on the specifics of her personal life, but I do know that when she was younger, she had a baby out of wedlock. She tried to raise the child on her own, but social services stepped in and took the child from her. I think this is her way of making certain that doesn't happen to the girls who come to her for help."

"Yet you still sound uncertain about her program."

"The truth is, Cutter and I don't know what to think. From what we gather, most or all the adoptions are handled privately. Private adoptions are a legal process and a far cry from baby trafficking, but after talking with Tatiana, it somehow left a bitter taste in our mouths."

"And why is that?"

"Tatiana said the expectant mothers seem to have money to spare. Enough for new clothes and new electronics. I know prospective parents pay for all hospital expenses and care associated with the mother's well-being, but new smartwatches and smartphones seem over the top."

"I agree," Madison said. "Expenses are one thing. Extras are another."

"I know it's enough to make Tatiana uncomfortable. So much so, in fact," Genny said, pausing to take in a big gulp of courage before confiding the rest, "that she's asked Cutter and me to adopt her baby. She just isn't comfortable going with the options Marcella presented to her."

The revelation stunned Madison. "What? She wants you to adopt her child?"

"I thought you were trying to have a baby of your own," Granny Bert put in.

"We are. But to be honest..." Tears misted Genny's blue eyes. "I just don't know if it will happen. I made an appointment to discuss fertility options with my specialist. I think Tatiana overheard my conversation, and I think that's why she came forward with her proposal."

Madison gently touched her friend's arm. "And this is something you're considering?"

"Yes. Cutter and I have discussed it, and we intend to meet with her this week to find out more details. Tatiana is a lovely girl, and she seems very bright. But she also seems very frightened. There's still something she's not telling us. Even if we don't end up adopting her baby, we want to help her."

"I admire you for that, Gen. I just don't want to see you getting your heart broken in the process."

The smile Genny offered wobbled on her face. "It may already be too late for that."

17

When Cutter and Genny arrived at the park, Tatiana was already waiting for them. It was a small park fashioned for a small town, with only a handful of picnic tables and benches scattered among the playground equipment. The only other people there at noon on a breezy February day were two older gentlemen who sat on a bench, sipping steaming beverages from their insulated mugs, and three women in jogging suits, making steady laps around the park.

Tatiana was bundled in a blanket and her denim jacket, waiting at a picnic table while holding an open book in her hands.

"Would you rather talk in our car?" Cutter suggested. "It will be warmer there."

The girl looked uncertain. "I feel more comfortable here," she said. "At least a public park could be a chance meeting."

"Sure," Genny said amicably. "That big playset blocks the wind a bit." She swung her legs over the bench and settled across from Tatiana. "How have you been feeling?"

"No morning sickness," the girl reported. "No crazy hormone swings, so I guess I'm lucky. I've seen some of the other girls really suffer, especially my friend Nicki."

It was one of the first bits of information she had volunteered without prompting, but Genny noticed how her face clouded after the admission.

"That's good."

"You didn't see any cars parked in weird places, did you?" the girl asked, her eyes nervously scanning the perimeters of the park. "Anyone who looked out of place?"

Cutter's reply came out sounding skeptical. "No," he drawled out the word. "But why do you think someone is watching you?"

"You just... you just never know."

"You must have a reason," Genny urged in a soft manner. "You said something similar at the inn. And you were beyond frightened at the coffee shop. What is going on, Tatiana?"

"I'm scared," the girl admitted.

"Why?"

Her eyes came back to pierce the two of them with their intensity. "This stays between us." Her tone said the words were non-negotiable.

"For now," Cutter agreed.

She didn't answer right away. First, she drew in a deep breath. "There's—There's things that have happened."

"What kind of things?"

"Dangerous things."

"It's not that we don't believe you—" Genny started.

"I know you think I'm paranoid," Tatiana broke in. "But they watch us. And when one of us steps out of line, there's a price to pay." She squeezed her eyes shut as she said the words. "There's been rumors... More than rumors, I'd say. I saw what happened to Nicki."

"And who is Nicki?" Cutter asked.

"My roommate. She did something stupid a couple of weeks ago and had to go to the hospital. It put her baby in danger, so they punished her. They cut off all her hair. It was long and blond and gorgeous, with just the right amount of curl." Her voice had a slight hitch to it as she finished on a sniff of tears. "It was her pride and joy, and now it's just... gone."

"They cut it short?"

"No. They shaved it off!" As horrifying as her words were, the next were worse. "If she had lost the baby, I have no doubt they would have killed her. She would have become like the others."

"What others?" Genny asked in a sharp voice.

"I never knew them," Tatiana admitted, studying the torn cuticles around her nails with exaggerated care, "but everyone knows *of* them. Not from the missus, of course, or any of the adoption people. But it's common knowledge among the girls."

Genny looked at her husband in confusion, but a slight shake of his head told her he was as lost as she was.

"I'm afraid we don't know what you're talking about," she told the girl softly.

"There's been a couple of girls before us who... who died." Tatiana looked up, her eyes again scanning the park. Her gaze zeroed in on the joggers. "How many times have those women circled the park? And why do they keep looking this way?"

"Probably my husband," Genny mumbled just under her breath. "He gets that reaction a lot."

While Cutter frowned down at her, Tatiana heard her and nodded in agreement. "A few of the girls were talking about him at the inn. They agreed he is pretty hot for a guy his age."

Cutter's head whipped around in surprise. "A guy my *age*? What am I, eighty?"

"No, but you are married," the girl pointed out.

His arm went to Genny's shoulders and pulled her close. "And happily so." He felt it important to make that much known.

"Yeah, Lyndie wasn't too thrilled about that," Tatiana said, almost in a teasing manner. It was the first time they had seen a genuine smile from her.

Genny was impatient to change the subject. "I don't think you need to worry about the joggers. They probably know how many rounds it takes to make two miles, or whatever their target range is." She laid her hand upon the picnic table in a calming manner, noticing how Tatiana kept hers in nervous motion. "Tell us more about the girls who have died. Was it from a drug overdose, you think?"

"No." She shook her head. "The missus doesn't allow drugs of any kind. We have regular drug screenings."

"What happened to the girls, then?" Cutter wanted to know. "What about their deaths makes you suspicious?"

"Who—Who said I was suspicious?"

"I hear it in your voice. And it's bound to be the reason you're so nervous about being seen talking to us. The reason you're so afraid."

The girl answered reluctantly, "The missus takes out a life insurance policy on us when we sign up. The word is that...uhm... they cash it in if a girl in the adoption program loses her baby."

"That's horrible!" Genny's cry was louder than she intended. The joggers were just close enough to hear her outburst and cast a worried glance back over their shoulders. "The policy is on you girls, right? Not your babies?" Genny pressed.

Tatiana nodded in silent agreement.

"First of all," Cutter all but growled, "why would she take an insurance policy out on you in the first place?"

"She explains it all when we sign the papers and name the inn as the beneficiary. It's to offset the cost of the program, in case the worst happens to one of us."

"I can see that," Genny had to admit. "But you said 'if' the girl was in the adoption program. Why just them?"

"Extra lawyer fees, I guess?" Tatiana sounded like she was reaching for straws.

Cutter chose his words carefully. "You said word has it that these policies are 'cashed in?' Deliberately?"

Clearly uncomfortable with his question, Tatiana didn't meet his eyes. She lifted one shoulder in an uncertain manner as she worried her cuticles once more.

Genny kept her voice soft and encouraging as she urged her to say more. "Why do they say that, Tatiana?"

"The girls who died... Both had miscarriages. A couple of weeks later, they were dead."

"Has anyone gone to the police?" Cutter wanted to know.

Fear moved into the teenager's voice. "No, and neither can you. You agreed," she reminded him in an accusing voice.

"I said for now. And before I knew someone had died."

"Daisy died in a car accident. I'm not sure about the other."

Genny felt a rush of relief. "So, it could have been a coincidence?"

The relief was short lived. A thunderstorm brewed in Tatiana's dark eyes. Her movements were jerky as she shook her head. "I wanted to believe that. I tried so hard. I convinced myself the rumors weren't true, even though I had seen the statues myself. But after seeing what they did to Nicki's hair... It was a warning. A threat."

"You need to leave *Cherubdipity*, Tatiana. Now." Genny's voice came out harsher than she intended.

Tatiana's sounded panicked. "I can't. Where would I go?"

"Your parents?" she suggested hopefully.

"Have six other kids at home." She shook her dark head again, her heartache obvious. "My dad just lost his job. They can't afford two more mouths to feed."

At a loss for what to say next, silence

descended upon the table, until Cutter broke it.

"Can you give us a few days to come up with a plan?"

"I guess it depends. Do you plan to adopt my baby?" the girl countered with a defiant gleam in her eye.

It was Genny who answered, "We'd like to."

Relief flooded Tatiana's features but was soon replaced with fear. "I don't know of any other girls who have gone outside the program to find parents for her baby. Everyone just uses the liaison provided." She twisted her hands in worry.

"And you're afraid it may not be safe to do so?" Genny guessed.

She nodded without saying a word, averting her eyes from theirs.

"We need time to discuss this, Tatiana," Cutter told her. "There's a lot to think about, a lot to consider. A lot of details to take care of. Can you give us a few days to come up with a plan?"

"You have a whole week. I won't have a day off again until next Thursday." Her voice was almost bitter. "If they suspect something is off, maybe not then."

"How can we reach you?"

The girl thought for a moment. "Be at *Antonio's* next Thursday at six pm. If I'm not there, ask to speak to Emilio. He'll know how to get in touch with me."

"We'll find a way to help you, Tatiana. I promise." Genny vowed softly.

"Remember your promise. This stays between us."

"Tati—"

She cut off any protest Cutter may have made. "If you don't promise, I'll sign the papers with the liaison." It sounded almost like a threat, until she added in a vulnerable whisper, "It's the only way I know I'll be safe."

With a look into his wife's pleading blue eyes, he finally nodded. "Meet us next week. We'll find a way out of this mess. We'll keep you safe."

Her voice clogged with unshed tears, Tatiana sniffed and nodded. "I should go. Wait a good ten minutes before you leave. Just in case."

"Please be careful, Tatiana," Genny whispered.

"You, too."

She never once looked back as she gathered her blanket and strode across the park.

18

Bethani watched the clock with dread, hating the way the hour hand slid ever closer to four. Trenton was due at her house any minute, which meant she had to put up with the dork long enough to plan their strategy for Mrs. Hathaway's class. It was a lame assignment, but Bethani was determined to get an A, just as she did in all her classes.

She hadn't bothered freshening up after school. Her hair was still pulled back in a messy ponytail and her tee-shirt was a bit rumpled. There was even a small mustard stain at the neckline, thanks to Josiah and Kevin messing around at lunch. She knew it was the equivalent to flirting in their minds, but sometimes teenage boys could be so childish with their silly pranks. Since it was only Trenton coming over, she wasn't concerned with how she looked. Her mom had suggested she invite the boy to stay for supper since Genny and Cutter would also be there, but she glared at her with blazing eyes and quickly shot down the suggestion. The less time he was there, the better.

Her only concern was to get this meeting over with as quickly and as painlessly as possible, and without anyone noticing his decades-old car parked in her driveway.

At two minutes till four, Bethani buzzed him through the gate and waited for the nightmare to begin. She had instructed Trenton to come through the gate, park around the back, and to use the kitchen entrance at the side of the house. Her feet were leaden as she moved to the door and opened it.

"Hey," the lanky teenager said, stepping over the threshold.

"Hey." Bethani felt a niggle of guilt as she rudely turned away from her guest. Without checking to see that he kept up, she left him to follow behind as she took the roundabout way to the entertainment room where they would study.

She traipsed across the homey farm-style kitchen, through the butler's pantry, skirted around the table and china cabinets in the formal dining room, crossed through the stuffy formal living room with its velvet couches, clicked over the shiny wood floor in the foyer, sailed through the ladies' sitting parlor, and, finally, entered into the very modern, upscale but casual family room.

Bethani finally turned to her guest, only to find that he was nowhere to be seen. With an exasperated roll of her eyes, she blew out a sigh and retraced her steps to find him. The house wasn't *that* big that he should get lost!

She found him back in the dining room, studying the murals that had been handpainted on the walls.

"These are amazing," he murmured. He didn't seem to hear her come in. He was mesmerized by the artwork, talking to himself about the play of light and dark, shadowing effects, and the story told upon the walls of the room.

"There you are!" she all but accused.

"Sorry," he murmured, even though he sounded anything but. "These murals are amazing. Handpainted many years ago, from the looks of them."

"Yeah, like a full century ago. They're original to the house." Bethani knew the television people had made a big deal out of them, but to her, they were just some old pictures painted on a wall.

"They're incredible," the boy said.

Come to think of it, these few sentences were the most she had ever heard him say. Occasionally, he pushed his black-framed glasses up on his nose as he stared at the walls. His expression was nothing short of awe.

"They're okay, I guess." She shrugged.

"Okay? How can you say that?" He turned to her in challenge, and for the first time, she noticed the color of his eyes behind the heavy frames. Clear, crystal blue, much like her own. "Look at the way the artist used shadows and light to make the images almost lifelike. Look at that meadow scene. The cows look like they could walk off the walls at any minute, right into the room."

Caught up in his fascination with brush strokes and technique, he stepped into her personal space as he pointed to another segment of the scene. He didn't dare touch the ages-old artwork as he called attention to a patent rail fence, its zigzag pattern interlaced with green vines bearing fruit.

"Can't you just smell those blackberries, growing fresh on the vine?"

When he smiled at her, she noticed that his braces were no longer on his teeth. In their place was a set of perfectly straight, almost blindingly white teeth, fully bared in what she belatedly realized was a *very* nice smile.

"Uhm, yeah. I guess," she answered, still distracted by his smile. How long had his braces been off? How had she not noticed before now? And did he *shave*? That looked like a little razor nick, right there on the tip of his chin. A strong, nicely chiseled chin, she decided.

And, yes, that woodsy scent was shaving cream.

An old memory ambushed her heart, bringing thoughts of when she was a little girl, giggling as she 'helped' her father slather his face with foam before he shaved it off in sure, even strokes. She hadn't thought of that in years, not until she caught a whiff of this same shaving cream.

Like most thoughts of her father, she wasn't sure if it was a happy memory, or a sad one. Her emotions were all tangled when she thought of her dad and the way he had betrayed them all in the end. At one time, he had been her knight in shining armor, and she had been his little princess, but somewhere along the way the fairytale had become twisted and tarnished. Some days, she didn't know if she loved him or if she hated him.

But she didn't want to think of such today, and

certainly not in front of dork-faced Trenton Torno. *Even though,* she acknowledged, *without the braces, he didn't look quite so dorky.*

"Sorry," Trenton said, just now realizing he had lagged behind. "I was blown away by this magnificent mural. This whole house, in fact. Look at that crown molding. And the lines of the house. The rooms flow together seamlessly." He tossed her another brace-free smile as he accompanied her into the living room, this time by her side. "You can probably tell I'm a fan of art and architecture. In fact, I plan to be an architect someday," he admitted.

Bethani had never heard him talk so much, but she decided she liked the sound of his voice.

"If you like these rooms, you'll probably like the staircase," she predicted.

Trenton not only liked the stairs, he went up them, caressing the hand-turned railing along the way. He didn't intrude onto the second-floor landing, simply turned around and came back down the steps with a goofy smile on his face.

Bethani found the smile oddly endearing with its unabashed honesty.

"I could spend a week wandering around in this house," he told her, his eyes darting from one architectural feature to the next. "The craftsmanship is outstanding."

"If my mom wasn't working, I'd take you in the library. It has a ton of woodwork and built-in cabinetry. Carved everything," she summarized, sweeping her hand toward the ornate woodwork they passed through en route to the front parlor.

She knew Nick Vilardi and the *Home Again* team had oohed and aahed about the very same features, but the praise sounded different when it came from Trenton.

"Maybe next time," he said.

"Sure," Bethani heard herself agree.

Why had she said that? She didn't plan for there to be a next time!

Did she?

"We can study in here. It's the media room slash family room, but it's a good place to study, too."

"Cool."

Strangely enough, Trenton seemed less impressed with the latest and greatest in media and home electronics than he did in the hundred-year-old carpentry details of the Big House. He was the first boy to cross over that threshold and not become starry-eyed at the sight of all the gadgets, screens, and surround-sound speakers that filled the space. Bethani couldn't help but draw a parallel between the underwhelmed Trenton Torno and the rowdy bunch of boys who had practically trashed the place two weeks ago. For the life of her, she didn't know what to make of the comparison.

When Trenton motioned for her to take a seat on the sectional couch before he sat, something fluttered to life inside her chest. It felt oddly like butterflies, but this was dork-face Trenton, not one of the handsome, popular guys as school.

Upon closer scrutiny, however, she couldn't help but notice that Trenton wasn't exactly ugly. In fact, he wasn't at all ugly. His face was nicely sculptured, and his skin was clearer than most teenage boys were, even if it wasn't very tanned. She still couldn't get over his smile, or the clear color of his eyes.

Come to think of it, he was kind of cute.

Not, she knew, that looks were everything. Even Jeff wasn't handsome in a conventional way, but his outgoing personality drew girls to him like a magnet. And somehow, she barely even noticed the acne on Drew Baines' face, even though he had a bad case of it. His easy laughter was what attracted her and every other girl in school to him.

Maybe if Trenton weren't so quiet and withdrawn, she would have noticed his blue eyes before now. Maybe if he joined in class discussions or hung out with the gang, she would have focused less on his braces and his glasses, and more on the pleasant timbre of his voice.

Bethani felt ashamed of herself. Maybe if she had given him half a chance, maybe if she had tried reaching out to him and including him in group discussions even one time, then maybe she wouldn't have so easily gone along with the crowd and referred to him as Dork Face.

Hypocrisy and her own unfair judgment of him made her face burn.

"Would you like something to drink?" she offered.

"I'm good. Maybe after a while." He pulled his backpack off so he could settle back against the cushions. "So, where do we start? I hope you don't mind, but I've already made a chart."

It didn't take long for Bethani to realize Mrs. Hathaway had done her a favor, pairing her with

Trenton. He had thought of several aspects she hadn't even considered yet, and with his quick mind and willingness to hear her ideas, she knew they would ace this project.

Soundproofing or not, tantalizing aromas wafted in from the kitchen.

"Smells like your dinner's almost done, so I guess that's my cue to leave," Trenton said politely. He started to put his papers and charts away.

Impulsively, Bethani asked, "Would you like to stay and have dinner with us?"

"Thanks, but my mom probably left something for me." When he saw the confused look on her face, he explained, "She had to work this evening, so she either left me something to eat, or money to order a pizza."

"Or you could eat with us." Without consciously realizing she was flirting, Bethani leaned in closer, her blue eyes twinkling. "You'll make seven of us, which means we'll eat in the dining room. You can stare at that mural as long as you please."

Trenton swallowed hard, unable to miss the way she tossed her ponytail and stared up at him with her big, wide, blue eyes. He might not even notice the mural at dinner, but he wasn't about to tell her that.

"Are you sure your mom won't mind?"

"Not if yours doesn't. She's big on getting other parents' permission."

"I'll text my mom and make sure it's okay," he said, pulling out his cell phone.

"If she says yes, I'll give my mom a head's up.

I'll even help her set the dining room table."

"I don't want to be a bother."

She waved his concerns away. "Nah. Half the time, we have someone else here, anyway. You never know who Blake's going to drag home with him, or when Megan will pop in. It's no biggie."

"Megan? Is she the redhead with purple-framed glasses?" he asked, reminding Bethani that he was still new to their school.

"Sometimes they're purple, sometimes green, sometimes zebra print. You never know with my stepsister."

"She's your stepsister?"

"Yep. Our parents got married almost a year ago. She lives with us part of the time, with her mom part of the time."

"That must be hard."

"Not really. Even before our parents married, she was here half the time, anyway. We've been best friends since we moved here after my dad died."

"My dad died, too," Trenton admitted, his face sad. "It sucks, doesn't it?"

"Yeah. It really did at first. And even though I don't go around telling him this—I don't want it going to his head or anything— I have a pretty great stepdad. He doesn't try to take my dad's place, so that helps, even though in a lot of ways, he's been more of a father to me than my own was." She blushed when she realized she had revealed such a private thing to him. She quickly changed the subject. "What about you? Did your mom remarry?"

"Nope. Just the two of us."

"That's gotta be rough."

"We manage."

Sensing he didn't want to talk about it, Bethani was relieved when his phone binged. With a glance down, Trenton reported, "My mom says it's fine. So, if your mom really doesn't mind..."

"She won't!" Surprised by her own eagerness, Bethani popped up from the couch. "I'll just be a minute. You could look up adoption agencies in the area while I'm gone, if you'd like."

"Good idea. We can call and ask them questions for the project." He was already tapping on his phone when she left the room.

Using the excuse of washing up for dinner, Bethani vaulted up two flights of stairs to her bedroom, where she took her hair out of the ponytail, brushed it free of tangles, and changed into a cute shirt the color of her eyes. She told herself it was because they were having company of dinner, namely Cutter and Aunt Genny. It had nothing, she assured herself, to do with Trenton Torno. Fresh makeup would be too much, but a light frosting of lip gloss wouldn't hurt. Wintertime could be so harsh on the lips.

Trenton insisted on helping her set the table. He seemed to enjoy choosing the pieces from the china cabinet and laying them out on the long, antique table.

"You can sit here, between Blake and me," Bethani said, adding the silverware.

"Blake is your twin, right?"

Her sigh was grievous. "Unfortunately."

"I think having a twin would be cool."

"At times it is," she admitted. "But at other times..." New noises and a bustling from the kitchen told her the other guests had arrived. "Sounds like we'll eat soon," she said.

As soon as Bethani made introductions, Cutter asked, "Is that your '69 El Camino in the driveway?"

"Yes, sir. It was my dad's car," Trenton replied.

"Sweet! I bet that baby really runs."

They started talking about engines, a subject completely foreign to Bethani. She left them to their car talk as she helped put the food on the table. When the men came in, Trenton held her chair for her, earning an approving smile from her stepfather.

Once seated, she looked at Trenton and apologized, "Sorry, but we have a tradition of holding hands around the table when we say the prayer."

"No problem," he said, reaching for her hand.

The butterflies took flight as her fingers snuggled within his.

After a round of polite chitchat and including the teenagers in their conversation, Brash and Cutter broke off into a topic of their own. Genny was describing the inn they had just visited, so it left the three teenagers free to talk among themselves. Bethani was surprised Trenton and Blake had anything in common, but she knew she was selling her brother short. He could talk to anyone about anything, getting his gift of gab from Granny Bert. And Trenton had held his own in the conversation with Daddy D and Cutter, so the easy camaraderie at the table shouldn't have surprised her.

"How's the project coming?" Madison asked as she brought out the dessert Genny had insisted on bringing. There was a chocolate layer cake and, at Blake's request, a full plate of Gennydoodle cookies.

"Good, I think," Bethani said, glancing at her partner for confirmation. "Trenton already had an adoption plan written for us when he got here."

"Adoption?" Genny squeaked. Her eyes darted to her husband's.

"We have this project at school," Bethani explained. "We have to pair up and pretend to be couples either expecting a baby, bringing home a newborn, or hoping to adopt. Believe me, adopting someone else's baby is more complicated than it sounds."

"Maybe I could help you," her 'aunt' offered.

"Really? You'd do that?"

"Sure. I like learning new things."

"Not to sound greedy or ungrateful," Trenton said, "but does your offer include more of these cookies?"

"It can."

"Then you're on!" the boy said with enthusiasm.

"Better run that by the little lady," Blake snickered from his left. He fully expected to be chewed out by his sister later that evening.

Trenton looked at the girl on his right, an apology in his eyes. "He's right. Bethani, is that okay with you?"

The teenager beamed up at him. "Sure. Can't

beat free cookies, right?"

Over his shoulder, she returned her twin's devilish grin. His attempt to torture her had failed.

It came as a surprise, even to her, but she no longer minded being paired up with Trenton Torno.

Both twins trailed Trenton out when he left. Blake wanted to see his car, and Bethani was oddly reluctant to see him leave.

Inside, the adults turned to a more serious conversation.

"Brash, did Maddy tell you about the girl we met at *Cherubdipity*?" Genny wanted to know.

"Not really. She said it was best I heard the story from the two of you." With a wink, he said, "I'm ready when you are."

They launched into the same story Genny had told Maddy, both adding details and their own impressions.

"What do you think, Brash? Are we crazy for considering this?" Even though ten years separated their ages, the two men had become good friends. Cutter valued Brash's insight into things, and vice versa.

"Adoption? Not at all. I can tell you from personal experience, you don't have to father a child biologically to love them as if they were your own. I couldn't love those two blond-headed kids out there more if they shared my own blood. I know Maddy feels the same about Megan."

Her head bobbed in full agreement.

"I think I hear a 'but,'" Genny worried.

Brash didn't answer immediately. "You hear a note of caution," he finally agreed. "Not with the idea of adoption. But maybe you should check out other sources, before you make a decision."

"Not a bad idea," Cutter agreed slowly, "but is there a particular reason you say that?"

"How much do you know about this girl?"

Reluctant to betray Tatiana's trust, Genny offered, "We spent some time with her this afternoon. She's bright and intelligent, and she wants what's best for her baby."

"And her boss?"

"I think she's equally as intelligent. I'm still undecided on where her concerns lay."

"I can tell how hopeful and excited you two are about this. And I don't want to discourage you," Brash said, leaning forward with both arms on the table, "but has it occurred to you that this could be a scam?"

"A scam?" Genny sounded shocked.

Her husband, however, nodded. "Of course, it occurred to me. That's why I hope you'll check out a few details for us. Run a background check, that sort of thing." He darted a look toward his wife. "Check out a few other things she mentioned. You have resources that we don't have."

"The fact that Marcella is so secretive sounds suspect to me," Brash admitted, "but maybe my job as a lawman has jaded me. That, and the way she insists on keeping her staff separated from her guests. Not to mention how she has the girls under her thumb, doling out their free time and their contact with the outside world. Either she's a control freak of the worst kind, or she's keeping them isolated for a reason."

"I built the fence in good faith," Cutter said. "I thought it was a simple perimeter fence. But Tatiana tells me it already feels like prison walls. I almost regret taking the job to begin with."

"I don't," Genny said, shaking her head vehemently. "If we hadn't gone there, we wouldn't have met Tatiana. Which means we wouldn't be able to help her now. Even if we don't end up with a baby, at least we'll have done a good thing, getting to the bottom of this." She looked at Brash earnestly. "And take my word for it. This thing runs deep."

19

"How do you feel about sharing date night with another couple?" Madison asked her husband the next afternoon over the phone.

"Bethani and Trenton? I thought they were just study pals. Although, I did see that little sparkle in both their eyes."

"You saw that, too? He seems like a good kid, so I wouldn't object, but no. It's not them."

"Cutter and Genny, again tonight? Not that I'd mind, but..."

"Not them, either."

"Please don't tell me it's my daughter."

"No, daddy dearest, it's not your baby girl."

"Then I give up. Just tell me."

"Do you remember a detective with the College Station Police Force by the name of Cade Resnick? According to him, you've met at a convention a time or two and once served on some panel together at another function."

"Young guy with short, blond hair? Big into team roping?"

"No idea. Never met him."

"Then why are we double dating with him?"

"Because his kinda-sorta girlfriend is a nurse at *Texas General*. From what I understand, it's complicated."

His sigh came through the phone line. "With you women, it usually is."

Ignoring his cynicism, she continued, "I told you about meeting her when Granny Bert was in the hospital."

"Lauren somebody?"

"Laurel. Laurel Benson."

"That's right. I recall the name now. But I still don't understand why we're sharing our date night with them."

"I asked Laurel to look into something for me, and she called earlier with some information. Since Cade speaks highly of you, and this is potentially a police matter, she thought that maybe the four of us could meet and have dinner this evening. She suggested we meet at that steakhouse you like so much on Texas Avenue."

"Steak?" Brash's voice perked up. "I'm in."

"I thought you'd say that, so I've already accepted. We're meeting them at seven fifteen."

"Okay, see you in a bit. Love you."

"Love you, too."

"Are you going to at least give me a hint as to what all this is about?"

Laurel allowed the handsome detective to take her coat and drape it over the back of the bar

stool. She waited for him to help her up—those
tall stools were murder on short legs like hers—
before answering.

"No. It will save time and energy to tell
everyone at once."

Cade Resnick settled onto the stool beside her.
"I knew you met the grandmother from that TV
show last year, but when did you meet the star?"

"When the same grandmother came back to
the ER a couple of weeks ago, this time as the
patient. Madison was with her, and we sort of hit
it off. We ran into each other a few days later in
the cafeteria, and she asked me to investigate
something for her. She's sort of an amateur
detective, you know."

"Great. Every real detective's worst
nightmare," he grunted.

Laurel glared at him. "Be nice," she warned.
"Madison is a very nice person, and her husband
is a well-respected officer in his own right."

"I never said she wasn't nice. But you have no
idea the havoc an amateur detective can wreak on
a case."

The server appeared to take their drink orders.
Cade motioned for Laurel to go first. "The house
chardonnay, please."

"Any dark beer on tap will be fine," he said,
turning back to his companion.

He wasn't clear if tonight was a date or not, but
he hoped it was. In truth, not much about their
relationship *was* clear. More than once, their
careers had put the two professionals at odds.
Laurel was a passionate and dedicated nurse who
took her job as seriously as he took his. Her

Momma Bear instincts came out when it came to her patients, even when her patient got caught up in one of his police investigations. He had the law on his side, but she had the best interest of her patients at heart. He could hardly fault her for that, even when it made his job that much harder.

The mutual attraction between them had only made things worse. There had been a few kisses with promise of something deeper yet to come, but so far, their schedules hadn't cooperated. They had better luck meeting for coffee or a quick lunch date, even though neither setting was nearly as romantic.

When she called to ask about this evening, he wasn't sure if it was her making the first move or simply what she claimed—a potential police matter she wanted to discuss with him and another interested party. Either way, he would have said yes, even before she sweetened the pot with news that the former football star turned fellow law officer would be joining them.

"Just do me a favor," Laurel said. "Withhold judgment until you hear everything we have to say. I think you'll find Madison has a very smart and inquisitive mind, even if she doesn't have the license to back it up."

"I'll try," was all he promised.

The deCordovas arrived just as their drinks did. The newcomers ordered their drinks before Laurel made the introductions.

"Madison, this is my friend, Detective Cade Resnick. Cade, Madison deCordova."

"It's nice to meet you, Cade. I think you may already know my husband, but honey, this is

Laurel Benson, a head nurse in *Texas General's* emergency department. Laurel, my husband Brash."

"I remember him from the show," the nurse acknowledged shyly. The handsome man was practically a legend, having first been a pro football player and then a star on the home makeover show. And she certainly couldn't forget all that hoopla that surrounded their marriage last year and that sexy photo of him shirtless. She thought her friend Shanae still had a copy of it tacked up in her work locker.

"It's a pleasure to meet you, Laurel." He smiled at the petite, curly-haired nurse. He released her hand to take her companion's in a firm grip. "Cade, it's been a while. About a year and a half, if I remember right."

"I wasn't sure you would remember me," the younger of the men replied. They were about the same height, but he was slender and lithe, whereas Brash's muscles were solid and thick.

"Of course I do. Good to see you again."

They made small talk until their table was ready, at which time they moved into the main dining room. It wasn't until they had settled in and ordered their food that the women explained the reason for their meeting.

"Cade, I'm not sure how much Laurel has told you," Madison began.

"Not a thing." He softened his brusque reply by laying his arm across the back of Laurel's chair and curling his fingers around her shoulder.

"And Brash, I didn't go into a lot of detail with you, either. Not until I had something a little more concrete. I'm assuming Laurel will supply those details next, but first, let me catch you up to speed."

She told the men about the overheard conversation in the ER and how it had made her feel. "Honestly, I wasn't eavesdropping," she defended herself when she finished, "but it was hard not to hear what they were saying. And once I heard it, I felt duty-bound to check it out."

Laurel picked up the story from there. "The girl wasn't my patient, so I'm afraid I wasn't much help. My friend Cami attended to the girl, and she confirmed what Madison suspected: the woman with her wasn't a parent, but she was listed as an emergency contact. Cami also had the sense that the two had more of a professional relationship than a personal one, and that the older woman wasn't very sensitive to the girl's emotional state."

Cade exchanged a loaded look with Brash, but both men remained silent as Laurel continued.

"At Madison's prompting, I did remember a similar case this summer. A girl who was three months pregnant came in with severe cramping after going swimming. She ended up losing the baby. There was a woman with her who, if I remember correctly, fit roughly the same description Cami gave me. What struck me most was that the woman left the room to make several phone calls. That isn't surprising, but it was the tone of the telephone calls and the way she criticized the girl for being so careless. I suggested we meet tonight because I did some digging and found out more about both girls. They both listed the same person as an emergency contact. I can't divulge names, but I thought it was worth noting."

"That can't be a coincidence," Madison protested.

"Definitely disturbing," Brash agreed.

"Just wait. I discovered something even more disturbing than that. One week later, the girl was back in the emergency room after being involved in a car accident. It was a hit and run and, unfortunately, she didn't pull through."

"That's terrible!"

Laurel agreed with Madison. "Another nurse remembered the incident, which she had discussed with a friend who worked at another hospital here in town. A similar thing had happened earlier in the year. A girl suffered a miscarriage and then wound up back in the hospital a couple of weeks later, hemorrhaging for no apparent reason. They were unable to save her. The official cause of death was listed as complications from a spontaneous abortion—or miscarriage, in layman's terms— but there was a lot of speculation about what really happened."

"I don't suppose this friend remembered if an older woman came in with the girl?" Cade asked.

"Interestingly enough, she did, although she never clearly understood the woman's relationship to the girl. What she did remember was that the woman seemed very upset when the girl died, but not in a teary sort of way. She seemed more irritated than brokenhearted, according to the friend."

Cade shifted in his chair, his expression turning dark. He leaned both elbows on the table to ask in a voice that wouldn't carry, "Prostitution ring? This woman is their pimp?"

Madison broke in before her husband could answer. "Laurel, do you know if the Franklin area falls within the hospital's service area?"

The nurse looked surprised by the question. "Yes, of course. We see patients from that area all the time. In fact—" She broke off abruptly, finishing with a stiff, "Yes. It does."

Madison read her sudden discomfort perfectly. "That's where the girls were from, isn't it?" she asked, eager to have found a solid link.

Laurel squirmed in her seat. "I can't really answer that."

Cade nodded in understanding. He asked the same question in a different way. "Would it be fair to assume that at least one of the three girls could have been from that area? And keep in mind that the hometowns of the two girls who died would be a matter of public record."

Laurel answered without doing so directly. "The third girl's hometown would be confidential, but I suppose you could make whatever assumption you like."

His brown eyes glittered. "So, that would be a yes. At the very least, the girl Madison overheard is from Franklin."

In reply, Laurel lifted a noncommittal shoulder, while Brash and Madison exchanged a silent communication.

"I don't think we're dealing with a prostitution ring," Brash told the detective. His mouth set in a grim line. "I think we're dealing with human trafficking. Namely, buying and selling babies."

Cade's face turned dark. "That's despicable!"

"Agreed. If it's what I suspect, it's not your average black-market deal. I think this is a very sophisticated program, parading under the ruse of private or independent adoptions. On the surface, it's all above board. Borderline noble."

"What could possibly be noble about selling a child?" Laurel practically spat.

Cade reached out and took her hand, a silent reminder to hear the other couple out.

Madison was the one to offer details. "There's a woman out of Franklin who runs a luxurious inn and spa. Our best friends just returned from there and are the ones who suggested there could be more to the business than meets the eye. On the surface, the owner created and operates an amazing community service project. She offers a job and room and board to young women who are pregnant. It's a very comprehensive, well-thought out program that requires the girls to take classes, make a plan for the future, and to save part of their wages as a head start once they leave."

"But, what? In exchange, they have to give up their baby?" Always passionate, the very idea made Laurel's blood boil.

"From what I understand, they have two choices. They can keep the baby and leave the program before their third trimester, taking references from the owner with them when they go. Or they can place their baby in a private adoption program, help choose the parents, and either stay in the program or graduate, so to speak, and move on."

"How is this program funded?" Cade asked.

Brash answered with, "That's the million-dollar question."

Laurel narrowed her eyes, not liking what was implied. "In other words, these girls are selling their babies!"

"That's what my friend Genny is afraid of. The minute she told me her suspicions, I thought of the girl in the ER."

"But where do the two questionable deaths come in?" Cade wanted to know. "We all agree, it can't be a coincidence that two women die under strange circumstances shortly after they've each had a miscarriage. In Houston or Dallas maybe, but we're in a much smaller community. The odds of such similar cases occurring within a year aren't favorable."

"I may have an answer to that. Maddy, even you don't know this part." Brash ignored his wife's raised eyebrows and explained, "Cutter wanted me to check out a story a girl from the inn told them, even though he didn't know any specific details. He didn't even know if it was urban legend or fact or fabricated simply to gain their sympathy. There was talk among the staff, however, that at least two girls who were in the adoption program had died after suffering miscarriages. He said one was killed in a car accident."

"That has to be these girls!" Madison gasped. "The story clearly wasn't fabricated."

"It sure sounds reliable," Cade agreed. Thinking aloud, the detective went on to murmur, "It's smart of them to use different hospitals. Less likely for someone to make the connection." He turned to the woman whose hand he still held.

"Do you know if the hit and run driver was ever found?"

"No clue."

His nod was thoughtful. "I can look into that easily enough. I can even look up the coroner's report on the other girl."

"Plus," Brash told the others, "Marcella Durant takes out a life insurance on the girls when they enter the program, naming *Cherubdipity* as the beneficiary."

Madison stifled a gasp. The implication was obvious.

"This is scary, Cade," Laurel whispered, her eyes wide. "It's horrible enough to think someone could take advantage of these young girls and profit from their babies. But to think they might resort to murder..."

When a shiver ran through her shoulders, he placed his arm around her once more and pulled her to his side.

Their plates arrived, bringing with them a lighter mood for the table. The couples enjoyed their meal while getting better acquainted.

"Dessert, anyone?" the server asked when they were done.

"No place to put it," Brash insisted, leaning back in his chair.

"That was a big steak," Cade agreed. "Ladies?"

"Not me!"

"No room."

With a unanimous round of nays, Cade told the server, "In that case, bring the check, please. All on one."

"We can't let you do that," Brash protested.

"Relax. I've got it," Cade insisted.

"I was the one who suggested it," Laurel argued. "We can at least split the check."

"Absolutely not. Besides, if this turns out to be something, I can always get the CSPD to foot the bill." The detective flashed a smile, even though his brown eyes were brooding. His mind was already at work, thinking of different angles of attack.

"The thing is, neither of us have jurisdiction in Robertson County," Brash pointed out.

Cade begged to differ. "If they're bringing their sordid business dealings to College Station, I do have jurisdiction. And I won't hesitate to exercise it."

20

A week after Madison and Brash were married, a tradition was born in their newly established household. On lazy Saturday mornings (should one occur), the kids would pile up on their parents' bed to rehash the events of the week.

Brash had once told Megan that love was like a rubber band. It could stretch to include many people, but it always held close those dearest to the heart. These Saturday mornings were a time to strengthen that band, and to strengthen their family as a unit. Together, they would work out solutions to problems, share accomplishments, discuss upcoming schedules, or simply relax and recharge.

Blake got up early to make a donut run, so breakfast on this Saturday was laden with sugar and yeasty deliciousness. Bethani washed a bunch of grapes to add a token statement of health consciousness, and Megan poured the milk. They piled it all on a tray and brought it upstairs, where Maddy and Brash had coffee waiting from their en suite coffeemaker.

"What's on the agenda for this week?" Maddy asked, pulling up the calendar on her cell phone to make notations.

"Scrimmage at Riverton on Tuesday. Practice every day but then and Friday," Blake said around a jelly-stuffed donut.

"I've got the night shift Thursday and Friday," Brash said. He made a point to take his turn in rotations at least once a month. With just himself and three deputies on the force, it seemed only fair. And Brash deCordova was nothing, if not a fair and just man.

"Friday is Mama Mike's birthday, so I'll be there for the night." The auburn-haired beauty picked through the pastry box to select a cinnamon-covered cake donut. "Beth, you're invited to go with us to eat. He'll probably pick Italian, so that means going to College Station."

"I will if I'm not working on that project."

"With Lover Boy Trenton?" Megan teased.

Bethani ignored the goading. "With my partner Trenton, yes."

"Is that like a life partner?" Blake scoffed.

"Not this again," Maddy groaned. "You two go easy on your sister. She has a class assignment and is trying to make a good grade on it. Blake, I trust you're taking your assignment just as seriously?"

"Not only that," her son agreed as he bit into a bear claw, his third selection from the boxes, "but I'm learning a good life lesson from it. Danni Jo and I may be a couple, but this assignment has shown us that we're too young to be parents. The only way to make sure that happens is to stay away from sex."

"Agreed, but stop there," this twin said, turning up her nose. "TMI."

Thrilled her son had come to this conclusion on his own, Maddy hid a beaming smile behind her donut. She nodded as she took a bite. "I think that was what your teacher had in mind when she said it was a safety measure."

"Danni Jo and I both have plans for college and careers. I'll be a pro baseball player, of course, and she'll be a horticulturist. She's gotten involved in her granddad's business. He said he may even leave *Marvin Gardens* to her one day." He shrugged as he downed a full glass of milk. "It wouldn't too be bad of a gig for me to do in the off season."

"Whoa, there," Brash said to the teen. "Since when are you and Danni Jo talking about marriage?"

"No time soon," he assured his parents. "We both want to finish college first. Marriage would be too distracting."

"Keep that line of thought, son," Brash advised.

Out of nowhere, Bethani asked, "Are Aunt Genny and Cutter planning to adopt a baby?"

It wasn't her place to say, so Maddy dodged the question. "Uhm, why do you ask?"

"She offered to help with my assignment like, out of the blue. And she seems really into it. She's made a couple of comments like 'Cutter thinks this,' or 'I'm looking for that' in an agency. Don't get me wrong. The help has been great. It just seems personal to her, like it's her own project or something."

"If you're going to do something, you may as well go all the way and do it right. But they would make excellent parents, don't you think?"

"For sure. Both are pretty cool for people their age."

"Excuse me, young lady. Genny and I happen to be the same age," her mother pointed out, "so tread carefully."

"You know what I mean, Mom."

Maddy couldn't help but smile. Her best friend *was* awesome. At any age.

"By the way," Megan remembered, turning toward her stepmother, "I did hear something you may be interested in. You know how I told you Elle's mother was a tech for *Barbour Foods*? Well, not anymore. They fired her."

"Really? I thought you said she was going to quit."

"She was, but they fired her before she had the chance. According to Elle, she stood up to her boss and told them she thought they were asking too much of their growers. The company made up all these insane rules and expected Mrs. Lomax and their other techs to enforce them. She said she couldn't, in good conscience, make them replace perfectly good equipment with an inferior product. They said no problem. She was fired."

"She actually said inferior product?" This fit into the narrative she was hearing from other sources.

"That's what Elle said."

Maddy's eyes narrowed in thought. "Do you think Mrs. Lomax would be willing to talk to me?"

Megan shrugged and popped a grape into her mouth. "Probably."

"Can you get a number for me?"

"I'll text Elle and ask."

"That would be great."

"There you go again," Brash teased. "Dragging the kids into your snooping."

"The Junior Division of *In a Pinch*," his wife reminded him with a sweet smile. "Speaking of that, Granny Bert lined up a few people for me to talk to on Monday. They're some of the growers who have had chicken houses the longest. Most of them are over in Milam County, but you know my grandmother. She has contacts all over the place."

"You're telling me!" Bethani said. "I told her about this assignment we have, and she popped off the name of two agencies for me to contact. She said one was reputable, one was iffy. I'm not sure what she meant about iffy, but it was the one her friend's daughter used."

"Do you mean Lana Kopetsky?" When the teen nodded, Maddy asked, "What was she talking about?"

"No clue."

"Aren't you taking Granny Bert back to the doctor this week?" Brash asked.

Maddy snapped her fingers. "Thanks for reminding me. I didn't put that on my calendar." Typing the information into her phone, she asked, "Anything else?"

"When I get home from the scrimmage, I could sure go for a big batch of Chunky Charlie cookies. Pencil me in for a dozen," her son said.

"What am I, a bakery?"

"That's okay. I'll make them," Bethani offered.

"Wait. What? You're actually volunteering to make cookies just because your brother asks for them?" Maddy eyed her daughter suspiciously. "Something's going on. Spill it, sister."

Bethani selected a handful of grapes with unusual concentration. "It was just an offer. You know I like to bake, and Chunky Charlies are easy enough. Throw in a bunch of different candies and nuts, mix them in oatmeal cookie dough, and voila! Ten minutes later, you have Chunky Charlies."

"So, you'd be okay with your brother and his friends eating every single one of them?" Maddy's tone was disbelieving.

The teen shrugged, still intent on her grape selection. "I might save a few. I've got a study session that night and all."

"Study session, my a—eyeball!" Blake said, quickly amending his choice of words. "You've got a study *date*. You're making those cookies to impress Dork Face, not for me."

"One, it's not a date," Bethani snapped. "Two, the cookies are for all of us. Three, his name is Trenton, not Dork Face. If you want to see a real dork, just look in the mirror."

"Why? You gonna be standing behind me?" he smirked.

"Maybe so," his sister shot back. "So, you'd better watch your back."

"Okay, you two. Knock it off." Brash's voice was just stern enough to silence them both. He tipped his auburn head toward his wife's phone. "But if we're putting in orders for the kitchen,

King Ranch Chicken sure would be nice on the nights I'm working."

Maddy typed in the request, making a side note to go grocery shopping. "Duly noted, my darling."

21

There were numerous chicken houses scattered around Milam and Robertson Counties, allowing Madison to multitask with one easy trip.

She called Genny to see if she'd like to tag along.

"I would," her best friend said, sounding out of breath, "but the doctor's office called and said they had a last-minute cancellation. As soon as Cutter gets home and takes a quick shower, we're headed that way."

"This is the fertility specialist?" Madison asked, dancing around the delicate topic.

"Yes. Even if we take Tatiana up on her offer, we still want to meet with the doctor. We don't want to stop with just one baby. The more the merrier, we say."

"Perfect. I'll let my three very quarrelsome teenagers spend the weekend with you and see if you change your tune. I don't know what has gotten into them, but they do nothing but bicker these days!"

"Really? Bethani couldn't have been sweeter

when she and Trenton dropped by the café to work on their project. Together, I think we all found some very helpful information."

"I think Bethani is suspicious of your motives. Do they know the real reason you're helping them?"

"Not from me, they don't. Then again, I'm not sure they knew I was there. I do believe I smell a romance in bloom."

"That's what the recent arguments have been about. Megan teases her about liking Trenton, Blake joins in, and Bethani blows up like a powder keg. I think she's still grappling with the reality of actually liking a boy she formally referred to as Dork Face."

"It's a cute face, though," Genny mused. "Oh, gotta go. I hear Cutter. Say a little prayer for us."

"You've got it. Keep me posted."

Setting out on her solo adventure, Madison met with four different chicken growers, hearing stories like the ones she had already been told.

One farmer wasn't concerned; his loan was paid in full and if the company messed with him, he would close the doors. His wife kept harping on him to retire, anyway.

One refused to play along with more of *Barbour's* games and had his farm for sale, even if it meant losing money. He claimed that, either way, he had the short end of the stick.

Two of the chicken growers were doing the upgrades and sinking themselves deeper into debt. They couldn't afford to lose the paycheck, even if another loan made it significantly smaller.

As she left each farm, Madison felt guiltier by

the moment. She had promised to help Lucy and her friends, but she was quickly losing ground. It seemed that *Barbour* had the upper hand, and there was no getting around it.

Fair or not, the contracts appeared ironclad.

Needing a break from the inn, Marcella suggested they meet at the coffee shop in town. As much as she loved her slice of paradise, sometimes she simply needed a change of scenery.

She was the first to arrive, beating her coffee date there by a good ten minutes. It gave her a chance to unwind from the pressures of the job and to mentally prepare for the clash sure to come.

Marcella never fancied herself as an innkeeper, but it suited her. She had been in college when she first met Gregory. Both had been focused more on their studies than each other. When she discovered she was pregnant, he informed her that having a child wasn't part of his seven-year plan.

What was she to do? Even though she told people her parents had disowned her, it was, in fact, the other way around; she had disowned them. A broken family in Baltimore didn't fit in with her aspirations for success. She had goals. A drug-dealing father and a mother in and out of rehab wouldn't help her achieve those goals. If anything, they would drag her down. And when she did manage to make something of herself—which she knew she would—her family would try to leach off her and use her as their own personal gold mine. No, the best thing to do was to leave them and her old life behind when she boarded that bus for Cambridge.

She had refused to give up her child, determined that she could be a better mother than her own had been. And she had tried. Lord knows, she had tried. She did without sleep, did without food, did without any shred of dignity. She managed to keep her scholarship intact, even when it meant leaving her baby with anyone who would take her. She couldn't hold down a job, attend classes, and be a mother all at one time, so she had done some things she wasn't proud of, just to make ends meet. She compromised herself on more than one occasion. If it meant a place for her and her baby to sleep for the night, or formula for Jessenia's bottle, she swallowed her pride and did what needed to be done.

By the time social services caught up with her, she was almost relieved. She loved her daughter, but she couldn't keep up this lifestyle. It was poison for both of them. And it certainly wasn't part of her plan.

Marcella was an excellent student, however, and very bright. Her grades wavered during those difficult months, but never faltered. After the social worker took her baby away, she had nothing to do but study. She threw herself into her schoolwork and soon, she was at the top of her class. Marcella graduated with honors and landed a job with one of Boston's top manufacturing firms. Soon, she was the head of their business department.

Marcella was at the height of her career, being wooed from one prominent company to another, when she ran into Gregory again. His seven-year plan had paid off well for him. He was now junior partner at a well-established New York law firm but was often in Boston on business. They picked up their relationship where it had left off, even though she knew he was married. She convinced herself it didn't matter; they had their careers and seven to ten days out of every month together.

It was enough, until it wasn't.

He had a wife. A family. An entirely separate life in New York.

She had a career and memories of a child she had loved and lost. *His* child, no less.

She noticed how Gregory always introduced her as his colleague, even though she had long ago moved from her own apartment and into the condo he had along the waterfront. She spent holidays alone, while he went home to spend time with his family. It took awhile, but Marcella realized she had become a 'kept woman.'

As humiliating as that fact was, that hadn't been the final straw. The final straw was the day his daughter showed up on his doorstep, eager to surprise her father and share her good news in person. She had been accepted into his alma mater to study law, just like her father.

The final straw was when she looked at the girl on the doorstep and realized it was like looking into a mirror. She stared at a face so like her own at the age of eighteen and knew a terrible truth:

Gregory and his wife had somehow adopted *her* daughter. Her daughter with Gregory. He had denied the baby when she was born and forced Marcella into a situation that had resulted in the child being ripped from her mother's arms, only to later welcome their daughter into his own home, his own life. A home and a life he shared with another woman. Not Marcella.

When the sordid details came out, they pushed Marcella to the edge of sanity. His wife couldn't have children of her own. She came from a wealthy family that needed an heir. Locating and adopting Gregory's biological child was the perfect solution and suited them all well. Everyone but Marcella. All those years Marcella had spent mourning the loss of her child and throwing herself into her studies and then her work, Gregory had spent watching the girl grow up. While she wondered what the girl looked like at the age of six, or ten, or at that wondrous age of sixteen, he had held her hand at the zoo and gone to her dance recitals and attended her high school graduation.

With the truth revealed, Gregory threatened to ruin her if she made waves in his perfect life. Until that moment, she never realized exactly how ruthless the man could be. Even though she had created a name for herself in the business world, he had enough clout, and enough money, to destroy her.

He strongly suggested that she leave Boston. He owned real estate in Texas, an investment property he had never laid eyes upon. He deeded the land and house to her as compensation for services rendered. Generous man that he was, he even paid for a one-way ticket out of town and all moving expenses.

She had been a disaster at first, banished and forgotten in the wilds of rural Texas. But as the beauty of the land worked its magic on her wounded soul, she slowly regained her fighting spirit. Even here, she could be somebody. She could make something of herself and salvage what was left of her life, different though it now was.

Marcella had never been afraid of a challenge; turning the property into a five-star resort had been that, and more. She was proud of what she had built and of the person she had become. Her new mission in life was teaching other women to take control of their futures.

Sometimes, however, the process was exhausting. There were days when the task seemed overwhelming. Days when she questioned her own leadership and wisdom. Those days came with more frequency, now that she had taken on a partner. Sometimes, she felt it all slipping out of her hands. Was she allowing someone else to control her destiny, the very things she warned her girls about?

Caught up in her thoughts, she didn't hear the jingle of the door chime, or the click of heels across the tiled floor. She never noticed the rustle of movement near her table, until the chair beside her moved and a toffee-colored hand waved in front of her face.

"Earth to Marcella. Anyone home?"

A smile of pleasure touched the older woman's face. "Jessenia. It's so good to see you."

The one saving grace from the debacle of her past life was the attractive young woman standing across from her now. When Jessenia had shown up unexpectedly on her father's doorstep in Boston, he had spun some tale about co-leasing the condo. There had been a mix-up in scheduling, he claimed, but the girl was too smart to fall for his lies. Even she could see the resemblance between the black woman and herself. She had always wondered about her heritage, and she saw answers in this woman who answered her father's door. Jessenia had taken it upon herself to search for Marcella. Without her father's knowledge, she had pursued her curiosity. The trail led her to a rural community in Texas and to a woman who was, without doubt, her birth mother.

These days, the up and coming young lawyer presided over the Dallas branch of her family's law firm. It had been her idea to venture out of New York and set up shop in the Lone Star State. It had been a hard sell to the staid board members and partners, her father in particular. Her secret weapon was her adoptive mother, who had the ultimate say as majority shareholder and chairman of the board. After learning that Marcella was still in her husband's life, she hated Gregory almost as much as Jessenia did. If Gregory opposed the expansion, she was all for it.

Jessenia was determined to make the Texas branch a success. She brought a team with her from Boston for support. They all worked long hours recruiting new clients and expanding the firm's horizons, but Jessenia worked the hardest of all. Not without coincidence, her first client had been the acclaimed *Cherubdipity Inn and Spa.*

Awards and accolades aside, it hadn't taken long for the attorney to realize the inn was teetering on the brink of collapse. Losing her very first acquisition to bankruptcy was out of the question; her father would forever taunt her with her failure. He still saw her move to Texas as a betrayal. Driven by determination and a fierce sense of independence, Jessenia convinced Marcella to take her on as partner. The cash infusions she provided gave the inn a new chance at survival.

"Have you ordered yet?" her daughter asked.

"Not yet."

The young woman pulled a file from her briefcase and thrust it toward her. "Look over these while I order."

Marcella sighed at the brisk order. Jessenia meant nothing by it, she told herself. It was simply her way.

As always, there were more papers to sign. Jessenia had an eye for investing and a strong opinion on how and where their earnings could be spent. She was all about diversification.

Returning with two oversized, stoneware cups and saucers, Jessenia didn't make time for pleasantries. "Did you sign them?" she asked.

Marcella eyed the papers in her hand. "Are you sure about this, Jessenia?"

Impatience edged the younger woman's voice. "Yes, Mammy, I'm sure. Have I steered you wrong so far?"

"No, but this is different from most of our

investments."

"How many times do I have to say this? The golden rule in real estate is location, location, location. The golden rule in investing is diversify, diversify, diversify." She took a sip of her chai latte and glared at Marcella over the rim of her cup. "You should know this. You majored in business."

Not for the first time, Marcella resented the tone her daughter often took with her. It was bad enough that she insisted on calling her *Mammy*. She called her adoptive white mother by the revered title of Mother, but not Marcella. The one time she mentioned it to Jessenia, the girl shrugged it off as being an affectionate nickname. Besides, she claimed, calling them both by the same name would be confusing. But Marcella often wondered if it weren't a dig about her race, even though the same blood ran through Jessenia's veins. Mixed ancestry had given her lovely skin and glossy, dark hair, but some of her traits revealed her African American heritage. Belittling that heritage didn't make sense to Marcella.

Then again, much of what her daughter did and thought didn't make sense to her.

In the end, Marcella signed the papers. Despite her misgivings, she knew that Jessenia was bright and ambitious. She had as much at stake as Marcella did, if not more. If she thought this was the right course of action for them, Marcella would trust her judgment. Her daughter was a good businesswoman and an even better attorney.

There was only one thing that bothered her. It

wasn't until they had become partners that Marcella discovered her daughter's most serious fault.

When it came to business, Jessenia was as cold and ruthless as her father.

As Madison drove through the small town of Franklin, she noticed the sign for *Cup 'o Love*. She could use a jolt of caffeine. She still had to take Granny Bert to her late-afternoon doctor appointment.

While standing in line to place her order, Madison tried finding a wormhole in the case against *Barbour*. So far, most of her efforts in helping the farmers had failed.

"I wish I could get through to speak with this J.D. Cockrell," she muttered. She had seen the signature often enough, scrawled across the bottom of the different contracts. "I'd definitely give that man a piece of my mind!" She knew *Barbour's* corporate lawyer was too busy and too important to be bothered with the likes of her, but she could always dream. Sometimes, she found that confronting a silent opponent in her head was almost as satisfying than going toe to toe with an argumentative, opinionated, flesh and blood adversary.

As she waited to order her vanilla latte, snippets of conversation drifted her way from a table behind her. Two women were having a heated discussion over some sort of business venture. Madison didn't intentionally listen to their disagreement, but their raised voices made it difficult not to hear.

"The golden rule in investing is diversify, diversify, diversify," the younger woman snapped in her Northern accent. "You should know this. You majored in business." A few more words floated on the air as Madison ordered and paid.

Solid investment... Right timing... Cumber-Tex... Again, diversity.

Behind her, a shuffling of chairs told Madison the women were leaving. One said something about driving back to Dallas. The other said she needed to get back to the inn.

Madison whipped her head around, but their backs were to her as they went out the door. They were both about the same height and build, but she guessed they were several years apart in age. Both were well dressed and wore their hair in a neat chignon, but one was streaked with gray, while the other was glossy and black.

When the barista handed over her drink, Madison asked, "Do you happen to know the two women who just left? They were sitting at that round table right there."

"Oh, sure. They're the owners of *Cherubdipity*, a fancy bed and breakfast just down the road. It was just featured on that Texas Bucket List show on TV." The girl at the register gave Madison a quizzical look before breaking into a smile. "Hey, I know you! You're from TV, too, aren't you? You have that big, old mansion they remodeled."

Madison offered a weak smile. "Guilty as charged."

"I loved that show! I wish they'd do another house around there. Your town is filled with hilarious characters!"

"They're characters, all right," Madison agreed, her tone less than enthusiastic.

"Crazily enough, your friend and her hot firefighter husband were in here not long ago, too. We didn't realize it was them until they left. Hey! You aren't doing another show around here, are you?"

"No, nothing like that. I was just in the area and thought I'd drop in."

"My mom owns the shop. If I'm not working the next time you come in, tell them Tamara said your coffee is on the house."

"That's very nice of you, Tamara."

The girl gave her a big smile. "You're like royalty. It's the least we can do."

22

The first two times the name flashed across his cell that afternoon, Douglas Townsend ignored the call. That name could only mean one thing—there was another 'hiccup' with the adoption, and they needed more money.

A few minutes later, his phone buzzed with a text.

> *If you want to welcome your baby into the world, meet us at Texas General ASAP.*

His hands trembled as he typed back a reply.

> *It's too early!*

Bubbles danced across the screen as he buzzed his secretary and told her to clear his schedule for the rest of the day. He glanced back at the message.

> *Tell that to the baby.*

Douglas stuffed papers into his briefcase and hurried out the door. He was as nervous as any first-time father, even though this wasn't his biological child. Taking the private elevator down to the parking garage, he ran through the checklist in his head.

As the elevator glided past the second floor, he realized he had forgotten the first line of action.

"Call Camille!" He slapped a palm against his forehead. "I forgot to call Camille!"

"This is rather strange," Madison murmured as they found seats in the waiting room at the hospital. "I've never been in a maternity waiting room when someone wasn't expecting a baby."

"I'm sure *someone* is expecting a baby," her grandmother pointed out contrarily. "It just isn't me, thank our sweet Lord and Savior! Been there, done that, half a century ago. I'm just here for a test."

"I guess I thought they'd have a different department for kidney sonograms than they did for baby sonograms. I'm not used to the hospital and clinic both being so small, or so close together."

"Makes sense, though, don't you think? Walk down a hallway, and you've left the clinic and are in the hospital. Good use of space and equipment, if you ask me."

"I suppose so."

A half hour ago, the doctor had examined the octogenarian in his office at the clinic. The test he ordered could be done immediately, so here they sat, in a waiting room designated for expectant families.

"That man yonder must be expecting a grandchild," Granny Bert said, nodding toward the distinguished-looking man in a suit and tie. He kept pacing the area, glancing at his smartwatch every few seconds.

"Could be the father," Madison mused.

Granny Bert clicked her tongue in disapproval. "Either he found himself a younger woman, or it was an uh-oh baby. And if that's the case, I pity his poor wife, putting her body through childbirth at this stage of life. Not only that, but by the time that child graduates from high school, neither parent will be able to even see the podium."

"He does look a bit older," Madison agreed. "He also sort of looks like the dean at Brazos College. The school has been sending literature to Blake, trying to lure him into their athletic program, and the dean's picture is on all the envelopes."

"I reckon a college dean can have grandchildren, same as the rest of us," Granny Bert reasoned.

"That reminds me. Bethani said you offered a few suggestions for her school project, but that one of the adoption agencies you named was questionable. What made you say that?"

"It's the one Lana Kopetsky used. Mark my words, something's not right about the way that girl adopted out her baby."

"What was wrong about it?"

"I'm not sure, but Wanda suddenly came into some money. It just doesn't make sense, unless there was some funny business going on."

"You told me you suspected a lawsuit."

"That was before she let something slip. She made a comment about *Heartstrings Adoptions* and how well they treated their mothers. Between what she said, what I deduced, and what I snooped around and discovered, I'd say they aren't quite on the up and up."

"Details, please."

"Wanda said something about Lana's baby fit the exact profile some family was looking for—parents with athletic abilities, above-average IQ, and at least one parent with blond hair." Granny Bert dipped her head and went on with a pointed look, "You know what Lana lacked in common sense, she made up for with book sense. She ranked in the top ten percent of her class. She was always good in sports, and her baby's father was some sort of physical trainer. But since when does a legitimate adoption agency let you pick and choose what child you get?"

"A private adoption agency, maybe?"

"Maybe," her grandmother said in a skeptical tone, "but that sounds mighty specific to me. Even if prospective parents are willing to pay to get the genes they want, what about the agency? How are they getting these made-to-order babies? They can't just place an order with a supplier and have one delivered to them. No pun intended," she claimed, but her smirk said otherwise.

"You know what you're suggesting." It wasn't a question.

"Call it what you like," Granny Bert said, "but what it boils down to is that these folks are buying and selling babies. Not to sound crass and unfeeling, but you can't fill a specific order like that without shopping from a huge inventory. Like everything else, at some point, it comes down to supply and demand."

Madison's nod was grim. "The more people who want red-haired babies, for instance, the harder those redheads are to find. I can see where unethical agencies might be willing to entice expectant mothers to go with them instead of others, but legit agencies wouldn't pay cash. They would attract their mothers with assurances their babies would get good educations, loving families, that sort of thing. Some even let the birth mother choose the adoptive parents and have an input in how the child is raised."

"Those are the ethical ones," Granny Bert pointed out. "But one of my sources told me that Lana is in some swanky mental facility. That costs big bucks. Suddenly, Wanda not only has enough for that, but now she has enough to go on a cruise and spring for a friend to join her. Joe Glenn tells me she was down at his dealership, looking at new cars. Tell me that don't sound fishy!"

"It does sound suspicious," Madison agreed.

A woman in scrubs came down the hallway and called a name from her clipboard.

"That's you, Granny. Need me to go with you?"

"Nah, you stay put. I probably won't be too long."

While Granny Bert went back for her test, Madison did a search for *Heartstrings Adoptions*. The company looked legitimate enough but, like *Barbour* and countless others, what they advertised and what they delivered were often two very different things.

As she perused the internet for more information on local agencies—there were surprisingly few in the area—she heard a commotion on the other side of the waiting room. A well-dressed woman had come through the swinging double doors, wearing a huge smile and a disposable hospital gown over linen slacks and Louboutin heels. Pearl studs peeked from beneath the blue cap covering most of her upswept, platinum-colored hair. Madison guessed her to be in her late forties.

"She's here!" she announced to the pacing man who bore a strong resemblance to the college dean.

"Really?" He caught her in a joyful hug before setting her back and insisting, "Tell me everything."

"Even though she's early, she has ten little toes and ten perfectly delicate fingers. They look long and dexterous, so we may have a concert pianist in the family! Her hair is thick and curly, and has the slightest hint of red."

I guess Granny Bert was right, Madison mused. She smiled as she watched them, finding their happiness contagious. *Even college deans can be grandfathers.*

The woman's next words derailed that line of thought. "We have a perfectly healthy, perfectly gorgeous daughter!" the woman said, throwing her arms around the man once more.

Ah, so he is *the father, but they're adopting*, Madison realized.

She didn't intrude on them, at least at first. She allowed them their time of celebration. They both shot off a few texts, amid laughing and planning and spinning dreams of the future. Only when she heard Granny Bert's voice drifting down the hallway did she dare approach the couple. It was now or never.

"Excuse me," she said, wearing a smile that was part timid, part delight at witnessing their obvious joy. "I couldn't help but overhear your good news. Congratulations!"

The couple gushed with pleasure, thanking her and sharing tidbits of their story. After twenty-plus years of marriage, they'd dreamed of this moment. Both were so proud and so happy.

"If it's not too forward of me, do you mind if I ask what adoption agency you went through? I have dear friends who are considering adoption," Madison explained. "Obviously, you've had a great experience, and I'm hoping for the same for them."

"Of course!" the woman said, all smiles. Beside her, her husband frowned. When he would have most likely made some comment about privacy, she missed his cautious expression and went on blithely, "We went through *Heartstring Adoptions*. They're new to the Brazos Valley, and we can't say enough about them! They've been absolutely a dream to work with!"

"I'll tell my friends," Madison smiled. "Again, congratulations."

She offered a parting wave as she joined Granny Bert and headed for the elevators.

"What was that about?" the older woman asked.

"Turns out, the couple are here with the birth

mother of their new daughter. And guess what adoption agency they used?"

"Since you look like the cat that just swallowed the canary, I'm going with *Heartstrings*."

"Bingo. The woman said the agency was a dream to work with, but the man's expression said something different. He looked a little green around the gills, so my guess is that they've been more of a nightmare, at least from his end."

"I suppose he could have hidden the facts from his wife," Granny Bert reasoned. "They look like the kind of couple who can afford most anything they want. If the wife wanted a baby, the husband may have done whatever it took to give her one. No matter the cost."

"I agree. Even though she seemed like a lovely woman, I doubt she bothers with things like budgets and account balances." A heavy realization pulled Madison's entire face into a frown. "Not so very long ago, I was the exact same way. I was content to let my husband handle our finances all on his own, instead of sharing control."

Stepping into the elevator and pushing the *down* button, Madison was honest enough to admit, "It's taken me a while to admit it, but I should have also taken some of the responsibility, as well. It wasn't fair to make Gray shoulder all of that on his own."

"Like I've always told you, girl. Marriage is a partnership. Like everything else in life, it requires a healthy balance. Not domination or submission but finding a happy medium. It's all about harmony and balance."

"Is that why you refuse to marry Sticker?" Madison teased as they stepped out of the elevator and into the lobby on the ground floor. "Is he too controlling?"

"Too stubborn is more like it. I swear, that man is as stubborn as a cross-eyed mule!" With a sheepish smile, she admitted, "Maybe I am a bit, too. Even if your grandfather wasn't such a hard act for him to follow, I've been a widow now for almost ten years. I've gotten used to doing things my own way. I don't need a man to come along now and tell me how to run my life."

"What about harmony and balance? Don't you think you and Sticker could find a happy medium?"

"I reckon that man has been married so many times, he's plumb forgot how a good marriage should be. I'm not sure there's enough time left for me to teach him, either."

"Speaking of good marriages, do you feel like stopping by the grocery store on the way home? I promised to make King Ranch Chicken one night for Brash, and Bethani wants to make a batch of Chunky Charlies."

"I could use a few things, myself. Even though," her grandmother was quick to point out, "I try to support the local market whenever I can."

"You can blame this transgression on me," Madison assured her with a grin. "For once, I can take the blame for being a bad influence on you, instead of the other way around."

The news Genny received from the fertility specialist was a mix of good news and bad news. Yes, there was a new procedure that promised favorable results for some patients. The bad news was that most of those patients were several years younger than she. With each passing month, Genny's ovaries sustained more damage and had less chance of recovery. While the doctor remained hopeful for the couple to conceive naturally, he tentatively brought up the subject of adoption, suggesting they keep their options open.

Genny shared the report with Madison the next day over coffee.

"I'm sorry, Gen. I know that's not what you hoped he would say."

"It's about what I expected," she admitted. "Sometimes, I think it's better to know the worse, than to keep hoping for the best and be disappointed. As much as I want to carry a baby, if I can't, I just can't."

"But he didn't completely rule out the possibility, did he?"

"No. He wanted to do another blood test for some reason, and maybe take a few images." She fingered the handle of the cup. "I don't know. Maybe I'm ready to accept the inevitable and move on. I'm serious about adopting Tatiana's baby. I think it will be a good, solid solution for all of us. Tatiana will know her baby will go to a loving home, and Cutter and I can start the family we've always dreamed of."

"Have you talked to Shawn Bryant about it?"

"Yes. He doesn't normally handle adoptions, but he said he would make an exception for us."

"That's wonderful!"

"Now if we can come up with a plan to get Tatiana out of *Cherubdipity* and somewhere safe. The first obstacle is finding a way to contact her, without putting her in danger."

"I don't have an immediate solution for that, but I do have some news to share. Has Tatiana ever mentioned the name *Heartstrings Adoptions* to you?"

"I don't believe so. Why?"

"Marcella may not be affiliated with them, but I do suspect the agency engages in shady dealings. I also believe it's the agency Miss Arlene used when Lana's baby was born. I don't think she intentionally chose a non-reputable agency to go with, but I can see her falling for their pretty lies and sugar-coated tales."

"What kind of lies?"

"I don't know for sure, but according to Granny Bert, Lana is in a very nice facility, and Miss Arlene now has money to spare. I know she likes going to Louisiana to gamble from time to time, but I doubt she won *that* kind of money at the casinos."

"Not without bragging about it, at any rate."

"This may be nothing, but I also met a very nice couple yesterday at the hospital. I took Granny for tests and had to wait in the maternity waiting room. I watched a very nervous, expectant father pace the floor, until the mother came out and announced they had a beautiful, healthy baby girl."

"Wait. The *mother* came out? After giving birth?" Genny's mouth hung open in surprise.

Madison's smile was as much an explanation as her words were. "The adoptive mother did. A very lovely lady in her late forties most likely, with pearls and jewels and a very nice pair of Louboutin heels."

"Ah, I see. The adoptive parents were wealthy and well established."

"*Very* well established. If I'm not sorely mistaken, the father was Dean Townsend from Brazos College. But the interesting thing is that I went over to congratulate them and happened to ask who they used for adoption. Guess what? They went with *Heartstrings.*"

Instead of sharing her friend's smile, Genny frowned. "Okay, I don't know what I find more disturbing. The fact that you randomly asked strangers who they used for adoption, or that a college dean would fall for an adoption scam."

"First, it wasn't exactly random. The wife shared the fact that they had been married for over twenty years and had finally resorted to adoption to have a child. I used the excuse of asking for a friend, namely you and Cutter. And second, I didn't say it was a scam. Just... shady."

"And you really think a college dean would go for that?"

Madison stretched her graceful neck and spoke with care. "I think," she said, choosing her words, "that sometimes people want something so badly, they're willing to overlook certain details. People want to believe what people want to believe. I have no doubt that *Heartstrings Adoptions* is a legitimate company. But there's a definite distinction between legitimate and ethical. It could be that they do a little of both; some adoptions on the up and up, some under the table. I don't know. But I think it's worth checking out."

"Have you talked to your nurse friend?"

"Naturally, she couldn't divulge any private information about the birth mother. She could, however, go up to the second floor and get a peek at the proud adoptive parents. She confirmed that it was Dean Townsend and his wife Camille. That's about all I know."

Genny narrowed her eyes in thought. "What does this dean look like?"

"Mid-fifties, balding... I don't know how to describe him. Look him up."

Genny typed his name into her phone's search engine. When his image came up, she nodded her head. "I can't be one hundred percent certain," she said, "but I think this is the man we saw at the coffee shop, talking to a very pregnant young mother. He gave her an envelope. I remember Cutter and I mentioned at the time that we imagined it contained a nice, fat check."

This time, Madison frowned. "He gave it directly to the girl? Then, how does the agency make their money?"

"Maybe it's part of the ruse. Make it look believable, like the money all goes to the mothers, and they aren't profiting off the deal," Genny suggested. "It's like you said. People want to believe what they want to believe. If he physically hands one check to the mother, he can convince himself that they all go to her. In his mind, he's doing a good thing, and he can justify anything that feels questionable."

"You're probably right."

"I'm also right about this: we need to do a little first-hand investigating." With a cunning smile, she announced, "And I know exactly the couple to do it!"

23

Two days later, as they approached *Heartstrings Adoptions* in downtown Bryan, Genny admitted to Cutter that, questionable background or not, a part of her wanted their inquiry to be real.

As suggested by the agency, they brought with them a list of questions to ask and had even filled out a preliminary application. Going through the motions felt so real, Genny wished they were. Even though Tatiana seemed sincere in her plight, they both knew a hundred things could go wrong before the final papers were signed, and the baby was born and delivered into their arms. With or without adopting her baby, if their own efforts for conception failed, they could very well be in this situation in earnest one day.

They met with a very helpful and knowledgeable man named Gilbert Lyn. He answered their questions with great confidence and without reservation, but when it came to making promises, he chose his words carefully.

"I have no doubt we'll be able to find a child

for you to adopt," he assured them. "If you have no preference of age, gender, or race, the odds are in your favor. If you're happy with any child between the ages of seven and seventeen, we could find you a son or daughter rather quickly. Placement is seldom an issue when all the boxes are checked. But the more specific your requests, the lower your chances are of finding a child. Newborns, especially, are quite difficult to find. That's not to say it's impossible, mind you," he softened his words with a smile, "but in the public system, it could literally take years. That's why we offer private adoptions, although it is a more expensive process."

"And why is that?" Genny asked, feigning ignorance.

He spouted off the general differences between private adoptions and those that were state-funded. He focused on the quality of health care options and the personal interactions between the birth mother and the adoptive parents that had become the hallmarks of privately funded adoptions.

"I must caution you, however, that unless you have a situation where you know the birth mother personally and have arranged for an independent adoption at the time of birth, there is still no guarantee of the timeliness or specific attributes of the child."

After a very thorough and informative meeting, Mr. Lyn thanked them for coming in and promised to be available, should they have more questions or want to proceed with the adoption process. He saw them to the door, where they shook hands and parted ways.

As they crossed to the front door with a packet of information and pamphlets in their hands, a dark-haired woman hurried from behind them, her manner hushed but urgent.

"Mr. and Mrs. Montgomery?" she called softly.

They turned in unison. "Yes?"

"I trust Mr. Lyn was able to help you with all your needs?"

"He gave us a lot to think about, that's for sure," Cutter commented.

"He may not have mentioned this to you, but if you have specific criteria you were hoping to fill, I head up our *Ties that Bind* department. We specialize in meeting your individual needs as best we can. If you have a minute, we can step into my office and discuss your options further."

Genny shot her husband a meaningful glance. This might be the 'something fishy' Granny Bert had sniffed out, and the reason Tatiana and the other girls were so afraid.

"Why, yes," Genny said with a bright smile. "That sounds like something we're *very* interested in!"

"Step this way," the woman encouraged.

She led them to a spacious office at the back of the complex. The accommodations here were much more elegant and posh than those in Mr. Lyn's office. As she invited them to have a seat on a velvet-upholstered settee near the softly glowing fireplace, she belatedly introduced herself.

"Forgive my manners," she said, offering a firm handshake to both. "I'm Cassandra Yoko, a senior liaison here at *Heartstrings*."

"Cutter Montgomery and my wife Genesis."

"You can call me Genny."

"It's a pleasure to meet both of you. Please. Sit," she urged. She took her own place in a matching wingback chair. "We realize that many prospective parents have a preconceived notion of the perfect child for them. Some are seeking children with special needs, feeling that they provide the unique love and attention required for such. Others hope to find a child that seamlessly fits into the image they feel their family projects. Whether that be through physical attributes, shared social statuses or ethnic groups, familial connections, or simply *whatever*, we do our best to match those needs. We have an extensive network of children already born and still in the womb, so with the proper guidance from you, we feel confident we can meet those needs."

Genny did her best not to flinch when she said the word "guidance." They all knew she meant "money."

Nevertheless, Cassandra Yoko went on with her smooth, graceful sales pitch. "I can't help but notice the two of you have a very All-American look, with your blond hair and fair coloring. Genny, you have such gorgeous blue eyes, and Cutter, you seem to be the athletic, outdoorsy type. Is a blond-haired child something you're hoping for?"

Cutter cut his eyes to his wife, willing her to play along. "Absolutely," he said, putting extra swagger into his voice. "And you're right. Any son of mine will be throwing a football by the time he's walking."

Not so long ago, Genny had played the part of a silly airhead to glean information from an overconfident con woman. It irked her to revive that role now, but she reminded herself it was for a good cause. She had yet to decide if Cassandra worked on her own or if the entire agency was dirty, but this woman was messed up in something evil.

"Now, honey," Genny said, letting a simper slip into her words, "we may get a little girl. She may be holding pompoms, not a football."

"As long as it's for SMU, it's fine by me." He used Southern Methodist University because it was the most expensive private university in the state and signified that money was no obstacle for them.

Cutter saw the spark of dollar signs warm Cassandra's eyes.

The liaison whipped out a notepad and pen neither had noticed before now. She jotted down their specific requests with a big smile, reading them off as she wrote. "Caucasian. Blond hair. Athletic tendencies."

"Oh, and high intellect," Genny said. "It would be nice to have another doctor in the family."

"Of course, of course."

Genny wondered if the woman was marking dollar signs beside each attribute, assigning them to a pricing scale the way reviews did.

Chicken entree/Athletic tendencies $$
Rib eye steak/Blond hair $$$$
Prime rib/ Blue blood $$$$$+

Playing her part to the hilt, Genny commented, "I can't help but notice you have a northern accent." She made certain her own accent rang true, boosting it with a touch of twang. "I want a Southern baby."

"Honeybunch," Cutter played along, "don't be prejudiced. If we raise the baby down here, it won't know it's a Yankee."

She crossed her arms and pretended to pout. "No. I want a Southern baby. A Texan." She jutted her chin out in defiance. "Preferably a fourth-generation Texan, just like you and me. You know the Montgomerys were part of Stephen F. Austin's Old Three Hundred when he settled the area that would one day become our state. I want to carry on that tradition of born and bred Texans."

It took all Cutter and Genny could do to keep from laughing. Cassandra's expression was priceless.

Born north of the Red River, she couldn't understand the pride these Texans felt in their home state. She had no idea who Austin and his three hundred were, or what difference it made where someone's great-grandfather was born. If he hadn't stepped off the Mayflower, what difference did it make? Understandably, her first expression reflected her confusion.

That confusion turned briefly to irritation at receiving such a ridiculous demand.

The moment her irritation turned to excitement was almost comical. It took the liaison all of three seconds to see the dollar signs surrounding such a specific and detailed request. This request was so specific, it didn't even register on her pricing scale.

She tried squelching the greed on her face, but

it reverberated in her voice. It fairly trembled with excitement as she cautioned, "You do realize that such a specific request will be difficult to fill."

"Doesn't matter," Genny said, shaking her head so adamantly that her blond hair swung through the air. "It sounds like you're from Boston. I want a Texas baby."

The airhead act must have been working, because Cassandra spoke to her as if she were a child. "Yes, Genny, I am from Boston, but we have local resources for our local families. I can assure you; we can get you a baby from Texas." Cassandra sat back and straightened her shoulders.

"However."

That one word said it all. Genny envisioned a dollar meter spinning above her head as she continued, "You should know that such a specific request will require extensive background checks, digging through family documents, certifying DNA results, and a hundred other extra details. I must be frank. It will require extra man hours, and we will be forced to pass that cost along to you."

"We have money," Genny assured her. "The price is the least of our concerns."

A wide smile spread across the woman's face. "Excellent, excellent. In that case, I can say with the utmost confidence that we can undoubtedly find the exact child you're hoping for."

"That's great news," Cutter said. He was already on his feet. He hoped the liaison read it as excitement, and not the revulsion he felt. He couldn't wait to get out of her office. "I'll call my accountant and tell him to free up some cash."

"That's an excellent idea, Mr. Montgomery. For the kind of specialized research your case requires, we will need to ask for a small retainer fee."

He raised an eyebrow but kept his voice neutral. "How small?"

"Ten thousand dollars should be a good start," she replied smoothly. "For expediency, we prefer outsourcing our research to independent firms."

Cutter knew he should reply, but he was stunned by the "small" amount she so casually tossed out. He managed a noncommittal, "That sounds smart."

"Do you have your checkbook with you? I'm afraid we can only take cash or checks for the research, and it's not included in any costs Mr. Lyn may have discussed with you."

"Sorry, I didn't think we'd need it just yet." He flashed her his most charming smile.

"We had no idea you'd be so helpful," Genny added, "or be able to move so quickly. We always heard the process took forever."

"This is just the initial search, you understand," Cassandra was quick to point out. "But I can see the two of you have given this matter a great deal of thought and know exactly what you want in a family. Many couples come in with questions but aren't ready to decide. Seeing how committed you are to adopting a child moves you to the front of the line."

She waited to see the expected smiles appear on the couple's faces. With a cunning undercut of her eyes, she added, "There are only ten or so families ahead of you."

"Ten? That many?" Genny's surprise was genuine. That hardly sounded like the front of the line to her.

"Well, only two of those are in priority status, so that still leaves you a path to third place."

"Priority status?" Genny questioned.

Cutter sounded more dubious. "Path?"

"Some of our clients are more eager than others," the liaison explained, "so we created our priority status. Again, moving with such expediency comes at a cost, but many of our families find it's worth it." She darted a sly look at Genny, even though she never broke stride with her words. "Some don't want to wait the standard months—even years—it often takes to adopt. They want to hold that baby close in their arms right now."

"Years?" Genny squeaked. She allowed her voice to warble over the word.

Cassandra shrugged. "We can't rush Mother Nature," she pointed out, a helpless expression painted on her face.

Genny could play along with the woman's sick game. She grabbed her husband's arm and demanded, "Honey, I want priority status. It may take another ten thousand, but I'm not waiting years to hold our baby!"

"Twelve, actually," Cassandra coed. "Another five would put you in second place."

"What about first place?" Cutter asked gruffly. "How much would that cost?"

"I—I really couldn't place you above the McAndersons," she claimed, adding just the right amount of uncertainty to her voice. "They've already committed so much to this process."

"Another ten thousand?" he asked. "Is that what it would take to get to the top of the list?"

Cassandra Yoko did a mental calculation in her head. "That would only be twenty-seven thousand. Definitely second place."

"What about thirty-five? Would that put us at the top?" Cutter ground out.

She looked thoughtful, seemingly torn with conflict. "I suppose the McAndersons could be nudged back a bit," she eventually decided. She sighed as if the weight of the world rested upon her shoulders.

She flung the weight away with a toss of her head. A cold light moved into her eyes, and her voice hardened. "But I'd need your payment in cash. No later than Monday morning."

Genny stumbled from the office building, feeling physically sick to her stomach. "That woman is despicable!" she spat.

The lines around Cutter's mouth were taut. "I agree."

"We have to stop them, Cutter. What they're doing is vile and disgusting! It's not only immoral, it's illegal. She was essentially selling us a baby. A made-to-order baby! That—That's..." She was unable to find words to describe the depravity of such actions.

Putting his arm around her waist, he swept her around the corner and away from any prying eyes that could still be watching. "Let's finish this in the car," he suggested.

"I feel so slimy, I may slide right off the seat," Genny predicted. She shook herself from head to toe, as if to shed any ill effects from being near Cassandra Yoko.

"My skin is still crawling," Cutter agreed. "I couldn't get out of there fast enough."

They hurried to their vehicle, where Cutter opened her door for her before going around to the driver's side and starting the engine.

"Knowing they probably milked their patients for all their worth, today I deliberately wore almost every diamond I owned," Genny said. "I swear, every time I moved, I saw the diamonds reflect in her greedy eyes."

"She was a piece of work, that's for sure. Thirty-five thousand dollars—on top of the adoption fees—just to do an initial search and put our name at the top of the list?"

"Think about the poor McAndersons. Now she'll go back to them and ask for more money, just so they can stay on top. I have no doubt it's a revolving door, and the only way to grease it is with more money."

"Who knows if she's even telling the truth? She may have taken one look at your diamonds and upped it a few thousand, thinking we were good for it."

"The fact that she's selling spots on the placement list is disgusting. What a horrible, horrible way to treat prospective parents!"

"She obviously has no conscience. No morals, whatsoever." His face was tight with disdain.

"We have to shut them down, Cutter. This has

to stop."

"I agree. But first, we have to prove what they're doing. That's going to be the iffy part."

"The day we were in the coffee shop, and Tatiana freaked out, was this the man we saw at the table?" She held her phone up, flashing Dean Townsend's photo his way.

"Yep, that was him. Who is he?"

"The dean of Brazos College."

"You're kidding. He's mixed up in this, too?"

"No. Well, I don't think so. I think he's an innocent bystander." She sounded less certain by the minute. "Or maybe not so innocent, but not exactly guilty, either. He and his wife used *Heartstrings* to adopt their baby. It just so happens it was the girl from the inn, so that's where it gets a little murky. But in all fairness, he may not have realized it's a shady organization."

"He handed the envelope to the pregnant girl. Surely, he thought that was suspect," Cutter pointed out.

"You heard what Cassandra Yoko just said. They claim to need money for research and background information. He may have truly believed he was paying for all the trouble it took to get those medical records you saw. And since he gave it directly to the girl, he may have convinced himself it was going directly to her and her medical or future needs. Like Madison said, people want to believe what people want to believe."

"Well, I for one believe these people need to be stopped."

"Me, too! Or, t-w-o."

"You know what else I believe?"

"What?"

"Whether or not the whole agency is corrupt remains to be seen, but it definitely goes beyond just Cassandra Yoko."

"Why do you say that?"

"Because that wasn't Cassandra we saw that day at the coffee shop. At the minimum, at least one more person is involved in this mess."

"Plus, Marcella," Genny reminded him. "I just wonder how long it will take before word gets back to her that we were at the agency today."

Cutter glanced down at his watch. "We may know soon. We're supposed to meet Tatiana at the restaurant in less than two hours."

The couple arrived at *Antonio's* well before six o'clock and lingered until the restaurant shut down at nine.

Tatiana was as no-show.

24

"I don't know how I'm going to break it to them."

Madison shook her head with dread before resting it in her hands.

Madison had worried over the situation for days. She had looked at the case against *Barbour Foods* from every direction she could think of. She had studied the contracts, spoken to the growers, questioned a former service tech, and done everything she knew to do to prove *Barbour* used tyrannical practices against their contract growers. In her opinion, they were nothing less than corporate bullies, using their weight and power to force subordinates to do their calling. But knowing and proving were two different things. Even after all her efforts, she had found nothing concrete to hold against them.

Overhearing her speak to herself, Derron asked, "Who's breaking what?"

"Me," she replied glumly. "I'm going to break Lucy Nguyen and all her friends' hearts when I tell them I can't find a solid case against

Barbour."

"Talking to the Lomax woman didn't help?"

"Nope. She suspects something bigger is happening in the background, but on the surface, it's all about bringing inferior farms up to par. They want to level the playing field for competition."

"Which isn't a bad thing, in and of itself," her assistant pointed out.

Madison had to agree. "*If* the growers weren't forced to make the upgrades at their own expense. Bullying them into compliance isn't the right way to handle the situation."

"So, what are you going to do about it?"

"What *can* I do about it?"

"What did GB have to say about it? She usually has all the answers."

"I didn't want to bother GB, as you call my grandmother. She's been sick and has enough on her plate as it is."

"Lucky for you, she called and said she's headed over. You can ask her about it when she gets here."

Madison wasn't certain she had time for the distraction, but it was too late. The outside camera showed the mile-long Buick pulling up now.

"Why is she using the office entrance?" Derron wondered aloud.

"Because she's still not feeling well, not that she would ever admit it. She probably figures I'm here in the office and knows this is the shortest route."

"Makes sense."

"I'm worried about her," Madison admitted. "She's getting feebler. And when I talked to her last night, she sounded out of sorts. Nine times out of ten, her grumpiness is just an act. She doesn't like people to know how soft hearted she is, but this time I think it's for real."

"Could be depression," he suggested.

Five minutes later, Granny Bert was settled in one of the wingback chairs across from Madison's desk, scowling as Derron handed her a cup of hot herbal tea.

"This doesn't have caffeine," she complained.

"Hey, don't shoot the messenger," Derron defended himself. "Or in this case, the server. I'm just following orders." He shot Madison a dark look, making it clear where those orders came from.

"You know the doctor said caffeine wasn't good for you." Madison deflected the blame as easily as Derron had.

"He also said weed was only helpful when used as an oil, but Wanda begs to differ."

Not willing to go there, Madison deftly changed the subject. "I hear Uncle Darwin is coming in to visit from Odessa. I know you're excited to see him, especially since he didn't make it for Christmas this year."

"Apparently, your other two uncles laid a guilt trip on him. Some nonsense about me not being a spring chicken anymore and needing to come more often. Blah, blah, blah."

"Are you sure that isn't *chirp, chirp, chirp?*" Derron snickered.

"Good one, boy," Granny Bert acknowledged.

Madison nailed him with a pointed look. "Don't you have some filing to do?"

"I don't think so. I thought we were going to consult with GB on the case."

While Madison drew in a sharp breath of irritation and shot daggers at Derron with her eyes, Granny Bert immediately perked up. "Case? What case? What do you need my help with?"

"It's nothing for you to worry with. I've about tied things up."

"What she really means is that she's throwing in the towel," her employee freely blabbed. "She can't figure this one out."

"Since when does a Cessna throw in the towel?" her grandmother demanded. "Or a Hamilton? Because you know good and well when a Hamilton sinks our teeth into something, we aren't lettin' go until something falls out. Our teeth or the truth, whichever comes first!"

"I'm not throwing in the towel. I'm just smart enough to know when I've been beaten."

"Beaten, or bested? You may be givin' up too easy, girl. Let me have a go at it, and we'll see if you still think that way."

As Granny Bert leaned forward with a gleam in her eye, Derron dipped toward Madison as he grabbed a file from her desk. "You can thank me later," he whispered in singsong. Madison rolled her eyes.

"What's the case?" the older woman asked eagerly.

"I think I mentioned it the other day. Lucy Nguyen and some of the other chicken growers think *Barbour Foods* is out of line, forcing them to make upgrades to their farms. But I've been over the contracts with a fine-tooth comb. So has Shawn Bryant. Legally, *Barbour* has every right to make such demands."

Her grandmother pinned her with a sharp gaze. "Is it moral?"

"I don't know about moral, but it's hardly decent. No one should treat their associates that way."

"Then they have no such right, legal or not."

"I agree, but I don't know what to do about it."

"Then it's a good thing you asked for my help."

Madison didn't bother pointing out that she hadn't asked for her help. That was on Derron.

"Where's your white board? Let's look at it and see what we've got."

As Madison slid the panel open to reveal her work aids, Granny Bert rubbed her hands together in anticipation.

"It's fairly cut and dry," Madison explained. "*Barbour* provides the chickens, the feed, the vaccinations, and all labor, transportation, and processing costs before the chickens arrive and after the chickens leave the farm. The grower provides everything the chickens need while in their care, including the houses, the electricity, and fuels needed to keep them cool or warm, etc., etc. If they run their farms and programs in accordance to company guidelines, the growers are well compensated for their hard work and tender loving care. The problem is that *Barbour* can change those guidelines whenever they please."

"And let me guess. It seldom pleases the

grower."

"Bingo."

"I've heard enough complaints to know that the grower is always out the dime to make improvements," Granny Bert said.

"Yes, but just like your brother's store, things are hardly a dime. We're talking hundreds of thousands of dollars. *Barbour* takes no responsibility to help pay for the upgrades. And what's worse, if the grower doesn't jump when they snap their fingers, *Barbour* simply jerks their contracts."

Granny Bert's nod was solemn. "I've seen it happen. Most times, *Barbour* makes up some excuse, claiming the grower broke this or that rule. I hear they hand out farm deficiency slips like they're candy. Makes it so hard for the grower; they give up in defeat, either selling out at a loss or selling their soul to the devil to stay in business."

"It makes you wonder who buys these farms, doesn't it?" Madison murmured absently.

"So? Did you check it out?" her grandmother demanded.

Surprised by the accusation in her voice, Madison twisted her lips. "Not exactly," she admitted.

"And why not? That could be your answer right there!"

"From what I understand, most of the farms are purchased by buyers from other countries. Primarily Vietnam, China, and that general area."

"What have I always told you, girl? What does that hunk of a husband of yours tell you, too?

Follow the money."

"I'm not sure that applies in this case. In fact, I think it has more to do with the equipment they're pushing people to buy, than it does to the farms being sold."

"How so?"

"From what I understand, the new specs for both Texas divisions call for equipment made exclusively by a company called HighRollers. The other divisions allow growers to choose from a list of approved manufacturers, but not Texas. More than one vendor has confirmed that HighRollers makes an inferior product to most of the others on the market, but that their price is the same, if not higher."

"A lesser product for more money? That doesn't make sense," her grandmother said with a frown.

"Exactly. Which makes me suspicious about their reasoning. Especially when I hear they're forcing growers to take out and destroy perfectly good equipment to make the switch."

"Somebody's getting a kickback."

"It certainly sounds like it, doesn't it?"

"Who's in charge?"

"The new manager for both Texas complexes is David Davison, newly arrived from *Barbour's* Georgia location."

"You dig up the dirt on this Davison fella?"

Madison shrugged. "There's not a lot of dirt to dig. He was born and raised in Cumberland, Rhode Island and studied poultry sciences at A&M. Entry-level jobs with two of the big names in poultry production helped him climb his way

up *Barbour's* management ladder. From what I
understand, he's headed to the top."

"Honey, there's always dirt," her grandmother
informed her. "Maybe you aren't using the right
shovel."

"What's that supposed to mean?"

"You said something about this last week,"
Granny Bert, stroking her chin in thought. "I
made a couple of calls, but I forgot to circle back
around and gather details. The only person to call
me back was Bill Gladstall, but I suspect you've
already talked to him. He told me he had an
interview with *Josie* Cessna and wanted to know
if we were any relation." She cocked a keen eye at
her granddaughter.

"You heard about that, huh?" Madison's reply
was meek.

"Sure did. And I couldn't be prouder! Sounds
like you're finally catching on, girl." She beamed a
proud smile as she dug her cell phone from the
pocket of her sweater and scrolled through the
call log. "Give me a minute, and I'll check back
with one of them now."

A few minutes later, Bertha Cessna thanked
the person on the other end of the phone,
promised to go parasailing with them soon, and
disconnected so she could give her report.

"Seems this Davison fella is younger than I
suspected and still a bit of a mama's boy. Shares a
big house with her in a swanky neighborhood.
House is big enough that they each have their own
wing, which is a good thing, since he has a serious
girlfriend. They've been together since they both
lived on the East Coast. They even started their

own company together. According to my source, he didn't go into poultry science out of any great love for feathered fowl. His real motivation was money. There were companies to conquer, money to be made, and an entire industry just waiting for his stewardship."

"You found all that out in one phone call?" Madison asked, clearly stunned.

"I imagine it took my source more than one call, but yes. I did."

Madison shook her head. "You never fail to amaze me."

"I'm not sure if that's an insult or a compliment, but I'll go with compliment."

"You do that," her granddaughter muttered. Shaking off her lingering astonishment, Madison's thoughts turned to the information gleaned. "This Davison sounds like a swell guy. Set your eye on the prize, step on however many backs it takes to get there, and care nothing about the industry itself, just the money it puts in your pocket."

"Maybe it makes Mommy dearest proud."

"Hmm. What kind of business did he and his girlfriend start, do you know? They don't by chance make poultry feeders, do they?"

"I think that would be a might too obvious, even for this joker. If he did have a hand in making the equipment, it would be buried behind a couple of shell corporations. Even I know to hide my tracks that well."

Madison gave her a wary look but didn't dare ask questions. Often with her grandmother, the less she knew, the better it was for everyone.

"And in answer to your question," Granny Bert said, "my contact didn't say what the business was. For all we know, they may be in cahoots with the Chinese government and helping them scoop up more and more of America, one farm at a time."

Madison knew better than to get her grandmother started on one of her rants. She hastily took a marker and wrote the name HighRollers on the board.

"We need to find out more about HighRollers. My preliminary search didn't bring up much."

Derron prissed over to her desk and presented a printout. "While you two were over here shooting the breeze, I was working these little fingers down to their nails." He wiggled the digits in question. "Here's a list of stockholders in both the *HighRollers Corporation* and *Barbour Foods*. You'll notice that there are several over-lapping names, which I have highlighted in yellow, in deference to baby chickens." Mention of the babies hijacked his attention, and his mind wandered.

"One time when I was young, Dragon Lady gave me three little baby chicks in my Easter basket. I named them Wynken, Blynken, and Nod. Blynken was dyed blue, Wynken was purple—"

"Derron, Earth to Derron." Madison called, waving her hand before his eyes. "You may have zoned out, but we're still here."

He shrugged a petite shoulder. "So much for Memory Lane. I never liked those chickens, anyway," he determined. "They had lice."

"Then why'd you dye your hair the same colors?" Granny Bert wanted to know.

His face looked stricken. A shiver worked through his body. "My God, you're right. I'll call Ramon and schedule an appointment." Spinning on his heel, he called over his shoulder, "FYI. I'll need the afternoon off, dollface."

If it meant being rid of the rainbow peaks, Madison was more than willing. "By the way," she said to his sashaying back. "Thanks for the printout."

"It's what I do."

"This is good," Granny Bert said, nodding to the list. "Could be the break you needed."

Madison didn't look convinced. "Only if it proves David Davison or someone in authority at *Barbour* is benefiting from the mandatory upgrades."

"Why else would they do it?"

"I'm sure the official version is that they're trying to be fair to all growers."

"Which is a bunch of hogwash! I know for a fact that many of the old houses still perform better than their brand-new counterparts. A good grower uses what he has to prosper. A bad grower squanders what he has to fail. That doesn't change just because you have a different trademark on your equipment."

"Which brings us back to why they want to make all these upgrades, and why the Texas division insists solely on HighRollers."

"Like I told you," her grandmother insisted. "Follow the money."

25

"I need a favor."

"Hello to you, too."

"Hello, dear friend of mine," Genny revised. Madison couldn't see the strained smile on her best friend's face, but she heard it through the phone lines. "I need a favor."

"Anything."

"I need you to ride with me to *Cherubdipity*."

"Sure. You've talked about it so much, I'd like to see it for myself. What day do you want to go?"

"Today. I'm getting in the car as we speak."

"Oh. Oh, well, okay. I guess that will work." She did a quick recap in her head. Bethani was going with the Aikmans to celebrate Matt's birthday. Blake and Jamal were double-dating and then staying the night at Jamal's. Brash would be getting up just in time to go in for the night shift. Granny Bert and Derron were already gone. "On second thought," she decided, "that works out perfectly. Let me leave Brash a note, and I'll meet you in the driveway."

"Don't forget your coat. It's getting chilly

again."

"Typical February. Up and down, up and down. See you in a few."

After leaving a note and grabbing her purse and coat, Madison found an impatient Genny waiting for her outside. She was barely in the car before Genny put it in gear and took off.

"What's so urgent that you left *New Beginnings* on a Friday during rush hour?"

"Tatiana. She didn't show for our meeting last night, and I'm worried."

"Where's Cutter?"

"He had an out-of-town job today and won't be in until late. I didn't want to wait that long."

"Did she get word to you that she couldn't make it?"

"No. That's just it," Genny said worriedly. "She said to ask for Emilio if she wasn't there. He knew how to get in touch with her. But he hadn't heard from her in a couple of days, and she didn't answer when he tried to text her on her tablet. I'm afraid something has happened. Worse yet, I'm afraid Marcella knows we went to *Heartstrings*."

"So? It's a legitimate service. Maybe not entirely ethical, but legit. She has no reason to think you've connected it to her."

"I don't know. She's a smart woman. She can put two and two together."

"Then why are we headed out there? What are you going to say?"

"I haven't figured that out yet. I just know I can't sit around and wait to hear from Tatiana! I'm worried, Maddy. I have a bad feeling about this. My stomach is all tied up in knots."

"Okay, okay. We'll come up with something. Let's think this through."

They tossed around a few ideas as they drove, but Genny's speedometer moved faster than their rehearsed lines. In no time at all, they had arrived at *Cherubdipity*.

"Wow. I see what you mean. This woman takes her cherubs seriously." From the moment they pulled through the gates, they were surrounded by angel statues in every size, shape, and form.

"This is only a sampling. You should see the rooms." She pulled to a stop near the front entrance and looked at her friend. "This is it. Ready?"

"Don't worry. We've got this, Gen. We've bluffed our way into—and out of— tougher situations than this."

Genny drew in a deep breath. "Here goes nothing."

The woman at the front desk greeted Genny warmly but was worried that she had somehow overlooked her name for a weekend booking. "Is that dashing husband of yours with you?"

"Unfortunately, I'm not here to check in. I was hoping to speak with Marcella. Is she in?"

"She is, but I believe she's with someone now. Why don't you two have a seat in the library, and I'll let you know when she's available. Would you like something to drink? Coffee? Hot chocolate? A cocktail?"

"Maybe you could send Tatiana or one of the girls in with a menu? My friend may want to sample some of your scrumptious desserts."

"Tatiana doesn't normally work the inn, but I'll

send someone over."

"That's not necessary. I'm good," Madison said.

"If you change your mind, you know where the bell is."

"Thanks." Genny led the way into the library and its warmly glowing fire.

"Imagine this," Madison murmured. "More angels."

"This was my favorite chair," Genny said, sinking into its comforting arms once again. "I liked to curl up here with a good book, or just to watch the fire burn."

"It's a lovely room," Madison agreed.

Instead of taking a seat, she wandered around in curiosity. She studied a few pieces of artwork, enjoyed the view from the window, and thumbed through a photo album resting on an ornately carved buffet. There were photos of happily smiling past guests, awards the inn had received, and pictures of weddings and parties thrown on the premises. As she closed the cover, she noticed a tabletop angel on either side of the book, each engraved with a name and date.

"I wonder if these were two of the brides who were married here?" she mused. "There's dates on them from last year."

Genny looked startled. "What are the names?"

Madison looked closer and read from the one on her right. "Daisy. It has a July date on it. And... Chelsea, dated March of last year." She looked up in time to see her friend's large, luminous eyes. "Genny, what's wrong? You look like you've seen a ghost!"

"Or—Or maybe an angel," she whispered. She got up and hurried over to where Madison stood, eager to see the statues for herself. "These are the girls who died," she said in a breathless voice.

In the middle of straightening one of them, Madison almost knocked the statue over. "Are you sure?"

"Tatiana said one of them was named Daisy."

Madison nodded slowly. "And the dates are right. Laurel said one was in the summer, the other a few months before."

Caught in their tangled and troubled thoughts, neither heard footsteps approaching.

"Genny! What a delightful surprise!"

Genny and Madison turned as one, their movement slow and filled with dread. It went through Madison's mind that they must look like Lucy and Ethel, caught red handed in one of Lucy's harebrained schemes.

"M—Marcella. I didn't hear you come in."

Marcella was dressed as impeccably as ever. She moved smoothly across the room and greeted Genny in a hug that wasn't really a hug. She held her arms wide but grasped Genny by the forearms, brushing the air with a side kiss. Even though Genny was a full-on hugger by nature, this modified version suited her just fine.

"And who do you have with you today?" Marcella wanted to know.

"My very dear friend, Madison deCordova. Maddy, this is Marcella Durant, the owner and innkeeper here at *Cherubdipity*."

"It's a pleasure to meet you," Madison said with a smile. "I've heard so much about you."

"Good things, I hope?"

"Of course. And you have a lovely home." Ignoring her tripping heart, Madison dared push her luck. "I was just admiring your photo album and these engraved angels. Were these some of the brides who were married here?"

A shadow crossed Marcella's face, and her smile fell. "No. I'm sorry to say, those are in remembrance of team members we've lost. It's always heartbreaking to lose a member of our family, but two in one year was particularly difficult."

"I—I'm so sorry," Madison said, because she was. She was also confused. Marcella seemed genuinely distraught, yet she had had a hand in their very deaths. Was it all an act? Lingering regret over something she felt must be done? Or, could they be mistaken? The evidence suggested otherwise, but what if Marcella weren't involved in baby trafficking? What if it were all coincidence?

Always be suspicious of 'coincidence.' Brash's advice rang in her head. *Question everything.*

As Madison's mind whirled, Marcella switched on a bright, happy smile. "How can I help you ladies this afternoon?"

Genny glanced around the open room. "Can we find somewhere a bit more private to talk? Your office, perhaps?"

A brief look of concern crossed the innkeeper's face, but she hid it well. She made small talk as she led them toward the back of the house and into a well-appointed office.

The first thing both women noticed were the

framed diplomas and awards parading along one wall. The institutions from which they came were impressive. Built-ins around the window held more awards, and a collection of random photos and snapshots.

One, in particular, caught Madison's eye.

"What a delightful view!" she said, stepping closer to the window. The move allowed her better access to a series of photographs, all featuring the same young woman with toffee-colored skin. It was a like a timeline of the woman's life, starting with a college cap and gown draped in honor stoles. She still looked young and carefree at the beach, arms wrapped around another girl and a dashing young man. The same man appeared in more shots, as the couple posed in front of familiar landmarks. They looked decidedly young at an iconic Cape Cod lighthouse and Newport's opulent Marble House, slightly older at the Centennial Olympic Park and Rock City Gardens, and both appeared wiser and more mature by the time they visited Paris. Some of the luster was gone from their eyes, dulled by the weight of responsibilities and adulthood.

It was a photo of the young woman holding a briefcase that originally caught Madison's eye. She was dressed for success in a power suit and elegant heels, her ebony hair pulled back in a sleek, sophisticated bun. She stood in front of an office building wearing a proud, triumphant smile. Something about the photo struck a chord of familiarity within Madison, but she couldn't quite put her finger on it. The best she could deduce was that she subconsciously remembered the burgundy briefcase from the coffee shop, when she had narrowly missed seeing the faces of *Cherubdipity's* owners. Did that mean this young woman was Marcella's... daughter?

Taking Madison's words at their worth, Marcella smiled. "Yes. I never tire from the view. Please, have a seat. Can I get either of you some refreshments?"

"We're good," Genny answered for them, taking a seat. Madison soon joined her. "I know you're wondering why we're here today," she began.

Marcella gracefully arched a sculpted brow. "It is a bit of a surprise."

Genny launched into the cover story they had come up with, recycling it from a former ruse they had pulled.

"Madison and I are co-founders of a small group we call *Sisters, Forever.* It's a modern-day version of the old welcome wagon when someone new moves to town."

That perfectly sculpted brow puckered in confusion. "I don't understand. We don't live in the same town."

"No, but we're all a part of the community as a whole," Madison was quick to point out. "The community of the greater Brazos Valley."

The innkeeper looked doubtful, but allowed a grudging, "I suppose."

"When someone new moves to The Sisters, we deliver a basket of goodies to them, much like the ones you give your guests here. Our baskets include coupons and discount offers for services within our community. Since *Cherubdipity* is within easy driving distance and is the nearest luxury resort to the towns, we thought you might like to be included in our program."

That much, at least, was true. Though the idea of *Sisters, Forever* had started as a ploy, they had liked the concept well enough to make it a reality. The next part, however, was pure fabrication.

"We do a newsletter every quarter, and Madison, here, acts as our 'roving reporter.' As owner of *In a Pinch Professional Services,* she also sponsors a 'What Makes Us So Special' award, highlighting specific people behind the places she writes about." Genny paused to bestow a grateful look upon her best friend.

Then she turned back to Marcella. "Anyway. I suggested we highlight *Cherubdipity,* and I even nominated a recipient for the award."

"Oh, how delightful." On the surface, Marcella's response could have passed as pleased. But the pleasure never reached her eyes. "That's very kind of you."

"I can assure you, the attention—and the award—is well deserved. Cutter and I had a delightful time here at *Cherubdipity,* and I'd love to share our experience with others."

"Again, that's so kind. We were thrilled to have you as our guests."

"I nominated a member of your staff because she went above and beyond, seeing to our needs and making certain our stay here was especially delightful. As I mentioned before, you have trained Miss Gomez well."

The announcement clearly took her by surprise. "Miss Gomez?"

"Tatiana," Genny clarified. "I believe I have the right last name?"

"Yes. Yes, that's correct. Tatiana Gomez."

Madison made a show of relief. "Good. The check is already made out in her name."

"Check? I'm afraid I don't understand." Marcella did, in fact, look confused.

"Part of the honor is the very generous $500 award presented to each recipient. We'd like to give the award directly to Miss Gomez, if you would be so kind as to have her step in here."

"Ah," Marcella hesitated, coming up with a lame, "I believe Miss Gomez may have the day off."

"I understood that Thursdays were her day off." When her voice came out more accusing than she intended, Genny softened them with a smiled explanation. "The only reason I say that is because we ran into her in town that Thursday we were here, and she mentioned she had Thursdays off."

"Yes, but sometimes I give the girls a bonus day off, just because. I like to reward good behavior and find it boosts morale, as well as productivity. If you'll leave the check with me, I'll see that she gets it."

Madison pasted a firm smile on her face. "No, this needs to be done in person. We take pictures for the newsletter and do a very brief interview. I promise, we won't take more than a few moments of your time."

Marcella's own smile never wavered. "As I said, Miss Gomez isn't available today."

"Tomorrow, then?" Genny pushed.

Even cornered, Marcella remained unflappable. "I'll have to consult the schedule, of course."

"Of course."

While Marcella tapped a few keys on her computer, Genny went for broke. "Would you like to know why I nominated Tatiana?" she asked.

The innkeeper never looked up. "Yes, of course."

"I was having a particularly difficult day, and Miss Gomez approached me to make certain I was okay. That shows a true sense of hospitality and caring."

Her words caught Marcella's attention, and she stopped what she was doing, focusing on the blond woman in front of her making the vulnerable confession. "I remember," Marcella said.

"What I didn't tell you that day... what I seldom tell anyone, other than my closest friends..." She paused, not only for effect, but because the words were more difficult to say than she thought they would be "...is that Cutter and I will probably never be able to have children of our own. I was making a difficult call, essentially admitting defeat in my ability to give birth."

Marcella's dark eyes filled with compassion. "Oh, Genny dear. I had no idea."

Her response took Genny by surprise, but she continued with their plan. She and Madison had agreed to throw out the bait and see if Marcella took it. "It's not something we talk about, so how could you? We're looking into adopting. In fact, we visited a perfectly lovely agency yesterday."

"Good. That's good," Marcella said, nodding her head in encouragement. "If you'd like, I'll be happy to put you in touch with the agency we use here at *Cherubdipity*. We've had such a warm, wonderful working relationship with them. The mothers who choose that route have been very pleased with their level of professionalism and compassion."

It wasn't the response Genny nor Madison had expected. They exchanged a wary look between them.

"Th—Thank you," Genny thought to say.

Marcella glanced back at the screen. "And it appears that Tatiana is working tomorrow, if you'd like to set up an appointment.'"

Genny was disappointed she couldn't see her today, but she took it to mean the girl was fine and expected back tomorrow. She was merely unavailable today, just as Marcella said.

"Uhm, yes. Yes, that's sounds good."

"Shall we say two o'clock?"

Madison nodded, looking to her friend for confirmation. "Works for me."

"Me, too," Genny agreed.

"I do hate to be rude," Marcella began, meaning she would be, no matter, "but today is an exceptionally busy Friday. I have a great deal of work yet to do..."

"Of course, of course. I'm sorry we barged in like this," Genny apologized.

"We like to capture the element of surprise," Madison pitched in. "It makes winning so much more exciting, don't you think?"

Marcella's cool smile was less than

enthusiastic, but she offered a half-hearted agreement. "I'm sure."

She stood and saw her impromptu guests to the door.

Just before leaving, Genny whirled around with one last thought. One last stab at making sense of all the mixed signals they received.

"Oh, and while we were here, a fellow guest mentioned how helpful another staff member had been." She put her hand to her lips, as if in thought. "They said she went above and beyond, as well. Maybe we could include her in the interview? I think her name was... Nicki? Do you have a Nicki who works here?"

Again, Marcella was caught off guard. Not waiting for her hostess to make up some excuse, Genny took a gamble and barged on, "They mentioned she may have been going through chemo treatments. Her head, I believe they said, was shaved. Do I have the right name?"

"Oh, yes, yes. You must be referring to Nicki Patterson. Lovely girl. With or without hair," she hastily added.

"We'll see all of you tomorrow?" Madison asked.

"Of course. I can't wait. Safe travels."

The words were barely out of her mouth before she shut the door behind them.

Firmly.

26

"Can't wait, my foot!" Genny fumed as they pulled out of the inn's circular drive. "What was all that nonsense? She sent more mixed signals than a drunk crossing guard on ice skates!"

"I'm thoroughly confused," Madison admitted, sitting back in the seat with a dejected sigh. "She said she was thrilled to have us stop by, but she saw us not just to her office door, but to the *front* door. Like she wanted to be certain we left."

"She doesn't want us snooping around. She's afraid we'll find out something. Something she wants to remain hidden."

"But, what? And if they're so doggone busy, why did she give Tatiana the day off? Why not all hands on deck?" Madison wanted to know.

"Rewarding good behavior?" Genny mocked with a sneer. "She was clearly *not* pleased that Tatiana took an interest in us! She chided the girl for her extra efforts. She even said this wasn't her first warning about 'fraternizing' with the guests. There's no way she would have rewarded her with an extra day off."

"But here's something else that doesn't make sense." Madison turned in the seat as best she could to face her friend. "If she's involved in this despicable baby-selling ring, why did she seem so genuinely upset over those two girls' deaths?"

"Guilt, I suppose."

"And why was she so sympathetic with you? Her concern looked sincere."

"The entire conversation was so bizarre," Genny acknowledged, worrying the side of her lip. "Why would she offer me the name of the adoption agency if she had something to hide? It doesn't make sense."

Madison's snort was one of scorn. "Just because she normally recruits the birth mothers doesn't mean she can't recruit the adoptive parents, as well. Without the parents, she wouldn't be in business."

"If it's like real estate, she could earn a commission off both ends," Genny muttered. She instantly sobered. "Oh, wow," she said in dismay. "When did I become so callous? This is a horrible, terrible, despicable practice, and I'm making light of the situation! If we're right about this, that woman is literally selling babies! She probably *does* make a commission. That is just so... so sick! Completely and utterly twisted."

"None of it makes sense, and yet it does," Madison said. "She has the perfect set up. Pregnant girls come to her looking for help, and she puts them in contact with *Heartstrings* and/or similar agencies. To keep them in line, they're rewarded for good behavior. But if they step out of line, particularly by putting their babies in danger, they're punished. You notice how she didn't correct your statement about Nicki's hair. It's easier and far more noble sounding to let you think she employs a girl with cancer than it does to admit she shaved the girl's hair off for reckless behavior. And don't even get me started on Daisy and Chelsea!"

"I'm serious. This entire situation makes me sick to my stomach. I think I'm going to puke."

Without further warning, Genny swerved to the side of the road and threw the car in park. She was out the door and headed for the wood line before Madison could unbuckle her seatbelt.

She gave her friend a few minutes before she approached with bottled water and the few napkins she had scrounged up. "Gen? Gen, honey, are you okay?"

Offering a sheepish smile, Genny stepped from the trees. "Sorry about that. I'm usually not so squeamish. But this whole business of buying babies makes me physically ill. It's just so wrong!"

"I agree. I feel the same way."

Genny took the offered water and rinsed out her mouth. She then took several long draws of the refreshing liquid before saying, "While I was puking in the bushes, I realized something."

"What's that?"

"We're on the backside of *Cherubdipity* property. I can see the girls dormitory from here. If we were of a mind to, we could walk through those trees there and get a good look around. Maybe we could see if Tatiana is here."

"You're forgetting one thing. Your husband just built an iron fence around the property. And these hips" —she pointed down at her slender silhouette, drawing a snort from her friend— "are not getting through those rails." She pointed at the fence in question.

"And you're forgetting my husband is a brilliant welder. This is only told on a need to know basis, but he builds a safety feature into all his fences. If you know where to look and what to do, he includes a secret latch on all his gates, so that no one is ever locked in and out of their property. All we have to do is find the nearest gate, and we're in."

Intrigued, Madison's hazel eyes twinkled with the proposed challenge. "Which way do you think it is?"

"Based on my loose recollection of the day he escorted me around to survey his handiwork, I think it's to the left."

"Then let's go."

"You think the car's off the road far enough? I know I pulled over at the last second."

"It should be fine. And I've already locked it, so we're good to go."

"Then, let's go."

They found the gate and secret latch easily enough. The two friends slipped through the opening and into the row of trees leading straight to the back of the buildings, where they found a small parking lot tucked between a maintenance shed and the dormitory. Genny saw a familiar battered Toyota among the smattering of vehicles, meaning Tatiana was most likely still on the premises.

Had Marcella lied, or was Tatiana enjoying a quiet day in?

"What, now?" Madison asked. "They probably have security cameras up, at least around the buildings."

"But if we don't go up to the door, how will we know if Tatiana is inside? I need to know she's okay. I can't bear to think she may have been punished or worse because of us."

"What if the door is locked?"

"I don't know. Maybe someone will come along, and we can ask them to let us in."

"Because random people are naturally welcomed inside the girls' personal housing unit," Madison said with heavy sarcasm.

"Hey, we're almost celebrities. It could happen," Genny argued. "Besides, someone may recognize me as a former guest."

As they waited in the trees, trying to decide their next move, they saw someone approaching via the hedge-covered sidewalk. "Do you recognize her?" Madison whispered.

"Unfortunately, I do," Genny said, mouth turned down in a frown. "Her name is Wendi, or Cindy, or something like that. She flirted unmercifully with Cutter."

A smile spread across Maddy's face. "Perfect. You have something to bribe her with."

Genny stared at her friend in surprise. "Since when did you become so cunning?"

Maddy answered with a shrug and two simple words, "Granny Bert."

Dimples appeared as Genny said, "I like it."

Genny found a small rock and tossed it on the front walk just as the girl stepped onto it. She looked up, startled, trying to find where it had come from.

"Pssst! Over here!" Genny whisper shouted. Because she didn't remember the girl's name, she omitted the first letter. "-indi!"

A series of emotions flashed across the blonde's face. Surprise. Displeasure. Then anticipation, as her eyes darted around for Cutter. Back to displeasure. Irritation. And, finally, fear.

"What are *you* doing here?" the girl all but spat.

"I need to talk to Tatiana. Is she here?"

"Maybe. But why should I tell *you*?"

"Because if you don't, I'll tell Mrs. Durant how you flirted with my husband."

The girl gasped. "I—I—I did no such thing!"

"Are you willing to bet your future on Mrs. Durant believing you, or me?" Genny asked in a cool voice.

The girl's hesitation was brief. "Fine," she sulked. "Tatiana's on the third floor. Last room on the left."

"Thanks."

Genny and Madison hurried into the building and up to the third floor, easily finding the girl's room. It was a no-frills dwelling, but the stairs were sturdy and the halls well lit.

Their knock was answered right away. An attractive girl opened the door, her face mirroring the surprise showing on Genny and Madison's faces. Even though they had heard about Nicki's infamous shaved head, they weren't prepared for the sight of it. Bits of blond fuzz were already sprouting new life in an uneven, erratic pattern across her skull.

Self-conscious about her looks, the girl shrieked and dove for cover, burying her head beneath a pillow on the nearby twin bed. Alerted to the ruckus at the door, Tatiana soon stuck her dark head around the corner.

"Miss Genny! What are you doing here? How did you get in?"

"Never mind that. When you didn't meet us last night, I got worried. I had to see for myself that you were all right."

"I—I am. I'm fine."

"You don't sound fine. Can we come in?"

"Umm..." She shot a look to her roommate, who was busy burying herself further beneath the covers.

Taking it as an invitation, Genny stepped into the shoe box of a room. There was barely room for two beds, a single chest of drawers, and two small desks with chairs, much less space to accommodate two extra bodies.

"This is my friend Madison deCordova. Madison, Tatiana Gomez. And Nicki, I presume."

"It's a pleasure to meet you, Tatiana. And Nicki, please don't hide on our account. You have lovely eyes."

"And such a smooth complexion! Gorgeous skin, just like Tatiana," Genny commented.

Slowly, the girl with no hair came out from the covers, her cheeks rosy with embarrassment but her eyes shining with appreciation. "Tat's always talking about you," she told Genny. "She says you may adopt her baby?"

"We're trying to work out the details," Genny admitted. "And you? Are you keeping your baby, or putting it up for adoption?"

"I wanted to keep it. So did my boyfriend, but... but we're too young to be parents! He's a sophomore in college and only has a part-time job. I worked at Dairy Delite until I came to work here. Neither of us made enough to support ourselves, much less a baby."

"We understand, Nicki. You don't have to defend your decision to us," Genny told her gently.

Nicki's smile wobbled on her face. "Tat's right. You're a nice lady."

"Thanks. Oh, and look. You have a lovely smile to go with your big, green eyes and your smooth complexion."

"When are you due?" Madison asked with an amicable smile.

"Not for another six months. I—I didn't think I'd harm my baby, going out and having fun. It was just bungee jumping at the mall. But they told me... they said..." She didn't finish her sentence. Instead, she ran her hand over her shorn head and bit back a sob. "They said blond-haired babies are in high demand. That if I lost the baby, losing my own hair would be the least of my worries!"

"Who said that, sweetie? Who threatened you?" Genny asked.

"The two of them. They both did." Now distraught, the girl dropped her face into her hands and sobbed.

Madison sat on the bed beside her to offer

comfort, silently urging Genny to say what she had come to say to Tatiana. The sooner they could get out of here, the better.

"Are you certain you're okay, Tatiana? They haven't threatened you, have they?"

"Not-Not exactly. They want me to sign my contract for adoption, but I keep stalling. Last night, when I left to meet you, the air was gone from all four tires. I think they know I've been talking to you."

"Do you feel you're in danger, Tatiana? Because if you do, we can take you with us right now."

"I asked for one more week. I promised I would make my decision by then."

Genny searched her dark eyes. "And you truly feel you'll be safe until then?"

The girl nodded. "Yes, I do. Andrew and I are both smart. Top of our classes. They—They like that. Smart babies are in demand. Plus, it's half-Asian. It might even pass as full Asian and be adopted by wealthy Asian parents who want an astrophysicist in the family. I think they want my baby badly enough to keep me safe, especially if I sign the adoption papers."

"And if you don't?" Genny was almost afraid to ask.

Tatiana refused to meet her eyes. "I can't think of that now," she whispered.

"When can we meet with you again? We're working the details out on our end. We've already spoken to a lawyer, and we're trying to come up with a solution to keep you safe."

"I'll try to sneak away Sunday evening after

dark. I'll be down by the road. There's a big oak tree in the first curve after the front gate. Pick me up there. If I can't make it, I'll try again on Thursday."

Genny leaned close and dropped her voice. "There's a secret latch on all the gates. There's one behind this parking lot that leads almost to the oak tree." She gave her the details. "Think you can manage it in the dark?"

"I'll manage."

"If you don't meet us by Thursday," Genny promised, "we're coming back for you. Guns blazing, if need be."

"I'll try to make it. If not Sunday, then Thursday for sure." The girl threw her arms around Genny's neck in an awkward hug. "Thank you, Miss Genny. You have no idea what it means to me, having your help. Knowing that you might be my baby's mother. It's what she deserves."

"It's what you deserve too, Tatiana. Never doubt that."

"I'm not rushing you, but you should go. It's not safe for you to be here."

"You'll take care of yourself? And the baby?"

"Yes. I promise."

A scant few feet across the room, Madison had a similar conversation with a quietened Nicki.

"I promise, Nicki. Genny, I, and our husbands will do everything in our power to help you. We want to protect you."

"It may be too late for me," the girl acknowledged, wiping tears from her face with the backs of her hands. "Just keep my baby safe. And Tat. She still has a chance to get out."

"We'll do our best. Stay safe. We'll be in touch as soon as we can."

After hugs and final goodbyes, Genny and Madison ran to the stairs and hurried down. Genny poked her head out the door and, finding the coast clear, led the way across the small parking lot to the edge of the tree line.

They almost made it, free and clear.

27

Intent on making it to the trees for cover, they were easy targets. They were ambushed from behind, tackled and roughly shoved to the pebbled, dirt-packed ground.

"L—Let me go!" Madison cried, but the words were muffled. The person straddling her back held her face to the ground, preventing her from turning her head. When her lips moved, grit pushed its way into her mouth.

"Don't make this uglier than it has to be," a rough, husky voice snarled.

"Get off me!" Genny demanded, only to have a knee slammed into her back. "D—Don't!" A twist of the knee, and her voice changed from angry to anguished.

Their captors jerked the women's hands behind their backs and tied them with pieces of heavy twine. Grabbing handfuls of hair, they forced Genny and Madison's heads down and straight forward, preventing free movement.

"Get up!" the husky voice demanded.

When Genny fumbled the effort, her captor

grabbed the back of her coat and hauled her unceremoniously to her feet. The seams dug into her armpits, but she refused to acknowledge the pain.

With her head down, Madison had limited vision. She tried in vain to see if anyone was within shouting distance, but her line of sight didn't extend far. She knew they were shoved along the edge of the parking area, onto a patch of concrete, and, without warning, over a raised threshold.

The maintenance shed.

Madison stumbled into the dark, cold interior. Her captor shoved her forward. There was the sound of something being dragged across the bare floor, screeching in her ears like chalk on a blackboard, and then a sharp, unwarranted chop to the backs of her knees. Madison went down, her bottom landing with a jolt onto a cold, metal bench. While she absorbed the shock of a sudden landing on the unforgiving surface, her captor hooked something to the twine around her hands.

One tug told her there was no wiggle room; she was there to stay. Before her eyes could adjust to the dark, her captor slipped something over her head. Her best guess was that it was an old pesticide sack. The smell was horrendous and gave her an instant headache, but at least she could breathe.

Meanwhile, Genny's captor pushed her roughly against the wall, pinning her there while tying a cloth over her eyes. With her hands and eyes now useless, the person jerked her around like she was a rag doll, repositioning her onto a low seat. The uncomfortable, round ledge biting into her flesh suggested it was the lid on a five-gallon bucket. She tried to stand and run but found it impossible. Something large and solid protruded above her head; she banged against it so hard, she saw stars. Plus, one ankle was now bound to a very heavy object that refused to budge.

"There's no need to yell," the second voice said in the darkness. "No one will hear you."

"What are you going to do with us?" Madison asked, fear making her voice higher than normal. She caught a whiff of something strong, perhaps diesel, and visions of a fiery death made her head swim. Or was it just fumes from the pesticide? Her brain was already fogged with chemicals and pain.

"Never mind," the first voice said. "We'll be back soon enough." The words sounded more of a threat than a promise.

After rustling sounds and shuffled feet, a door closed and there was silence.

Genny and Madison filled the emptiness with their cries for help, but a loud racket on either side of the small building roared to life, drowning out any noise they might have made. The clamor nearest Madison sounded like a lawn mower. Hadn't she seen one of those fancy, zero-degrees, industrial mowers parked nearby? Brash had one, so she knew from experience how loud one could be. The other noise could have been a second mower, or perhaps a motorcycle. She couldn't rule out a semi-truck idling on the other side of the thin, metal walls, either. The din was that loud.

"We may as well save our voices," Genny said. Even inside such a small space, she had to practically yell.

"My person wasn't Marcella." Madison's voice was muffled.

"Mine had on a tweed jacket. Marcella was wearing lined linen."

"Could it have been a coat?"

"A goat? Don't be ridiculous!"

Inside the paper bag, Madison's voice came out distorted. She spoke louder, if not clearer. "A coat! Maybe she wore a tweed coat."

"It wasn't Marcella," her friend insisted. "The perfume was wrong."

"But they were both women."

"Who are they?"

"I detected a Boston brogue from one of them," Madison said.

"I've never heard of a Boston broach," Genny said, again misunderstanding her words. "But Cassandra Yoko had a Boston accent."

"The other voice sounded familiar..." Madison murmured, racking her brain to think where she had heard it.

"Hounded? What are you talking about?"

Madison shook her head, even though her friend couldn't see. In doing so, the bag over her head caught on something behind her. The bag pulled taut, and Madison initially panicked, thinking she might suffocate. When she realized she was still alive and breathing in the rancid stench of stale pesticide, she worked to free the bag from its snag.

At first, the ripping sound didn't register in her

chemically intoxicated brain. She tugged again and heard another rip, almost freeing the bag from its unseen nemesis. As understanding dawned, she reversed her actions and rammed her head back against the wall. She banged against it harder than intended, but what was a little more pain if it freed her from the noxious smell? Her reward was the sound of another rip as she turned her head to one side.

"What are you doing?" Genny asked.

"Hold on."

"Are you finding a way to get free? Because my person knows how to tie a knot! There's no budging. My right ankle is tied, too."

While Genny complained about the knots and how uncomfortable her bucket was, Madison meticulously ground her head from side to side, unmercifully tangling her hair in the fray. The bag tore a little more with each move, ripping a few strands of silky brown along with it. Tears stung her eyes, but she continued to work her head back and forth and up and down, until finally the bag was ripped down the center.

Unfortunately, it still draped over the top of her head.

Madison tried blowing it off.

"What is that sound? It's not a gas leak, is it?" There was a note of panic in Genny's voice.

"It's me."

"What did you *eat*?"

"Not. Gas." It was difficult to talk, as she was using all her wind to blow the bag off her head. It moved but refused to fall.

"I suppose that could have been Cassandra,"

Genny said from across the room. "She and Marcella are obviously working together. They're about the same age, too. Who knows? They may have known one another in Boston, and that's where they came up with this horrible scheme to begin with."

While Genny rambled, Madison worked to be free of the bag. She wiggled her shoulders this way and that, inching the bag upward one minuscule degree at a time. She tried leaning forward, but whatever she was hooked to didn't allow much movement. She twisted and turned until she was out of breath, and still the bag remained perched atop her head. She leaned her head back to rest for a few minutes, surprised when the bag tipped forward.

She tried again, wiggling and writhing, grunting and grinding, until she had a crick in her neck. Releasing an exhausted breath, she dropped her head back in defeat.

Just like that, the bag tumbled off her head and fell away.

Madison wanted to weep with joy, but the feeling was short lived. The room around her was still as black as ever. At least the air was fresher and flowed more freely into her lungs.

Unaware of the battle her friend waged, Genny still thought aloud, "Did you notice the pictures in Marcella's office? Most of them had the same girl in them. I think that must be her daughter, but I wonder how she reconnected with her, after all these years? The state took her away when she was little. There was a snapshot of the girl on the desk. She wore a high school cap and gown, but I recognized the man behind her. He was some hotshot lawyer for the Morgans. I vaguely remember he often had a black woman with him, but he introduced her as his associate."

Madison regained enough strength to speak in something longer than one-word sentences. "You think the woman was Marcella? You think they had a daughter together?"

"It would explain the girl's coloring."

"But not why the man was at her high school graduation."

"Hey, I can hear you better now," Genny realized. "Your words aren't as muffled."

"They put a bag over my head, but I finally got it off. Fat lot of good it did me, though. There's no windows, so no light. Everything is pitch black."

"There's a rag over my eyes, and it reeks like it was soaked in oil. It's all I can do not to throw up again."

"Concentrate on something else," Madison suggested. "I saw the pictures, too. They seemed to cover a span of several years, from graduation into adulthood. A lot of them had a younger man in them, too, so I guess he's the daughter's husband or boyfriend. They must like to travel, because there were photos from a lot of touristy places. Mostly New England and Georgia, but some in Paris."

When Madison fell silent for a long moment, Genny called out in concern, "Maddy? Are you still there?"

"Yeah," she answered distractedly. "Just thinking. There's something that keeps nagging at me, but I can't put my finger on it. Something about the pictures."

"What is it?"

"I don't know. But something... Oh. And I think the daughter, if that's who she is, is Marcella's partner."

"Really? Why?"

"That day in the coffee shop, the girl said those were the *owners*—plural—of *Cherubdipity*. I think one of them carried a burgundy briefcase, like the woman in the picture. And both women had northern accents, even though Marcella's isn't so pronounced."

"She's lived in the South long enough to knock the hard edges off," Genny surmised. After a pause, she further deduced, "So, that was the *daughter* who ambushed us and left us here?"

Madison thought about it, comparing the voices the best she could. "I think it was," she decided.

After a moment of silent worry, Genny dared to ask, "Wonder what they plan to do with us?"

"I'm afraid to." She wasn't sure her low voice carried over the roar of the motors outside, but it was just as well. Genny already sounded scared, without adding her own fears into the mix. After a long moment, she changed the subject. "Any luck on getting your hands free?"

"No. And I think she tied my ankle to an elephant, because I can't move whatever it is I'm attached to."

"My eyes have adjusted a bit to the dark. I don't see an elephant, but I see a lump that could be you."

"Gee, you flatter me so."

"If that's you, there's something big on the other side of you. A big piece of machinery, maybe? A huge motor?"

"Something that takes oil," Genny muttered above the rumble. Madison couldn't see it, but she envisioned her friend wrinkling her cute little nose in distaste.

Madison's mind circled back around to the women who had ambushed them, and why.

"Maybe the daughter is an accountant, or a lawyer like her father. That day in the coffee shop, they were discussing business. Investing, to be specific." Something else tickled her mind, but Madison couldn't isolate it. Everything was a blur in her mind, still stinging from the acrid burn of the pesticide. "Maybe we're getting too close and threaten to topple their empire. Marcella may want to keep her hands clean, so she sent her business-minded daughter and the adoption liaison after us. They have as much to lose as she does."

"They aren't going to just turn us loose," Genny pointed out. "We have to *do* something. We have to get out of here."

"I'm working on it. Whatever I'm hooked to has a hard edge along one side. I'm trying to saw my hands free, but it's a slow go."

"Even if my hands were free, I don't think I could get away from my elephant."

"Leaving you behind isn't an option and isn't going to happen," Maddy told her friend.

It became a moot point the minute the door handle moved. They had just run out of time.

The bright glare of sunshine was as blinding as

the blackness. Madison couldn't see as their abductors stepped into the shed, but she assumed they were at the same disadvantage. That had to be worth something.

"Let's make this fast," the one with the husky voice said. "Davy is done with the car."

"Give my eyes time to adjust, and I'll administer the dose," the other said.

"Dose?" Despite the clatter of motors outside, Madison's sharp ears picked up their low voices.

"No need to worry yourself over it. It will all be over soon."

"Not really," Genny answered in a bitter voice. "You'll still be buying and selling babies. How can you live with yourself, doing such a despicable thing?"

"We're giving those children a chance," the husky-voiced woman argued. "At least their new parents want them. They want them so badly, they're willing to *pay* for them! Handsomely, I might add. An investment on that scale guarantees those children a better life."

"You may tell yourself that, but surely even you are bright enough to spot the lie," Genny spat. She knew she goaded them, but she couldn't stop herself. What they did was too vile to ever defend.

The other woman, most likely Casandra Yoko, responded, "I have to say, you're a good actress. You almost had me fooled yesterday, going on about Southern babies and wanting to adopt a fourth-generation Texan." Her statement confirmed her identity. "But you don't think we would accept you into our program, do you, without fully investigating you? You, Little Miss

Goody Two-Shoes, are nothing but trouble."

"I should have known that," the first said, roughly grabbing her arm and pulling her coat down, "the moment I saw you talking to Tatiana in the coffee shop."

"That was you? Wait. Wha—What was that? I felt a prick! What did you just do?" Genny's voice rose with hysteria.

Across the room, Madison could see just well enough to tell that both women stood over her friend. Genny bucked and tried twisting free but to no avail.

"I just gave you a little shot," Cassandra informed her breezily. "Something to thin your blood. Nothing to be concerned over."

"Not unless you had a mega dose," the other woman added. "Or should you get in a wreck. That could present a real problem." Her threat almost held a teasing note.

A cold realization hit Madison. "That girl last year. Chelsea. That's how you did it, didn't you? She hemorrhaged to death after a miscarriage." Horror filled her voice. "You made it happen! You gave her blood thinner and deliberately killed her!"

"She became a liability," the woman said without feeling, her voice even more coarse than before.

Angered by her flippant reply, Genny drew back her free leg and kicked like a mule. The attack took the crouched woman by surprise, and she stumbled backward, crashing into some unseen object. A string of obscene words flew from her mouth.

She came up fighting, her hand striking Genny across the cheek. When she would have done worse, the older woman stopped her.

"Jessenia!" she said sharply. "We don't have time for this. We still have to deal with the nosy one."

"Yes," Jessenia with the husky voice sneered, "the nosy one."

Madison sensed, as much as saw, Jessenia stalking toward her. She could see little else, but she swore she saw angry flames shooting from the woman's eyes.

"You just couldn't leave it alone, could you? You had to keep on and on and *on*. Now my father is demanding spreadsheets, my birth mother is asking questions, my adopted mother is pissed, and this one—" Madison imagined she hooked a thumb to the other woman— "thinks she's calling the shots. If that's not enough, thanks to you, the company is asking questions, and Davy is under review. Why couldn't you have just left well enough alone?"

"I don't know what—" Madison stopped, unable to finish her sentence.

With a sudden flash of clarity, she *did* know what the woman was talking about. It all became clear to her now.

"David Davison," she said, her voice somewhat breathless. "He's the man in the pictures," she realized. "Of course! That's why there were so many pictures of you along the East Coast and Rhode Island. That's where he's from. I couldn't place one of the locations, but I realize now it was Kyle Field, before they expanded the stadium.

David went to Texas A&M, where he studied poultry sciences. And then he moved to Georgia, where the other pictures were taken. It all makes sense now."

"Are you waiting for applause?" she asked nastily.

"No, but an explanation would be nice." Anything to keep them talking while she found a way to get free. "Why?"

"Why, what? Why do I hate my father? Because he used me, that's why. He had no use for me—let them take me from my birth mother and put me in foster care, where I went through five homes in as many years—until it suited his purposes. When he couldn't inherit his wife's fortune without an heir, he suddenly couldn't wait to claim me as his own. He pretended we were a happy little family, but the whole time he was keeping my birth mother on the side, shacked up with her in his Boston condo. He used us both!"

Her voice took on an air of superiority. "But I found out, and then I turned it around and used it against him. I may have pressured him to hire me at Cockrell, Abrams, Cockrell and Cockrell, but I *earned* my place there. With Mother's help, I convinced him and the rest of the board we should open a law office in Texas—"

"That's the other picture!" Madison interrupted on a gasp. "That's how I knew the building. It's in Dallas!"

"—with me at the helm." Jessenia continued as if Madison had never spoken. "My very first client was my birth mother Marcella Durant. Or were you asking why I hate her, too? That would be because she's *weak*." She spat out the word as if it left a bitter taste in her mouth.

Madison continued to saw as Jessenia raged.

"She let me slip into the system. Even after making a name for herself in the business world, she fell back into her same old pattern. She allowed my father to use her again. It went on for years, but she was too weak and too cowardly to stand up for herself. He banished her to Texas, and I thought there was hope for her. She managed to make something of herself without him, which I admired. Her vision was to save the world, one pregnant teen and one baby at a time. But a social experiment on such a grand scale required money, and she didn't have nearly enough. As her lawyer, I advised her to take on a partner. Never mind that *I* am that partner. She should have stood up to me. She shouldn't have allowed the money to change her vision. She should have stood up for herself and what she believed in. I detest weak women."

"And David? Do you hate him?" *It seems likely,* Madison thought. *This woman is filled with hatred.*

"Of course not! David understands me. We want the same things in life, and we know how to make those things happen. We're partners. In life, and in business. He understands what drives me to be the best. He allows me to be strong." A bitter laugh seeped into her words. "Ironic, isn't it, that he's so weak when it comes to his own mother? He can't quite cut the apron strings, and so here we are, still living with Mommy Dearest."

Madison was confused about who she

referenced, until Cassandra spoke up. The woman had slipped upon them in the shadows and was surprisingly near. "Face it, Jessenia," she snapped. "Without me, you wouldn't be where you are today. I was the one who told my son about the money to be made in the poultry business. I'm the one who gave you the idea about specialized adoption services. Without me, the two of you would still be investing in penny stocks, with only pennies to show for your efforts!"

Even when she thought she had it figured out before, she had been wrong. At least about part of it. Madison couldn't believe she had missed so many clues.

"*Cumber-Tex*," she mumbled. They were close enough to hear her words over the clattering motors. "*Cumber* for Cumberland, where he grew up. And *Tex* for Texas, where you would stake your future. You're the majority stockholders for HighRollers equipment!"

"That's right. And the majority stockholder in the Liaison Group."

"I—I don't know who that is," Madison admitted, but she sensed they were important.

"The group who's been buying up all the foreclosed farms, that's who. The contracts may be in other names, mostly Vietnamese so no one is the wiser, but we control them. We thought it was a touching name, given that Cassandra here is a liaison for *Heartstrings Adoptions*. And she's right. If it hadn't been for her third late husband— funny how they all have died from heart complications and blood loss— we would never have known about the lucrative chicken business. Naming our group after her seemed the least we could do."

If Madison's hands had been free, she would have smacked herself in the forehead. Instead, she murmured, "Cockrell, Abrams, Cockrell and Cockrell. You're Jessenia Cockrell. J.D. Cockrell, the lawyer for *Barbour Food's* poultry division."

She thought she saw a smirk cross her face, but it was difficult to make out details in the murkiness. "It's almost been too easy," Jessenia complained. "Not nearly as challenging as I had hoped, given that I'm the company's lawyer, and Davy is David Davison, division manager for the Texas division. It's been like taking candy from babies, forcing the growers to buy our products or, essentially, sell us their farms at a tremendous loss. Either way, we've made a fortune. Is that the *why* you meant? Why I took full advantage of a good thing? Because it's made me a very rich woman, that's why!"

While Jessenia raged like a mad woman, Genny worked to free herself from her binds. Somehow, when Jessenia had fallen earlier, it had loosened Genny's ties to the elephant. She wasn't free yet, but with more work, she might manage it in time to escape these two lunatics.

"And make no mistake," Jessenia went on, "we're the money behind the *Cherubdipity* partnership, too. Cassandra's years with CPS may have sparked the need for specialized adoption services, but I was the one to recognize how it fit perfectly into Mammy's social experiment. *Cumber-Tex* allowed it all to happen. Without it,

Cassandra would still be in Boston, and Mammy would be in the poor house. And none of those babies would have a proper and loving home!"

"Specialized adoption services?" Genny spat out the words. "Is that what you call buying and selling babies? Is that what you tell yourself so you can look yourself in the mirror each day?"

Madison was so caught up in Jessenia's altered sense of reality—did she really believe she was helping— that she forgot about Cassandra. Without warning, the woman jabbed a needle into her arm. It hurt like heck, but more than that, it made Madison mad. Why hadn't she remembered to keep an eye on the older woman? Obviously, this was hardly the first time she had killed by way of the vial.

"I don't know how you got the sack off your head," Cassandra said, "but the pesticide would have sped things along. It contains additional anticoagulants, perfect for getting rid of unwanted pests like yourself. When you bleed out at the scene of the accident, no one will be the wiser."

"What makes you so sure we'll be in a fatal accident?"

Cassandra's voice was cold enough to freeze hell itself. "David may be weak in many ways, but he always does what his mother tells him. Take my word for it. There *will* be a fatality."

Madison and Genny both knew that if the women delivered them to David, they wouldn't survive.

They had to escape. Now.

28

Genny tugged and pulled, but her ankle was still anchored in place. Through all her twisting and turning, the bucket had shifted, pushing her further from the elephant and putting her leg in an awkward position. With hands tied behind her and the monstrosity overhead, her range of motion was severely limited. She attempted to scoot forward, but it only made matters worse. The bucket shot out from under her, her bottom hit the ground with a solid thump, and her bound hands hung painfully on something behind her, tangled in part because of her coat. It felt like her arms had been wrenched from their sockets. As tears stung her eyes, she couldn't help but cry out in pain.

The roar of the motor outside swallowed up her cry. Jessenia and Cassandra paid her no attention, their focus still on Madison. It was hard to hear what they were saying, but she had other things to worry about now. Namely, what was that hot, searing pain she felt down one wrist? Almost immediately, something trickled down her arm.

Was it blood, or a spider? How fast did injected anticoagulants work? If it was blood, would she bleed to death right here on the shed floor? If it was a spider, was it poisonous?

You're being melodramatic, Genesis, she chided herself. *Stay calm. Panicking won't do either of us any good.*

She heard the thud as much as felt it. Within seconds of the searing pain, her arms broke free from their impediment, smacking her bound hands against the concrete floor at her back. She moaned and instinctively pulled her hands forward to ease the discomfort in her shoulders.

It took a full two seconds for her to realize that her hands had moved. Independently.

Whatever caught her arms not only ripped her skin, it tore through the twine binding her hands together. Her hands were free!

She slid out of her coat and jerked the blindfold from her eyes. She lost no time working to free her ankle. She found the knot and worked at it furiously, knowing time was critical. Any minute now, the women would march her and Madison outside to their death. Somehow, they would get them into her car and on the road, forcing an 'accident.' No one would be the wiser. Officially, cause of death would likely be blamed on 'deep lacerations sustained in the accident.' A tragic accident that was no accident at all.

It seemed an eternity, but she felt the knot loosen, ever so slightly.

Across the room, Madison kept Jessenia talking, trying to buy them more time.

"Does Marcella know you're selling the babies

to the highest bidder?"

"Marcella is an idiot," Cassandra answered. "She has some lofty notion that her good deeds will save the world. She's so convinced she's doing something righteous, she's blind to what's happening right under her own nose."

"If she had put as much thought into my upbringing," Jessenia added bitterly, "I would never have gone into foster care in the first place."

"Nor would you be so driven to succeed," Madison pointed out. "In a weird way, you owe your success to her."

"And to show my appreciation, I'm funding her pet project," Jessenia reasoned. "It's a win-win for everyone. She gets her social experiment paid for, parents get the babies they want, babies get the homes they deserve, and we get more money. Everyone wins."

When Genny didn't cry out with indignation—what about girls like Daisy and Chelsea, and the fact that buying babies was morally and legally wrong—Madison knew her friend had a plan. She might even be free by now and biding her time to make her attack. Madison had to keep their captors' focus on her. She had to keep them talking.

"Is the *Heartstrings Agency* real, or one of your investment shells?"

"Oh, it's real. Cassandra knew of them through her CPS connections and heard that they were struggling financially. *Cumber-Tex Investments* stepped in and funded their needs, creating the very lucrative *Ties that Bind* department, which Cassandra oversees. Again, win-win."

321

A shadow moved behind Cassandra, and Madison knew it was her friend. With her own hands still bound, she only had her legs to use as a weapon. Lucky for her, they were long, lithe, and strong.

Genny was shorter than Jessenia, but she had the element of surprise. She raised her arms high and brought them down over the other woman's head, her coat's belt pulled taut between her hands. She tugged it tight against Jessenia's neck and managed to cross the ends, even as the woman fought back. Genny held on for dear life, tightening her hold with every twist and turn.

Madison had no time to see what happened. Her feet shot out and kicked Cassandra's legs out from beneath her, knocking the older woman to the ground. Cassandra came up dazed and sputtering, but Madison managed to lock her long legs around the woman's neck.

The liaison tried standing, dragging Madison upward with her. With her hands securely fastened behind her, Madison's long body was stretched out like a slinky, but she never released her hold. She squeezed tighter, cutting off the older woman's air supply. Cassandra faltered and fell back to her knees, all the while clawing and tugging at the legs around her neck. She managed to gouge Madison's skin, but not to dislodge her hold. Madison locked her knees, determined not to lose the battle. Their lives depended on it.

Genny and Jessenia's tussle had moved to the floor. Younger and stronger than her opponent, Jessenia had a physical advantage, but it paled in comparison to Genny's dogged determination and sheer will to live. Any weakness on her part would surely lead to their deaths, and she wasn't about to let that happen. She vowed right then and there to adopt Tatiana's baby, and to be the best mother she could possibly be.

Jessenia fought like a cage fighter. She was like a slithering serpent, twisting and gyrating, trying anything to escape the belt around her neck. She was on her back, Genny squashed beneath her, using any means of attack. She jabbed Genny with sharp elbows, used the strength in her legs to kick backward, and pounded her hips against hers, over and over.

But even a cage fighter was no match for a mama bear. With thoughts of her baby fueling her, Genny took the abuse and never turned loose of the belt.

The door opened with a loud and sudden bang, reverberating against the side of the wall as it was flung aside. Daylight flooded into the space. Silhouetted against the brilliance of the sunshine beyond, Cutter looked like a giant. An angry giant.

His eyes focused on his wife, assessing the situation in the blink of an eye. He roughly jerked Jessenia to her feet, captured her arms at her sides, and flung his iron-hard arm around her middle, hauling her back against the wall of his chest. Weakened and gasping for air, she still managed to fight.

With the other hand, Cutter helped Genny off the floor.

"Genny! Are you okay?"

She heard the fear in his voice. Exhausted and out of breath, she nodded her head and managed to assure him, "F—Fine. Don't l—let her go. Evil."

"Evil? *You're* evil! You nearly killed me!" Jessenia shrieked. She kicked and fought to be free, trying to get to Genny. Even though she aimed for his wife, her heel caught Cutter's shin.

In response, he held her tighter, cutting off her air supply. "Stop it! Stop it right now!" he commanded.

Jessenia was foolish enough to lash out once more. "I'm going to kill her," she threatened, her husky voice a growl of hatred. She tried kicking her way free.

"I've never hit a woman before in my life," Cutter told her through gritted teeth. "But so help me, you kick me again or make one more threat against my wife, and I will make an exception. Be. Still."

Trusting she would heed his words, he looked over at his wife. He touched her face gently, ran a concerned eye over her to make sure she was in one piece, and saw the blood.

"It's nothing," she said still breathless. "Help Maddy. I'll look for a light."

She found a string hanging from a bare bulb in the middle of the small room. One tug, and seventy-five watts of light lit the space.

"Oh, wow. That wasn't an elephant, at all," she murmured, seeing the large compressor she had been shackled to. The ledge she banged her head on was nothing more than a shelf.

Cutter went to help Maddy, dragging Jessenia along, willing or not.

"Hold up there, Maddy," he told the long-legged brunette. She sat on the edge of a narrow bench, her arms bound behind her and her body in a position that had to be uncomfortable. Her knees were unwavering in their chokehold around Cassandra Yoko's neck. The liaison sat on the ground, disheveled and defeated after what must have been an exhausting battle. "Don't choke the woman to death."

"I'm—I'm tempted, believe me!" Madison was as winded as the others.

Never loosening his hold on Jessenia, Cutter leaned over and spotted the problem. "You're anchored to a pulley." He unhooked the frayed twine from the massive hook, instantly freeing her. "Honey, untie Maddy's hands while I do something with this wildcat."

He dragged Jessenia back across the room. She dug in her heels like a stubborn child, but he was stronger and simply pulled her along, breaking one heel off her shoe as it scraped against the concrete.

"My Jimmy Choos!" she lamented.

"You won't need those in prison," he assured her.

When he leaned down to retrieve Genny's coat belt, Jessenia attempted a dash for freedom. He had no choice but to tackle her face down on the ground, where he tied her up like a roping calf, both wrists bound to both ankles. She might flounder around like a fish, but she wasn't going anywhere. Her skirt bunched up around her hips so, being the gentleman that he was, Cutter threw Genny's coat over her for modesty. When she cursed him up one side and down the other, he found the oily rag and used it as a gag.

With the bigger threat taken care of, he went back to Cassandra. He found more twine to bind her wrists around the leg of the bench, leaving her on the cold floor as well. One look at her wearied face said she didn't have it in her to try an escape.

"Want to tell me what's going on?" Cutter asked, propping his hands on his hips. By now, even he was winded.

"First, how did you know to come here?" Genny asked.

"Tatiana. She sent me a weird message. I thought it was a mistake at first, but then I realized it was in code. I dropped everything and got here as fast as I could." He pulled out his phone and showed her the brief but effective text.

Dear Guest, You left a valuable item here at the inn. Please come ASAP to assure its safety.

Instead of a signature, it had a lowercase "t" at the end. It could have been a typo, but Genny knew it was the girl's way of plausible deniability, should the message be intercepted.

"She's a smart one," Genny said with pride. "That's why I've decided I definitely want to adopt her baby." She was rewarded with her husband's wide smile of approval. Warmth blossomed in her heart, but she wasn't finished. She shot Cassandra a disdainful glare and added, "Not because he or she is a born and bred Texan or the next brain surgeon, but because his or her mother is a good, decent, honest person. Something the two of you know nothing about, but something normal people recognize and appreciate."

Madison peeked over her shoulder to read the message. "Thank God you were working not far from here," she told Cutter, handing him back his phone. "Otherwise, you may not have gotten here in time."

"I called Brash and told him something was up, but you need to give him an update. Knowing him, he's already halfway here. I need to call 911. These ladies have a date with a jail cell."

"These aren't ladies, Cutter. They're cold-blooded killers."

"And they have an accomplice," Genny remembered. "A man named David Davison. He has my car and plans for our fatal 'accident.'"

"Not anymore," Cutter said with a grin. "I came upon your car along the road and saw a man sitting inside. When I asked if he was having trouble, he made up some bull about running out of gas and having a buddy bringing him more. I wasn't sure what was going on yet, but I wasn't taking chances. I tied him up with rope from my truck and stuffed him in the trunk. I'll let the sheriff know where he can find him."

"You did that?" Genny's eyes were wide. "What if it turned out to be nothing?"

"He was sitting inside a car I knew you would have locked, so that's not nothing. And I figured the worst he could do was bring charges against me for tying him up. Like I said, I wasn't taking any chances. I walked in from the back gate and found Tatiana and a few other girls standing outside the building, afraid to go in, but afraid something bad was happening inside."

Genny looked beyond the door and, sure enough, there stood Tatiana, Nicki, and two other girls she vaguely recognized. They kept a safe distance away, but Genny noticed they were armed. Tatiana and one of the girls held shovels, Nicki a hoe, and the fourth girl had the blunt end of a rake aimed for action. Belatedly, Genny realized the roar of the engines were silent, and she could hear Tatiana's hesitant voice.

"Miss Genny? Are you okay? Did they hurt you?"

Genny held her arms out in welcome, and they met in the doorway for a hug. "No, sweet girl. Thanks to you and your quick thinking, they didn't. You may have saved our lives."

"Thank God!" the girl said, sobbing. "I was so afraid for you. I didn't know what else to do. We— We weren't going to let them get away, though. We were going to stop them." She motioned to her rag-tag team of warriors and weapons.

"Thank you, all of you." Genny smiled. "You were very brave." She hugged Tatiana again. "How can I ever repay you for what you did?"

Tatiana leaned back and gave Genny a soulful, melancholy look, her voice tremulous. "You can give my baby the parents and the home she deserves."

Tears rolled down Genny's face. "Yes," she said with a vigorous nod. "We've already made our decision. We want to adopt your baby, Tatiana, because we know she'll be every bit as brave and strong as her mother." She offered another dimpled smile and a shrug. "Or he. Could be a boy."

Dark curls tumbled around her shoulders as Tatiana shook her head. "No, my heart says it's a girl. And my heart is happy, knowing she'll have an awesome mom like you."

Behind her, Cutter's voice roared, "Genny? What's this about an injection? We need to get you and Maddy to the ER. Now!"

It was a crazy, eventful afternoon. The sheriff's department arrived and took Jessenia, Cassandra, and David into custody, and Marcella in for questioning. Two ambulances weren't far behind, whisking Genny and Madison away to the hospital. They requested Texas General. Cassandra refused to say what strength anticoagulant she had given them, but it was safe to assume it had been far above the normal dosage.

Tatiana, feeling partially responsible for their plight, asked to go along and make sure they were safe. She rode with Cutter to the hospital, where Brash was already waiting. Detective Cade Resnick was there, too, his face grim as Cutter gave him the initial details.

"Am—Am I in trouble?" Tatiana asked, her dark eyes full of fear.

"Why would you be in trouble, Miss Gomez?" the detective asked in a quiet voice. "You did nothing wrong."

"But I... deep in my heart... I knew something wasn't right. I suspected something was wrong."

Her hands twisted in her lap.

"And you told us about it," Cutter assured her, gently touching her arm, "so that we could help. Because of you, Tatiana, these horrible people were caught and stopped. And Genny and Maddy are alive because of you."

"That makes you a hero in my book," Brash assured her warmly. "You're definitely *not* in trouble."

"You're not in trouble," Cade reiterated, "but we could certainly use your help in understanding how this operation worked. Would you be willing to do that?"

She nodded in agreement, even though she was obviously frightened at the thought. "I'll do whatever I need to do. Those women are evil."

Normally, nurses didn't come out into the waiting room, but the head nurse made an exception. "Brash? You may come back now," Laurel announced

Cutter was on his feet, trailing right behind. "What about me? My wife came in at the same time. Genesis Montgomery."

"You must be Cutter." The petite brunette smiled.

"Oh, sorry," Brash apologized, running a hand through his dark-auburn hair. "Cutter, this is Laurel Benson. Laurel, Cutter Montgomery." With introductions barely done, he asked eagerly, "Are our wives going to be okay?"

"Come see for yourself."

"Me, too?" Cutter wanted to know.

"Your wife is still having her picture taken," Laurel said, her teasing manner meant as assurance for the anxious husband. "As soon as imaging brings her back to her room, I'll be back for you."

True to her word, Laurel was back just a few minutes later. Cutter strode down the hallway amid murmurs and looks of appreciation, similar to those Cade received, especially when the detective wore his jeans and spurs.

Laurel smiled. *There was just something about a cowboy that women couldn't resist.*

They passed Madison's room, where the low murmur of Brash's deep voice rumbled with concern.

"I'm just thankful you're okay, Maddy. I don't know what I would have done if something had happened to you."

"Just hold me," she replied.

Which was exactly what Cutter planned to do when he reached his wife's room.

"Are you okay, Genny darlin'?" he asked. "What did they say?"

"Nothing, yet. They haven't read the results yet." She patted the bed beside her, encouraging him to have a seat. "Relax, Cutter. I feel fine. Excited, even."

"Excited?"

"We shut down a despicable baby-trafficking ring. Even better than that, we committed to adopting Tatiana's baby. We're going to be parents, Cutter!" Her blue eyes sparkled with delight. "Aren't you as excited as I am? You meant it, didn't you, when you nodded? We're really doing this, aren't we?"

He took her hand, his own eyes as bright as

hers. "Yes, darlin', we're doing this. We're starting our family."

She did a little happy dance in the bed. When her heart monitor beeped in protest, she merely laughed. "Tatiana says she just knows it will be a girl. Do you have a favorite girl name?"

"Sure. Genny."

"Genny, Jr?" she laughed. "I don't think so!"

"We still have some time to decide."

"Fine. But on the way home, we're going shopping. I want to buy our baby's very first gift."

Cutter didn't look as thrilled as she did, particularly when he said, "One thing we're buying is a new car. I don't know what that David joker did to yours, but I don't care. We're getting a new one."

"We'll need it, anyway, for a car seat," Genny said dreamily. She named off all the other things they would need, and Cutter resigned himself to being broke for the rest of his life.

"Knock, knock," Tatiana said a few minutes later, waiting for permission to be invited in. "They said I could come back now."

"Tatiana! I'm so glad you're here." Genny's smile was wide and sincere. "We've just been talking about the baby. We're going to buy a new SUV, so there will be plenty of room for a car seat."

"This woman already has me in the poorhouse," Cutter complained affectionately.

Tatiana's brave smile wavered a bit. "That's exactly why I know you'll be excellent parents. You know what to buy and have the money to do it. I could never give her all the things she needs."

Hearing the sadness in her voice, Genny held out her hand. "Does it bother you to hear us talk about this, sweetie? Because if it does..."

"No. No, it actually helps." She sniffed, trying hard not to cry. "I know I'm doing the right thing. It hurts, but I know it's for the best. I like hearing the excitement in your voice."

"Oh, Tatiana, I am *so* excited! I think I've already fallen in love with the baby, and I've never even seen her! I can imagine what a beauty she'll be, though, with your dark coloring and sweet smile."

"Her father is very handsome, too." The girl's voice caught with emotion.

Trying to lighten the mood, Cutter grinned and did his best Elvis imitation. "Thank you. Thank you very much."

Tatiana rolled her dark eyes and 'whispered' loud enough for Cutter to hear, "Don't tell the old guy, but he's kinda cute. I heard the nurses whispering."

The curtain moved again, admitting Doctor Joe Renaldi. "Hello there, Mrs. Montgomery. How are you feeling?"

"Fine. Truly, I feel fine, but they insisted I come in to be checked out."

"Do I need to go?" Tatiana offered.

"No, stay. You're family now." Genny beamed at her.

"I remember you from that TV show," the doctor told his patient. "With all that delicious food you cooked, what made you decide to sample rat poisoning?"

"I didn't by choice!" she assured him. "And I

didn't eat it. It was injected through a syringe."

"It was a large dose," the doctor acknowledged. "Luckily for you, you got here quickly, and we were able to reverse the effects before any real damage was done. That cut on your wrist bled a little more than normal, but a couple of stitches and a pressure pack took care of it. The important thing is the baby is fine."

"The... The baby? What baby?" Genny asked.

"What are you talking about, Doc?" Cutter wanted to know.

Doctor Renaldi looked at the couple in surprise. "You don't know?" he asked.

"Know what?" Cutter asked, getting aggravated at his evasive answers.

He looked back at Genny. "Mrs. Montgomery, you're pregnant."

29

It was said that God moved in mysterious ways.

It wasn't for Genny to question why or how, but it would forever remain a mystery to her why He chose to make them the parents of almost-twins, born a mere two months apart.

After trying unsuccessfully for a year to have a baby, it came as a huge surprise to know that, just as they had committed themselves to the idea of adoption, she finally turned up pregnant. The specialist called later that evening, reporting the same results from the tests he had run. He sounded as surprised and pleased as she did.

Tatiana assumed this meant the couple wouldn't adopt her baby now, but once the initial shock wore off, they assured her that wasn't the case. Genny had meant it when she said she had already fallen in love with the baby. She had her heart set on a dark-haired, olive-skinned child. Best of all, Cutter could still have the blonde he had hoped for. It was too soon to know what color eyes either child would have, but it didn't matter.

Their parents would love them, no matter what they looked like.

Cutter bought an SUV the very next day, making certain there was plenty of room for two car seats, a double stroller, and all the assorted necessities required by two traveling infants.

In the wake of the investigation, Marcella Durant was found innocent of any wrongdoing. She hadn't known the details behind Jessenia's financing, how it was funded, or that Daisy and Chelsea's deaths were orchestrated. She was horrified to know she had unwittingly helped her demented daughter turn innocent babies and their mothers into a cash commodity. The strict house rules and obsession about 'fraternizing with guests' were simply part of her controlling nature.

Cumber-Tex had their hands in many different ventures, some legal, some borderline, and some, like *Ties that Bind*, horrendously evil. While Jessenia and David had quite a system with *Barbour Foods*, they weren't to blame for all the food giant's dirty deeds. Orders to upgrade at the owner's expense came directly from corporate. *Cumber-Tex* and *The Liaison Group* simply took advantage of a bad situation and profited where they could.

Madison gave Lucy and the other growers back their money, unable to keep it with a clear conscious. With the spotlight on the Texas Division, orders to upgrade were put on a temporary hold, but Madison knew they would eventually be reinstated. Either someone in corporate had their own hands in the till somewhere, or the company simply had no compassion for the growers who sustained their company from the ground up.

Much to Marcella's surprise, Gregory Cockrell stepped up and did a decent thing. He found a legitimate financial backer for her well-conceived 'social experiment,' so that she could continue to have a positive impact on young women's lives. *Heartstring Adoptions* closed its doors, but a reputable adoption agency took its place, offering to place the babies in good and loving homes.

There was no evidence to prove the adopting parents were aware of the trafficking scheme. They had been victims, too, paying inflated prices for imaginary fees and services. Like Douglas Townsend, some may have suspected something wasn't right, but what Madison said was true: people wanted to believe what people wanted to believe.

The dean did, however, step down from his position. His official resignation slated his desire to spend more time with his family.

And so, spring came, and then summer, each season bringing with it more of God's mysterious wonders and ways.

Trenton Torno became a regular visitor at The Big House. After he and Bethani aced their health assignment, he found various reasons to stop by for a visit. Bethani initiated their first date, inviting him to a celebratory dinner when she and Megan made the cheerleading team again. She publicly acknowledged her interest in him by saving him a seat at lunch every day and holding his hand in the hallways. By summer, they were going steady.

As Derron's relationship with Ramon cooled, so did his desire for multi-colored hair. He kept his color to a minimum, choosing only one at a time for accents: Irish green for spring, ocean blue for summer, and, as fall approached, pumpkin orange.

Tatiana chose to stay at *Cherubdipity* until her third trimester, at which time her family welcomed her home. A sonogram proved that she was, indeed, having a girl, but the baby's birth father was officially out of the picture. He and his parents moved away unexpectedly, cutting off all means of communication.

Cutter and Genny visited the Gomez home often, getting to know their baby's birth family so that they could share her heritage with her as she grew older. After the baby was born, Tatiana had plans to start a new life for herself. She was accepted to a college in West Texas, where she could focus on her studies and make a fresh start. They left the lines of communication open, however. Even though the child would be legally and solely theirs, they knew she might one day have questions concerning her birth mother and other blood relatives. They wouldn't deny her that connection.

After all the help they had received from Laurel and Cade, Genny and Cutter threw a small dinner party to show their appreciation. It was just them and the deCordovas, which turned out to be the perfect number. On another occasion, the six met for dinner at *Antonio's*, with loose plans to meet again soon. Since the nurse and the detective weren't exactly a couple, making too many plans was a bit dicey.

Trenessa Green still needed improvement with her filing skills, but she had come a long way since the first of the year. By summer, she had become an integral part of the *New Beginnings* team. Genny still hadn't worked out the logistics of how motherhood would look as a restaurateur, but the further along she got in her pregnancy, the more tired she became. Having Trenessa there allowed her more time to rest and to prepare for the arrival of not just one, but two bundles of joy.

And even though Genny thought she was prepared for the first of the two "Big Days," still she wasn't.

One Saturday morning in late September, she and Madison went to an estate sale at the late Alpha Bodine's grand old Victorian. Genny was looking for something special to go in the nursery, some heirloom from the past to remind their children to always appreciate history. She didn't have anything specific in mind, but she would know it when she saw it.

Madison had discovered a canvas painting that caught her fancy. She was trying to decide where it would look best in the Big House when Genny's phone rang.

"It's time!" Tatiana's frantic voice said. "My water just broke!"

Genny froze, suddenly unable to remember the checklist she had made for just this purpose. *Think, Genny. Think.*

"Uhm, okay. Take a deep breath and just breathe. Try to relax."

They both practiced the breathing exercise,

and Genny visualized the list they went over at least once a week.

"Do you have your suitcase?"

"Yes. It's in the car."

"Is the car full of gas?"

"Yes. Mom has it running."

"Have you called the doctor?"

"Yes. He'll meet us there."

"Have you called Genny and Cutter?"

"Uh... yeah. I'm talking to you now."

Genny laughed at her own foolishness, but the sound came out in a quiver of nerves. "Oh, yes, how silly of me. Okay, let me grab Cutter, and we'll meet you at the hospital."

"Got it. Oh, and Genny?"

"Yeah?"

She could hear the bittersweet smile in Tatiana's voice, a mixture of sadness and joy that this moment had finally come. Nevertheless, the girl squealed with excitement. "You're about to be a mommy!"

THANK YOU for reading and allowing me to entertain you.

I'm sorry to leave you here, but I couldn't squeeze the birth of *two* babies into this story. That comes in *Murder Worth a Thousand Words*, along with a brand-new "old" mystery, available this fall. Wish me luck that things don't go like they did while writing this book. (See Intro Note: Who Knew?)

If you liked Head Nurse Laurel Benson and Detective Cade Resnick, they have their very own series, Texas General Cozy Series of Mystery, and would love to show you around their hometown.

And, as always, if you liked this or any book and would like to keep them going, please, please, *please* show your support by leaving a review! Amazon, Goodreads, and BookBub are the big three, but all feedback helps.

After leaving your review, please feel free to drop me a personal note. (This is the best part of being an author!) Here's how you can reach me:

beckiwillis.ccp@gmail.com

www.beckiwillis.com

https://www.facebook.com/beckiwillis.ccp/

Again, thanks for reading!

ABOUT THE AUTHOR

Becki Willis, best known for her popular The Sisters, Texas Mystery Series and Forgotten Boxes, always dreamed of being an author. In November of '13, that dream became a reality. Since that time, she has published numerous books, won first place honors for Best Mystery Series, Best Suspense Fiction and Best Audio Book, and has introduced her imaginary friends to readers around the world.

An avid history buff, Becki likes to poke around in old places and learn about the past. Other addictions include reading, writing, junking, unraveling a good mystery, and coffee. She loves to travel, but believes coming home to her family and her Texas ranch is the best part of any trip. Becki is a member of the Association of Texas Authors, the National Association of Professional Women, and the Brazos Writers organization. She attended Texas A&M University and majored in Journalism.

Connect with her at http://www.beckiwillis.com/ or http://www.facebook.com/beckiwillis.ccp?ref=hl. Better yet, email her at beckiwillis.ccp@gmail.com. She loves to hear from readers and encourages feedback!